The armored personnel carrier began rolling toward the center of Times Square

The Executioner made his decision. He checked the 100-round drum in the Ultimax and fell in behind the moving vehicle. As the myriad flashing, strobing neon and high-intensity lights blinked above him, Bolan noted the shadows and observed his opposition.

Beyond the police barricades, crowds of New Yorkers gawked, watching the scene unfold with no knowledge of just how dangerous the battleground was about to become. The APC rolled slowly onward. The police officers inside were similarly unprepared for the firestorm that awaited them.

The signal came and a shot rang out from somewhere in the crowd. The bullet burned into the back of the APC just over Bolan's shoulder.

Hellfire erupted.

MACK BOLAN ®
The Executioner

The Don Pendleton's
Executioner®
KILLING TRADE

A GOLD EAGLE BOOK FROM
W💥RLDWIDE®

TORONTO • NEW YORK • LONDON
AMSTERDAM • PARIS • SYDNEY • HAMBURG
STOCKHOLM • ATHENS • TOKYO • MILAN
MADRID • WARSAW • BUDAPEST • AUCKLAND

First edition March 2008

ISBN-13: 978-0-373-64352-3
ISBN-10:   0-373-64352-7

Special thanks and acknowledgment to
Phil Elmore for his contribution to this work.

KILLING TRADE

A sword is never a killer; it is a tool in the killer's hands.
—Lucius Annaeus Seneca the Younger 4 BC–AD 65
The Art of War

A man with a gun is just a man with a gun. When he chooses evil, he becomes a predator and that means he'll face me.

—Mack Bolan

THE
MACK BOLAN
LEGEND

Nothing less than a war could have fashioned the destiny of the man called Mack Bolan. Bolan earned the Executioner title in the jungle hell of Vietnam.

But this soldier also wore another name—Sergeant Mercy. He was so tagged because of the compassion he showed to wounded comrades-in-arms and Vietnamese civilians.

Mack Bolan's second tour of duty ended prematurely when he was given emergency leave to return home and bury his family, victims of the Mob. Then he declared a one-man war against the Mafia.

He confronted the Families head-on from coast to coast, and soon a hope of victory began to appear. But Bolan had broken society's every rule. That same society started gunning for this elusive warrior—to no avail.

So Bolan was offered amnesty to work within the system against terrorism. This time, as an employee of Uncle Sam, Bolan became Colonel John Phoenix. With a command center at Stony Man Farm in Virginia, he and his new allies—Able Team and Phoenix Force—waged relentless war on a new adversary: the KGB.

But when his one true love, April Rose, died at the hands of the Soviet terror machine, Bolan severed all ties with Establishment authority.

Now, after a lengthy lone-wolf struggle and much soul-searching, the Executioner has agreed to enter an "arm's-length" alliance with his government once more, reserving the right to pursue personal missions in his Everlasting War.

1

Mack Bolan surged to his feet from the folding chair, knocking it backward as he overturned the circular alloy table. Someone nearby screamed. As the Executioner crouched behind the dubious cover of the dented table, a steady stream of 62-grain steel-core ammunition punched merciless holes through it. Bolan swept aside his windbreaker and drew the Beretta 92-F from the holster inside his waistband. Rolling away from the table, he brought the weapon up in two hands as he crouched on one knee. He shot the gunman between the eyes, the 9 mm hollowpoint round coring through the man's head. The gunman staggered and dropped, his heavily accessorized AR-15 clattering to the pavement. Bolan pushed to his feet, knees bent, scanning left to right with the Beretta before him, searching for more targets. Around him, panicked citizens and tourists ran for their lives, overturning the outdoor furniture as they went.

Bolan took stock. This was New York City, not Baghdad, but the scene had gone to hell faster than most. He was likely outnumbered and, because he'd tried to keep a low profile, outgunned. The Beretta in his hands was a fine weapon, but offered nowhere near the firepower of the select-fire Beretta 93-R or .44 Magnum Desert Eagle that were his normal field kit.

The instructions from Stony Man Farm had been clear enough, the scenario straightforward. Several high-profile shootings in New York City had raised flags at the Farm because of their technical details. Someone was using new small-arms ordnance on the streets, explosive high-penetration rounds that could chop through vehicles and body armor with startling ease. Aaron Kurtzman and the Farm's team of computer jockeys had traced the ammunition to a dealer trying to broker a large sale in Manhattan. The Executioner, posing as a buyer, was to meet this man. The time and place were set in advance.

It was crucial not to spook the dealer. The arms network in the city could extend to any number of people. To find and destroy the source of the dangerous rounds, Bolan had to track it through this contact. He had loaded down accordingly, going armed but not heavily so, balancing preparation with the image he was trying to project to the arms dealer.

Now, that lack of firepower might prove fatal. Hal Brognola, director of the Justice Department's Sensitive Operations Group, had stressed to him the delicate nature of the situation, the political sensitivities in a city only too recently the target of the world's worst terrorist attacks. It was a calculated risk, but it had seemed reasonable enough. Bolan was to meet the dealer, find out what he knew and trace him back to his sources.

The contact failed to show. Whether he was dead, missing or had simply been scared off didn't matter. In the man's place had come an assassin.

Bolan spared the fallen gunman a glance. The dead man's weapon had all the bells and whistles—tactical light, vertical foregrip, red-dot scope. Going only on the hardware and the man's clothing, it was possible the would-be murderer was a mercenary, of the type that Brognola and the Farm had warned Bolan to expect at some point.

The arms dealer, a man named West, was formerly employed by a large munitions developer called Norris Labs International. NLI, among other activities, kept a security contractor on retainer—the type of private paramilitary force a company, if just corrupt enough, might field to cover its bloody tracks with more bodies. If the intel and the Farm's theories were correct, NLI was eager to prevent its involvement with the explosive ammunition from becoming known. They were therefore highly motivated to stop West and kill anyone connected with him.

Their death list now seemed to include Bolan.

The second shooter was not far behind the first. He engaged as he moved, firing a Heckler & Koch .45 as he ran, too eager to acquire his target. The man was clearly pushing the envelope of his own skills. Bolan held his ground. Heavy slugs scraped the pavement at his boots. The Executioner aimed calmly and dropped the second man with another clean shot to the head.

Bryant Park had become a killing ground. The Executioner, no stranger to the Big Apple, was equally familiar with the fog of war. As more armed professionals closed in from two sides, Bolan sought the only cover he could find—the Josephine Shaw Lowell Memorial Fountain. Putting the fountain's pink granite between himself and the gunmen approaching from the north, he targeted the contingent closing from the east and opened fire. It was a delaying tactic, aiming a suppressing field of fire at the enemy.

The Beretta barked a dozen times and locked open, but Bolan was already up and reloading on the move, running through the short pause created by his bullets. There were crowds of pedestrians nearby, and the Executioner knew he could not afford to put them in danger. It was no small feat in such a crowded city, but Bolan managed to plot a route away from the killzone that did not put anyone else in the line of fire. He paralleled traffic on Forty-Second Street as he ran, careful to stay as far from both people and vehicles as he could.

Horns blared as spectators, watching him go, voiced outrage or encouragement—Bolan could not tell which. Behind him, the swarming groups of shooters converged but held their fire. Clearly they were not willing, just yet, to ignite a war in full view of witnesses, but Bolan didn't trust his luck or their restraint to hold forever. In his head he heard the numbers falling. The NYPD and maybe even a task force of Emergency Service Unit personnel could arrive at any time. New York City was a lot of things, tough among them, but a full-blown gun battle in Manhattan would draw an overwhelming law-enforcement response.

Brognola wasn't going to be happy.

The soldier's black-clad pursuers, all bearing Colt assault rifles and an assortment of handguns, overcame their reluctance and began to chase the Executioner with their fire. Bullets chewed the sidewalk behind him and narrowly missed clipping his feet. Out of immediate danger but bearing wide-eyed witness to the coming carnage, the closer drivers leaned on their horns.

As the Executioner moved, the OD canvas messenger bag slung over his shoulder slapping against his left hip, he whipped shots behind him. He took one gunman in the thigh, toppling him, before punching a trio of 9 mm bullets through another. The shooter went down, but there were more to take his place.

Bolan weighed his choices as he ran. He could not bull his way through the dense New York pedestrian traffic, nor could he endanger the vehicle traffic on the street. He wouldn't use innocent people as shields. It was bad enough that there were plenty of people, far too many, to see just what was happening. This low-profile meeting had turned into a high-profile disaster. The hostile team was hot on his heels, moving up both sides of the street. With no other options and with no choice but to get the innocents out of harm's way, the Executioner ran for the twin stone lions guarding the New York Public Library.

There were crowds of people everywhere. There was only a moment to get them moving before his pursuers would be in range. His face grim, he did the only thing he could. Aiming the Beretta down and at the angle least likely to send ricochets spraying the area, he started shooting.

"This is a terrorist attack!" Bolan shouted. "Everybody get

out of here!" He punctuated the order with another pair of gun-shots. "Move! Move!"

There was more screaming, but not much, as those within range hustled to put space between themselves and the big, dark-haired gunman in their midst. New York, a city hardened to terrorist attacks and near-misses since September 11, was still standing and still vibrant, despite the best efforts of count-less enemies, foreign and domestic. New Yorkers, even many of the tourists, were a hardy breed, inured to violence and to its threat, proud of their city. They weren't stupid, but neither were they cowed. Bolan saw more than a few hard looks as people ran from him. One man, a twentysomething with a shoulder bag and wearing a 5.11 tactical vest, almost looked as if he might go for a weapon under his clothing. Bolan eyed him hard and the young man backed off, looking through what he thought was his enemy, unblinking. The Executioner watched until the man rounded the corner, his hand still fingering the edge of his vest.

Bolan counted himself lucky. In a city where mere mortals couldn't get permits to carry guns without a great deal of wealth and political influence, more than a few who valued their lives over petty politicking had made the choice to go armed illegally. The Executioner would not have been surprised if one of the lo-cals had taken a shot at him. Bolan changed magazines and took cover behind one of the stone lions, covering the street as the hired shooters closed on him. The timing was going to be tight.

As they moved up on either side, Bolan crouched low. Gun-fire pocked the pedestal of the stone lion. Then a group of four men made their move, trying to flank the Executioner and get a clear shot at him as he engaged the others. Bolan, again on one knee, took a careful two-hand grip on the Beretta, sighted and fired.

He took the point man in the head, the hollowpoint round doing its deadly work as it punched through the gunman. Bolan fired several more times, taking the second man in the chest and driving the others back. The remaining two began to backpedal, moving smoothly on bent knees. They fired as they went, almost gliding. They were well-trained. Bolan's bullets chased after them, but when he was certain they were backing off, he returned his attention to the main group. Above him, the statue took several high shots, spraying him with stinging debris.

Reloading again, Bolan drew a bead on another enemy as the man crouched behind a suddenly abandoned pickup truck. The gunman, tucked behind the protection of the engine block, nevertheless exposed too much of his bent arm and gun hand. Bolan's bullets shattered the man's elbow.

The Executioner had time to watch a pair of men advance to back up their fallen comrade. Each one carried a slightly longer AR-15, the heavy match barrels of the stainless-steel weapons gleaming in the afternoon light. Bolan ducked back behind the lion's pedestal as they opened fire.

The Executioner flinched as a quartet of shots punched through the stone of the pedestal. His eyes wide, Bolan watched as tiny fires flared up in gaping exit holes in the stone. He barely had time to throw himself from behind the pedestal as a fusillade of heavy slugs split the pedestal and broke large pieces from the lion above. Several bullets dug into the stone of the library steps, sparking more small fires that burned with unnatural intensity. Bolan rolled, feeling the heat, squinting against the grit and debris that coated him. He shoved the Beretta forward, slightly canted in one fist, burning through the magazine as fast as he could. The angle was bad, but the shots forced the gunners back behind the pickup truck.

The slide of Bolan's pistol locked open again. Bolan's support hand slapped the ejected magazine away from his body where it couldn't end up under his feet. He brought the last of his spare magazines from the holster at his belt, slapped it home and racked the slide briskly as he advanced smoothly, knees bent, in an aggressive isosceles crouch. As he pushed the gun to full extension again, ready to engage his attackers with his last fifteen rounds, he finally heard the sirens through the ringing in his ears.

The first of the NYPD cars roared up, tires squealing as they cut through the chaos of Manhattan's traffic. Bolan's eyes narrowed as he watched the gunmen, already backing off and buttoning up, their weapons disappearing under long coats or simply held behind their bodies as they faded back in the noise and confusion. Bolan hit the magazine release on his Beretta and racked the slide as he stood, moving out into the middle of the library steps. As police officers with Glocks and shotguns drew down on him, screaming commands at him, Bolan let the Beretta swivel out of his grip, dangling from his finger by the trigger guard. He held it high over his head as he settled to his knees, his free hand behind his neck.

No, Hal Brognola was not going to be happy—but Bolan wasn't finished yet.

He was only getting started.

2

Bolan sat at the small table in the corner of the coffeehouse, an insulated cup of overpriced coffee untouched before him. Checking the heavy stainless-steel watch on his wrist, he sat back in the wooden chair. Brognola had managed to straighten things out, more or less, and much more quickly than Bolan would have thought. The local authorities hadn't detained Bolan long before cutting him loose, though it was clear they were not happy about it.

After conferring with the Farm following the shootout at the library, the big Fed had started pulling strings and pushing buttons, hard. The Farm had identified the person most likely to be of use to Bolan in his search through the city—Detective Len Burnett. Burnett was head of a multijurisdictional drug-trafficking task force operating in the greater New York City area, with the authority and the connections Bolan would need. He was on record concerning investigations into several of the shootings that had flagged the Farm's interest. He was also a veteran officer with a good record, by all accounts. Brognola had arranged to have Burnett assigned as liaison to Bolan. He knew that wasn't likely to go over well with Burnett or his bosses, but it couldn't be helped.

The Executioner couldn't blame NYPD for resenting his presence. He hadn't started the war—it was raging long before Bolan had arrived for his most recent tour of the Big Apple— but he'd brought it boiling over onto their front steps within view of countless civilians. Fortunately, despite waging a running firefight in midtown Manhattan, Bolan's attackers hadn't killed anyone. The property damage was extensive, but the cost in lives was zero.

So far.

The bad news was that Bolan could see no way this wasn't simply the opening salvo of a much bloodier battle.

The soldier watched the entrance to the coffeehouse. He did not wait long before a man matching the description he'd been given pushed open the door and let it slam none too gently behind him. The newcomer was male, late thirties to early forties, with an unruly mop of curly, receding brown hair, three days' worth of beard stubble and a paisley tie at half mast. He was a large man, standing a couple of inches over six feet, with a slight paunch and a lanky, big-boned frame. He wore an off-the-rack suit that actually fit him quite well, the jacket of which didn't quite conceal the bulge of the gun on his right hip. He quickly surveyed the coffeehouse and zeroed in on Bolan without hesitation. The soldier's corner was secluded enough, the ambient noise loud enough, that the men could speak in reasonable confidence on what was, Bolan calculated, neutral ground. He did not intend to antagonize Burnett if he could help it, given that he needed the man's assistance.

"Matt Cooper?"

"That's me," Bolan nodded, standing to offer his hand. Burnett took it and returned a firm handshake.

"Burnett," the man said pleasantly. As he sat, his expression hardened, his smile bearing all the joy of an undertaker. "Would you mind telling me," he asked with feigned mildness before his voice went completely cold, "just what the fuck you think you're doing in New York?" He spoke quietly, but the menace in his tone was real enough.

Bolan looked at him blandly. "That's need to know."

"Well," Burnett said, leaning forward, "I damn well need to know."

The Executioner regarded him for a moment, saying nothing.

Burnett wiped one hand down his face, shaking his head. "Look, Cooper," he said, using the cover Brognola had supplied and that Bolan's Justice credentials listed, "I want to believe we're on the same side. Chief Vaughn told me he's been getting calls from high-powered types in Washington all morning. That's the only reason you're not up on every charge in the book and a few off the books, as far as I'm concerned. You've got connections. Okay. I can live with that. But I won't have you burning down this city around my ears!"

"You're right," Bolan said simply.

"What?" Burnett asked.

"We're on the same side," Bolan offered. "At least, we ought to be, depending on what your stake in all this is."

"Drug interdiction's my stake," Burnett said. "If your people knew to ask for me, you know what I do. My task force is focused primarily on violent crime related to cocaine trafficking."

"Crack?" Bolan asked.

"The crack dealers are the small-timers, these days," Burnett admitted. "It's the big gangs and the organized-crime families moving hundreds of kilograms of cocaine that concern me." He turned and stared into space for a moment, looking out the picture window at the busy city street beyond. He sighed. "Cooper, I've lived in New York all my life. I've watched crime come and go. I've seen how bad it can get. As a rookie, I watched the city nearly eat itself alive in the late seventies. Then there was the backlash. Remember those movies, all the vigilante flicks about cleaning up the Big Apple? There was that subway shooter…and that didn't stem the tide. Things got worse until the last bunch of cronies in city hall decided to clamp down, clean up the joint. We started to turn a corner."

"It's never that easy," Bolan commented.

"No," Burnett said, turning to face him, "it isn't and it wasn't. Now we're seeing the worst of the violent crime surge again. I've got Colombian and Dominican gangs, with a few minor Mexican players for flavor, pushing into Manhattan, of all places. Midtown Manhattan, Cooper! All it takes is one good massacre on Broadway, a hit on the street in front of the United Nations, or, God help us, a frigging war in front the New York Public Library, and we'll be lucky to see so much as another nickel in tourism. They'll be rolling up the bloodstained sidewalks by the time we're done. This city will be the wasteland they were all predicting it would become, back in the bad old days. I want to stop that before it can happen, Cooper."

"It's more than drug interdiction and drive-bys," Bolan told him.

Burnett paused. "That's right," he said. "A few months ago, we had an officer shot in the line of duty. Tragic as the death of a good cop is, that wasn't so surprising. What had us up nights worrying was that the patrolman was shot after taking cover behind the engine block of his Crown Vic."

"Shot through cover, you mean," Bolan guessed.

"Exactly," Burnett nodded. "The rounds—9 mm, forensics tells us—went through the heaviest part of the car like it wasn't even there. Maybe a .50-caliber rifle could do that. But 9 frigging mm? Show me small-arms ammunition that can do that!"

"That's why I'm here," Bolan admitted. "That wasn't the first such case."

Burnett's eyes narrowed. "That's right," he said. "There have been almost a dozen shootings, some large-scale, some minor drive-bys. In each one, witness accounts or the evidence and the bodies we found afterward point to something nobody's ever seen before. The lab couldn't make much of it, other than to say it was like a miniature depleted uranium round. We sent some samples to the FBI, what we could find, but we haven't got anything yet."

"You have," Bolan told him. "You got me."

"You're FBI?" Burnett asked. "I thought you were with the Justice Department."

"It's more complicated than that," Bolan told him. "Let's say for now that the samples you sent raised the right flags in the right departments. Word of what you're facing made its way to the right people. They're working on it right now. That's also why I'm here. That's what I'm after. Depleted uranium ammo in the hands of violent drug gangs in New York City? That's volatile business. The fire's got to be stopped before it spreads."

"Fine," Burnett said, growing impatient. "But you weren't shooting it out with any coke-runners yesterday. My men on the scene tell me they saw paramilitary commandos of some kind."

"Did your people intercept any of them?" Bolan asked.

"No," Burnett said, his face reddening. "We pursued several of them but lost them. They shot up a SWAT van, among other things, making their escape."

"Some of them," Bolan said, "were using the ammunition we're looking for. Not all, but at least two."

"What's the connection?" Burnett asked. "How did it go down? Why were they shooting at you?"

"We'll get to that eventually," Bolan said, putting him off. "Tell me about the gangs you're working," Bolan said.

"Why?" Burnett demanded. "How do you fit into this?"

"Trust me," Bolan told him.

"I guess I don't have much choice," Burnett said. He thought about it for a moment and then continued. "We've got two gangs at war right now, both of them moving into Manhattan to prove something to the others—and to city hall, if you ask me. One's the Caqueta Cartel, headed by Luis Caqueta. They're the Colombians. The other is El Cráneo, the Skull, a Dominican gang fronted by a charming character named Pierre Taveras."

"How does the trade play out?" Bolan asked.

"Caqueta moves large quantities of cocaine through Atlanta, using a variety of small-time Mexican groups to move the coke from the southwest. The Mexicans completely control the West Coast and the Midwestern markets, but here on the East Coast,

El Cráneo and Caqueta are fighting for control. It's been getting bloodier and bloodier as they try to outdo each other. A lot of the coke originates in Colombia, where your people in Washington have been cutting aid to drug interdiction for years now. The pipeline is getting wider and the distributors on this end are getting more brutal as they fight over rights to distribute their poison in the Northeast."

"Bloodier and bloodier," Bolan repeated, "meaning, the street wars are escalating and the hardware is, too."

"You know it as well as I do," the cop said.

"Yes, I do," Bolan confirmed. "Initially, my involvement was supposed to be low profile," he confided. "Our people—"

"Which people are those?" Burnett interrupted.

"Our people," Bolan said again, ignoring him, "put me on the trail of one Jonathan West, thirty-four, a technician formerly employed by a company called Norris Labs. Have you heard of it?"

"Norris Labs International." Burnett nodded. "They do all that contract work in places like Iraq, right?"

"Yes," Bolan said. "There are only a few corporations larger. NLI has its hands in everything from pharmaceuticals and arms development to contracted military services ranging from catering to armed security. They retain a privately owned firm called Blackjack Group, whose contractors guard convoys and even sign on for field operations in Iraq, Afghanistan and other hot spots."

"And that's relevant because…"

"We believe NLI developed the depleted uranium small-arms ammunition," Bolan stated. "My people are analyzing it, but initial examination of the recovered fragments you originally sent to Washington correlated with some patents and weapons trials linked to NLI. They've been working, apparently, to miniaturize the depleted uranium ammunition currently in use in heavy weaponry, while increasing its antipersonnel potential."

"Where does this West guy fit in?" Burnett asked.

"West tried and failed to broker a deal for a large quantity of DU small-arms ammunition six months ago. His contact, he thought, represented a drug gang based in West Virginia. The gang's inquiries were part of an FBI sting.

"Domestic chatter had it that the ammunition was available. Several months of Internet chats and e-mails established that this fictitious group was looking for heavy armament, at which point they were contacted by Jonathan West. West quit or was fired from NLI several months prior to that—he says one thing, while they officially say another—which makes him a disgruntled employee with access to either the ammunition or plans for it."

"If you were trailing him here," Burnett said, "I gather the sting didn't go as planned."

"It fell through," Bolan admitted. "The FBI and a few associated agencies have been tracking West since, recently placing him here. He was using an Internet service to transfer money electronically from a credit account to what he thought was a safe drop, a post-office box here in the city. Once we knew where to look, we found more Internet traffic pointing to West trying to move the DU cartridges locally."

"And?"

"We created another fictional group looking for heavy firepower," Bolan said. "A white supremacist group based here in the greater New York area. A meet was arranged with West to discuss terms and prices. I was here to keep that meeting."

"Let me guess," Burnett said. "In Bryant Park."

"Exactly," Bolan said. "The rest you know."

Burnett shook his head again. "I don't know *jack*," he complained. "How does meeting West become a full-blown war?"

"There was no attempt to make contact before I was attacked in force," Bolan said. "That tells me either West sent them to intercept me and eliminate me—which wouldn't make much sense, unless he had reason to suspect me—or there's something much more complicated going on."

"Meaning what?" Burnett asked.

"Meaning, that I suspect those men were operatives for Blackjack Group—paid mercenaries, judging from their equipment and tactics."

"Why would NLI and their security firm risk open war in an American city?" Burnett asked.

"Think about it." Bolan nodded at the street beyond the window, at the people passing by. "You're a controversial corporation with ties to the military-industrial complex, as they say. Not the best public relations already. Now your experimental and very deadly ammunition is finding its way onto the streets of a city that's had its nose bloodied one time too many in recent memory. This goes way beyond the usual political posturing, cries for gun control, that kind of thing. If you were NLI's management, would you want your company linked to endangering the lives of innocent civilians on American streets? If it comes out that NLI is or did produce the munitions used, we're likely to see congressional action. To some people, that would be worth killing for to avoid."

"Do you have any proof of this?"

"No," Bolan said. "That's what I'm looking to find. West may or may not still be out there. If NLI and Blackjack sent those shooters to silence me, chances are good they're looking for West, too, if they haven't gotten to him already. If I run him down, I'll either get what he knows, or find a link to who took him out. Either way, it gets me closer to the source of the DU."

"I don't know exactly what connections you have, Cooper," Burnett said reluctantly, "but word has come down from the highest authority. I've been instructed to offer you every assistance in the pursuit of your objectives. Until you're through in New York, I'm your shadow."

"Which means you'll help me," Bolan said.

"It means," Burnett informed him, "that I'll drive."

3

Burnett piloted the unmarked Crown Victoria through canyons of glass and steel, flooring it whenever a clear straightaway offered itself in the congested mess that was Manhattan traffic. Several times he came so close to surrounding vehicles that Bolan thought one of the mirrors would be sheared off, but the car remained intact. At each stoplight, pedestrians flowed around the car like a river raging against worn rocks. All around them, the city throbbed with noise and activity, as millions of people went about their business.

Somewhere among those millions were people Bolan sought.

The Executioner's secure satellite camera-phone began to vibrate in his pocket. "Cooper," he answered, so whoever was listening at Stony Man Farm would know he was not alone and could not speak completely freely.

"Striker." Barbara Price's familiar voice spoke in Bolan's ear. "How are you holding up? We got an earful from Hal yesterday. He was fit to be tied."

"I don't doubt it," Bolan said. "When you get a chance, explain to him that there was no other way."

"I will, if he ever gets off the phone with the local, state and federal authorities in New York," Stony Man's honey-blond, model-beautiful mission controller said over the scrambled line. "I wouldn't hold my breath."

"I won't," Bolan acknowledged. "What have you got?"

"Some of the information you requested—technical specs and some dossiers per this morning's request."

"Go ahead," Bolan told her.

"All right," she said. "First, the DU rounds. Samples recovered from crime scenes in New York correspond to 9 mm, .45 and 5.56 mm small arms."

"You spoke with Cowboy?"

"Yes," Price said, knowing Bolan meant John "Cowboy" Kissinger, Stony Man's armorer. "Per your request last night, he's got a care package on its way to you. He also left me some specifications. He says the rounds are, as near as we can tell, depleted uranium cores sandwiched in tungsten shells and tipped in an accelerant that makes them explosive. They're incredible penetrators but also mildly radioactive and plenty poisonous. Get hit, and if the bullet doesn't kill you, the toxic shock might. Cowboy tells me the rounds are pyrophoric."

"Meaning they'll start fires where they hit?" Bolan asked.

"Very probably, because of the DU, the accelerant or both."

"What will it take to stop them?" Bolan asked.

"Nothing short of heavy vehicle armor will make a difference," Price informed him. "And we're not talking light protection like on an up-armored Humvee or even most armored personnel carriers. In heavier calibers, this would be an antitank round at the very least. It would take a tank to stop the small stuff. Stay out of the way of them, Striker."

"I'll do my best," Bolan said. "What have you pulled up concerning personnel?"

"I've got a possible address for Jonathan West, linked to a credit card that was recently used to purchase a variety of computer equipment. It's on the Upper West Side."

"Shoot," Bolan said.

Price gave him the address and the soldier passed it on to Burnett, who adjusted course accordingly. "We're rolling now. What else have you pulled up?"

"I've got photos and bios for Luis Caqueta, head of the Ca- queta Cartel. Also for his half brother, Carlos 'Eye' Almarone, and one of his lieutenants, known only as 'Razor' Ruiz. Their opposite number includes Pierre Taveras, leader of El Cráneo in New York, and two operatives whom we believe are in his inner circle—Julian 'July' de la Rocha and Jesus Molina."

"It's coming through now," Bolan confirmed, glancing at the color screen of his satellite phone and noting the data- transmission icons.

"Anything else?" Price asked.

"Just tell Bear and his team to keep working on that NLI data," Bolan said. "I need to know what and who I'm up against there. I'll have follow-ups as needed."

"Will do."

"I'll be in touch once we find West, if he's there," Bolan said.

"Be careful, Striker."

"Always," Bolan said. He closed the connection.

"Your mother?" Burnett said, eyes on the road.

"Something like that," Bolan replied.

"Yeah." Burnett almost chuckled. "Assuming that was your boss, or your people or whomever, we can cross-reference what you have with the task force's files." When Bolan said nothing, Burnett finally pressed, "Cooper, what is your story? How are you so connected in Washington? Just what are you after?"

"I want the same thing you want," Bolan told him. "I want those DU rounds off the streets. I want to stop the escalating war between El Cráneo and the Caquetas. And I want to find the men responsible for setting it all in motion."

Burnett regarded him for a moment before dodging a taxi and cutting off a panel truck to take position in a slightly less con- gested lane. He tromped the accelerator as soon as he had the shot. The Crown Victoria roared forward.

"Who are you, Cooper?" Burnett asked.

"Just a man," Bolan told him. "Just one man. Like you."

"Yeah," Burnett scoffed, "just an ordinary guy who runs around in a black commando suit under his jacket, hoping nobody will notice his odd fashion sense."

Bolan said nothing. The formfitting blacksuit he wore beneath his windbreaker was subtle enough that most people wouldn't notice it, but Burnett wasn't stupid. They both knew Bolan, whatever relationship he had to the Justice Department, was no ordinary government functionary. Bolan hoped the cop's respect for authority would keep the lid on his curiosity. It didn't hurt at all to have a local professional, somebody familiar with the battleground that was New York, to help Bolan with his search. If Burnett became a liability, however, Bolan would have to go it alone.

The two rode in silence for the remainder of the trip. Burnett parked in front of a fire hydrant when they reached their destination. They exited the vehicle and paused to look up at the five-story brownstone.

"What floor?" Burnett asked.

"Fifth," Bolan told him, patting himself down and checking the Beretta in its holster. "We'll have to search, once we get up there. Do you carry anything heavy in the trunk of this?" He gestured back to the unmarked car with his thumb.

"I've got an 870," Burnett told him.

Bolan nodded to the car. Burnett took the hint, unlocked the trunk and freed the Remington shotgun from its rack. He checked its loads and then scooped a handful of double-aught buckshot shells from a cardboard box in the trunk, dropping the shells into the left-hand pocket of his suit jacket.

"You expecting trouble?" Burnett asked.

"I always expect trouble," Bolan told him.

A woman in a frayed housecoat watched them from the steps of the brownstone, where she sat knitting something and drinking from a bottle in a paper bag. Bolan nodded as he passed her on the steps.

"Ma'am," Burnett said, carrying the shotgun close to his body and tipping an imaginary hat with his free hand.

Inside, the lighting was dim compared to the sunny autumn day outside. Bolan squinted and paused in the small entryway, letting his eyes adjust. Outside, the brownstone looked almost charming. Inside, the wallpaper was peeling and the interior was obviously divided into a warren of studio apartments. Burnett scanned the mailboxes mounted flush with one interior wall. Only a few had names, none on the fifth floor.

"I guess it wouldn't be that easy," Burnett said. The shotgun in both fists, he made for the stairs. Bolan followed. The rickety stairs creaked under their weight. As they climbed, Bolan drew the Beretta, his thumb swiping up the slide safety out of long habit. The stairwells smelled of urine. As they passed the third floor, they could hear someone screaming. Bolan paused only momentarily. It sounded like a domestic squabble. Shaking his head, Burnett looked upward and Bolan nodded. The two men finally made the fifth floor without incident.

"Now what?" Burnett asked quietly.

"Try these apartments nearest the stairs," Bolan told him. "I'll start at the other end. Stay sharp. If I flush him to you, try not to kill him."

"Right," Burnett said dubiously. "Because I was planning on shooting the suspect as soon as I saw him."

Bolan looked at Burnett hard. "Don't get yourself killed, either."

"I'll do my best," Burnett said. Bolan marched off. The two men started rapping on doors, both of them staying well clear of the doors themselves. Bolan had been on the receiving end of more than a little gunfire through locked doors before. Burnett either had experienced some of the same, or he was just good at his job. Either way, Bolan was glad not to have to hold his hand; the man was a veteran officer and knew his way around.

Bolan was on his third door, having received no answer and

hearing no movement at the first two, when the hollow-core door flew open.

"What the hell is it?" The woman who answered was slim and not unattractive, despite the heavy black eye makeup she wore. Her bottom lip pierced by several silver rings. She wore shorts and a halter top, her bare midriff covered in Celtic tattoos. Bolan, his gun held low behind his right leg, nodded to her.

"Miss," he said. "I'm looking for someone."

She smiled up at the Executioner. "What a coincidence," she said, one hand sliding idly up and down the door frame as she leaned in the doorway and eyed Bolan up and down. "So am I."

Bolan produced a small photo from the inside pocket of his windbreaker. "I'm looking for this man," he said, letting her get a good look at the photo of Jonathan West. "He might not look like this. He may have changed his hair color, or grown a beard or done something else to disguise himself."

The woman frowned through a lip full of metal. "You a cop?"

"No," Bolan said truthfully. "It's very important—"

Several shots rang out two doors down, as bullets peppered the thin wood of the apartment door on which Burnett had been knocking.

Burnett jacked the pump on his Remington 870, pressing himself against the wall beside the door. "Police!" he bellowed into the corridor. "This is a lawful entry!"

The door practically disintegrated under a withering full-auto blast, peppering the plaster of the opposite wall. Bolan tackled the woman before him, throwing her down through the doorway onto the scarred hardwood floor of her apartment. He stayed on top of her until the shooting stopped. Burnett's shotgun sounded like a cannon in the narrow corridor outside as the lawman fired back.

Bolan checked the woman beneath him, who looked at him with a mixture of fear and excitement. The Executioner nodded to the large windows at the end of the small studio, beyond which he could see a fire escape.

"Does that go all the way across the front of the building?" Bolan asked sharply.

She thought about it for a second. "Yes," she said, as Bolan got to his feet, his Beretta in a low two-hand grip. "It connects all the apartments on this side."

"Stay low," Bolan told her. "Don't go out until the shooting stops. And call 9-1-1!" He was moving before she could say more, throwing open the window and stepping outside. Wind tugged at his hair as he crept along the rusted metal fire escape. From the apartment two doors down, more gunfire erupted. It was the unmistakable chatter of an Uzi, punctuated by more of Burnett's shotgun blasts.

Wincing as his combat boots rang on the metal fire escape, Bolan slowed and dropped to his knees as he neared the window he wanted. Then he threw himself on his back, using his legs to shove himself forward as he stared skyward, concealing himself between the window ledge and the floor of the fire escape. Below him, New York City continued to bustle, temporarily oblivious to the slaughterhouse within the unassuming fifth-floor walk-up on the Upper West Side.

There was another lull in the automatic gunfire. Bolan popped up, his pistol held compressed against his chest in both hands. He fired twice, punching spidery holes in the window glass, then lowered his shoulder and dived through. He came up, still targeting the shadow he'd seen through the glass—a single, relatively small man with a submachine gun in his fists. The gunman was shoving another stick magazine into the grip of the weapon.

"West!" Burnett called from the hallway. "Stop!" The small man charged the door. Bolan dived aside as a shotgun blast from the doorway peppered the rear wall of the apartment. Then Burnett was down, tackled as the Uzi fell to the floor. The two rolled into the corridor. Bolan closed on the doorway, his Beretta leading, unable to get a clear shot.

"Cooper!" Burnett called, wrestling for his shotgun.

As Bolan approached he could see blood soaking the khaki shirt the small man wore. Burnett's blast hadn't been a complete miss. The cop used his size advantage to muscle his way to his feet, shaking the smaller man back and forth as the pair fought each with both hands on the Remington.

Bolan aimed the Beretta two-handed, trying and failing to acquire his target. He lowered the weapon, then raised it again as first Burnett, then the small man moved into his line of fire. "Down!" he shouted.

Burnett took the cue and dropped onto his rear, falling back and slapping his arms. The small man, who had been pushing against Burnett's resistance, flew forward with the shotgun in his hands. Bolan fired once, low, catching the gunman in the thigh. The man grunted and stumbled over Burnett down the corridor, out of Bolan's view. The shotgun fell from his fingers.

"Stop!" Burnett called. From the floor he clawed for the gun holstered on his hip. Bolan reached the doorway as the wounded gunman rammed the door of the woman's apartment two doors down. It opened and the woman screamed.

"Shit," Burnett cursed, pushing to his feet with a .40-caliber Glock in his fists.

"Back! Get back!" the gunman shouted. He reappeared in the corridor, one arm around the young woman's neck. He held a folding knife to her face, the serrated S-curved blade just barely below her right eye. His face was ashen. A pool of blood was forming where he stood.

Bolan advanced, the Beretta high in his line of sight. Burnett backed him as the two men crept forward.

"I said stop, damn your eyes," the small man said. He spoke in a clipped, British accent. "Come any closer and, I swear, I'll carve this bird's eye out."

The woman's eyes widened at that, but to her credit she remained still. Bolan's gaze found hers and her expression hardened with resolve.

"You're going into shock," the Executioner said. "You won't be on your feet for long."

"Get back, I said!" the wounded man shrieked. "I'm walking out of here, you lot, and little missy here is coming with me. If I start to go, I'll cut her throat as I do. Now, drop the hardware!"

Bolan nodded, almost imperceptibly.

The woman jerked her head to the side, away from the knife. It was just enough. Bolan's shot drilled through the man's eye. The body collapsed, a puppet with its strings cut, the folding knife still clutched in one dead hand.

The woman screamed.

"Easy," Burnett said, holstering his Glock. He went to her and put one arm around her shoulders as she started shaking. "Easy," he said again. "It's okay. We got him. We got him."

Bolan stepped around them and leaned over the corpse. There was a lot of gore, but most of the face was still visible. He took his phone from the inside pocket of his windbreaker and checked the photo viewer, examining the small image on the color screen.

Burnett, still calming the distraught woman, caught Bolan's frown. "Is it him?" he asked.

"No," Bolan said, steadying himself on one knee. He activated his phone's built-in digital camera, snapping a couple of shots of the dead man. "I'll transmit these—"

"To where?" Burnett queried.

"I'll send these," Bolan said evenly, "for analysis." He nodded to the woman. "Get her back to her apartment and call in before we're buried in units responding to the gunfire. I'm going to check West's apartment."

Burnett nodded and ushered the crying woman past the body and through her doorway. Bolan backtracked, unclipping the SureFire combat light from his pocket. With the Beretta and the light together in a Harries hold, he swept the cluttered and dim studio, wary for West or someone else hiding in ambush.

The studio was a wreck. Apart from the bullet holes just added to it, and the litter of empty pizza boxes, soda cans and other bags of garbage, what little furnishings it held had been torn apart. The sofa cushions had been cut open, as had the mattress sitting without a box spring in one corner. A set of bookshelves had been knocked over and many of the books torn up as whoever had tossed the place—probably the dead man in the hallway outside—searched for hiding places. A rolling computer desk bearing a state-of-the-art desktop unit was relatively unscathed, but the computer itself had been gutted.

Bolan checked near the desk and found the hard drive on the floor. It was badly damaged. No computer technician himself, Bolan was not sure if its data was retrievable or not, but he placed the drive in a pouch of his blacksuit nonetheless.

Behind the desk, on the floor in the far corner of the studio, Bolan found Jonathan West.

The image in his phone's data file confirmed it. It was Jonathan West and he was quite dead. The smell hit the Executioner as he examined the body, finding nothing in the man's pockets and discovering a small-caliber wound behind the dead man's left ear. Judging from the condition of the corpse, West had been murdered at least a few days previously.

The Executioner frowned again. The gunman he and Burnett had intercepted hadn't been here to kill West, at least not that day. That meant he'd had some other purpose in mind. Bolan's eyes fell on the gutted computer again. He would have the hard drive couriered to a mail drop for the Farm, where Aaron "The Bear" Kurtzman and his team could take a crack at it. Stony Man's wheelchair-bound computer expert and his assistants had worked similar miracles in the past. If anyone could manage it, they could. It might be nothing, of course. But it might just be the case that the dead man in the corridor had come to destroy the computer, which meant the information on it might be valuable.

Bolan was no cop and he had no interest in playing detective. He did, however, need to find the source of the DU ammunition. Without West, there was no telling where it might be, where it was coming from, or how much more of it could be waiting to hit the streets and turn them red. If West could not tell the Executioner his secrets, perhaps West's computer could.

"Cooper!" Burnett's voice was agitated as he called from the doorway to West's apartment. He held a wireless phone to his ear. "We may have a break."

Bolan holstered his Beretta. "What have you got?"

"The department called. It's Caqueta. The cartel wants to deal."

4

Burnett parked the Crown Victoria illegally, checking his Glock unnecessarily as he and Bolan exited the vehicle. As they crossed the street, a horse-drawn carriage clopped past, the tourists inside staring about happily. Both men paused for a hurtling yellow cab before taking the asphalt-covered path into Central Park.

"I hate leaving the shotgun in the car," Burnett said as they walked.

Bolan said nothing. He had his messenger bag slung over his shoulder across his body, his windbreaker covering the Beretta and his spare magazine pouches. Behind his left hip he wore a SOG Pentagon dagger in a custom Kydex Sheath inside his waistband. The guardless, double-edged, serrated dagger had a five-inch blade. There'd been no need for the weapon before now, but he'd worn it since arriving in New York and recovering the Beretta and his other personal items from the courier drop at the airport.

"That was good shooting back there," Burnett offered.

"You didn't do too badly yourself," Bolan said.

"Yeah, whatever." He looked back at the car as they left it behind. "Cooper, I'm bringing you in on this because I don't figure I can keep you out of it if I want to."

Bolan looked at him as joggers, power walkers and various people on bicycles passed the two men. He was uncomfortably aware of the number of innocents who might be caught in the line of fire. "If the Caquetas are part of the street war in New

York, the one West or someone else has been using as a market for the DU ammo, he's a legitimate target. He's also a potential source of information."

"Exactly," Burnett said. "Though I don't know as I would have listed them in that order." When Bolan said nothing, Burnett forced a chuckle. "I guess I still wouldn't mind having a little more firepower."

"Neither would I, but then, I said as much already."

"Don't go there." Burnett laughed genuinely this time.

Back in Jonathan West's apartment, Bolan had briefly considered taking the Uzi from the dead intruder in Jonathan West's apartment, but the idea had made Burnett too nervous. The weapon was evidence in the shooting, as was the knife the intruder had used. Burnett had assured Bolan that he'd be able to borrow suitable hardware from the department, given his pull with the powers that were. Bolan had in turn given Burnett an address to which they had driven before coming to the Caqueta meet in Central Park. There, at what was a government agency safehouse, they had shipped the hard drive to the secure mail drop that would, though Burnett didn't know it, get the data to Stony Man Farm in a matter of hours.

"Listen, Cooper," Burnett said soberly, "Caqueta is an animal. He's the elder statesman of the cartel now, but he used to get his hands plenty dirty, especially when he was clawing his way up the chain. We couldn't nail him on it, but early on in his stewardship of the Caqueta Cartel he killed an undercover narcotics agent with his bare hands. Beat him to death. His greatest hits, if you'll pardon the pun, include garroting a woman he suspected of cheating on him, using what used to be his favorite piece of piano wire stretched between two pieces of broomstick. He is also widely believed to have personally pulled the trigger on the family of the Colombian prosecutor who took him on in the late 1990s, trying to pin the Caquetas down at home. Shot the man's kids in front of the mother, then kneecapped her.

Had his lieutenant, Razor Ruiz, cut the eyes right out her head, so the death of her children would be the last thing she ever saw. She couldn't testify against him because she killed herself before the trial. Drank oven cleaner. It was ugly."

Bolan didn't comment. Caqueta and his people were no different than countless other thugs he'd battled in his War Everlasting. Luis Caqueta was a means to an end. He was also a predator whose people had shed gallons of innocent blood. He would not get any more chances to prey on New York or any other city, when the Executioner finished with him.

The two men followed the trail to the designated spot. There, on a park bench, sat Luis Caqueta. Bolan recognized him from the file photos.

Caqueta was a bit thick around the middle, with curly white hair cut close to his head. He was in good shape for a man his age, though, with strong, muscled forearms crossed over a silver-tipped walking stick. He wore a linen suit that was completely unnecessary in New York in autumn, but which would have looked right at home in Colombia. His face was smooth, almost peaceful, with subtle features that belied the monster staring out from his large, brown eyes.

The man standing behind the bench to Caqueta's right was also someone Bolan and Burnett recognized. Tall, painfully thin, with gaunt features and hollow, sunken eyes, Razor Ruiz stood almost at attention by his employer. He wore a lightweight dark trench coat over a black T-shirt and slacks. Bolan didn't like that at all; Ruiz could be hiding anything under that long coat.

There were no other men in sight. Bolan took in the landscape with one sweeping glance. There were several park buildings nearby, not to mention more than a few civilians going about their business. Some were sitting and reading. Others were playing with dogs or simply walking. Any of them could be plants to back up Caqueta. He could have troops stationed nearby, too.

It would not be the first time the Executioner had walked into an ambush to trigger it before rolling right over the top of it.

Ruiz had his hands in the pockets of his trench coat as Bolan and Burnett approached. They stopped a few feet from the park bench. Caqueta leaned forward on his cane but made no move to rise.

"So, Detective Burnett," Caqueta said, smiling like a shark. "You have come." His voice was a rich baritone, slightly accented. "And you bring a friend. Who is this large fellow?"

"That's really not—" Burnett began.

"You were instructed to come alone," Caqueta said sharply. "Yet you bring another. Explain to me why I do not simply leave now and let you take your chances."

"Cooper," Bolan told him. "Justice Department."

"Justice?" Caqueta's eyes widened. "And what would you know about justice, Mr. Cooper? Is it justice that my people are gunned down in broad daylight in the most prosperous part of this, the crown jewel of the East Coast? Is it justice that I must take ever more drastic means to protect them, to protect my family, to protect myself?"

"Spare me the tale of woe," Burnett said scornfully. "You and El Cráneo have been trying to take each other out for years. Now you've found a way to do it while endangering even more people. It's not enough for you that innocent men, women and children get caught in the line of fire while your family and Taveras's people gun for each other. Now you've got weapons guaranteed to cut up anyone within sight of your murders."

"Ah," Caqueta said thoughtfully. "You speak of the special bullets."

"No shit, Caqueta," Burnett said. "I speak of the *special bullets*. I know your organization isn't faring well in your war with El Cráneo, either. That's why you're not going to do anything but sit right here and tell me what you wanted to tell me. You wouldn't have called if you weren't desperate."

Caqueta shifted uneasily on the edge of the bench. Behind him, Ruiz bristled, his dark eyes flitting angrily from Burnett to Bolan and back again. Bolan watched as the detective worked Caqueta verbally. The man was good. Bolan's already high estimation of Burnett rose accordingly.

"It is true," Caqueta said reluctantly, staring at his feet, "that my enemies conspire against me and use El Cráneo to do this terrible thing."

"Meaning, they're beating you," Burnett interpreted.

Caqueta looked up at him sharply. "No, they are not," he said. "They have, however, successfully convinced the supplier of the bullets to sell the lion's share to them, those sons of pigs."

"So you're outgunned," Burnett said.

Caqueta shrugged. Behind him, Ruiz continued to glare. It was obvious he did not approve of the meeting.

"What do you want, Caqueta?" Burnett asked bluntly. "You called and said you wanted to deal. Well, deal. What have you got that I want?" Bolan looked from the tall detective to Caqueta. The answer was obvious.

"I can tell you how and where I purchased my supply of the bullets," Caqueta said. "Of course, this is all hypothetical. I would admit to nothing. I know of no bullets, none at all, when it comes to…to the record, you see?"

"I see," Burnett said grimly. "We look the other way and you help us put the supplier away."

"More or less." Caqueta nodded. "I can lead you to a certain fellow who brokered the sales with me and with Taveras, and he will lead you to your precious bullets."

"What assurances do we have that your information is legitimate?" Burnett asked.

"I have little choice," Caqueta said frankly. "To compete with El Cráneo my people must have weaponry to rival their own. Our supply—the supply we do not have, of course—of the ammunition is dwindling. Taveras has increased his own stockpiles.

El Cráneo is planning something, something very big. It is the way they think, the way they operate. They plan to show me, to teach me—me!—a lesson. They will also show you and your people that you are powerless to stop them."

"Give me a name," Burnett demanded.

Ruiz turned to his boss. "Jefe, no! Give them that, and—"

"Silence!" Caqueta roared.

He turned back to Burnett. "The man's name is West."

"Too late," Burnett told him. "We're ahead of you. West is dead."

"Is he, now?" Caqueta said, unimpressed. "Not much of a surprise. A man like that, a man meddling in so many different affairs of life and death. Such a man must have many enemies, no?"

"You have nothing for me, then," Burnett said.

"Do not be so quick to dismiss me," Caqueta said, his voice hard again. "Either your people are not as thorough as mine, or NLI is not as forthcoming with the law as it might be."

"What do you know about Norris Labs?" Bolan put in. Caqueta eyed the big soldier, his expression stern.

"I know that this West quit some time ago, some months before my people made the first purchases of his very useful, very powerful bullets for our weapons. And I know that he quit after another man, a much more significant man, was fired. This fellow was a researcher, a developer of arms. It would seem, my sources tell me, that this man was full of great and useful ideas. He was unappreciated by his employers, and when he complained of as much, they deemed him too troublesome and sent him away. West was his assistant at NLI. It would seem he was loyal to the man, not the company. Or perhaps he was loyal only to money, and was offered more than his former employers would give. That is often the way, is it not?"

"Why do you know all this?" Burnett asked.

"Would you not look into the men on whom you staked the

fate of your family, your business, your honor?" Caqueta
shrugged. "West contacted us after the first sales were made to
El Cráneo. He arranged for a demonstration. He asked that I send
one of my bulletproof limousines—and a driver of whom I was
not terribly fond. He found some piece of street trash, gave him
a magazine full of bullets for his pistol. When my driver arrived
at the meet, he was killed immediately. The bullets passed
through the armored car and through a fire hydrant nearby."

"So you had no choice but to escalate the war," Burnett said
skeptically.

"None," Caqueta said. "West told me in no uncertain terms
just how much ammunition my enemies had purchased. It was
only a matter of time. We—hypothetically, of course—armed
ourselves accordingly. But a few months later, he stopped an-
swering our messages. El Cráneo grew bolder, more vicious. I
lost more men even as I took down theirs. We are running out
of the special bullets. El Cráneo had obviously cut a deal with
West, offered him more than I could."

"They're winning the war," Burnett said.

Caqueta shrugged again. "They do not have to. You can stop
this. Things can be…shall we say, much more calm. More like
they used to be."

"While you continue shipping your poison," Burnett said.

"I do not force it up anyone's nose or into anyone's veins,"
Caqueta said. "I am interested in business, not war."

Burnett sighed. "Like you," he said, "I don't know what
choice I have. Let's get this straight, though. I'm not making any
promises, Caqueta. If I could nail you to the wall, I would do
it."

Caqueta laughed. "But of course you would, Detective Burnett. That is what makes you safe. You are predictable. As long
as I am not stupid enough to give you evidence you can use
against me in court, you are no threat to me. And as long as you
have no such evidence, I am no threat to *you*."

"All right," Burnett nodded. "We understand each other. Give me the name."

"The man you seek," Caqueta said, "is—"

Something caught Bolan's attention. Reflexes honed over years of battle kicked in. Whether it was a simple shift in the wind, or some other subconscious cue, something was wrong.

"Down!" Bolan yelled. He tackled Burnett, just as Luis Caqueta's head exploded.

They heard the gunshot as Caqueta's nearly headless body fell forward onto the ground before the bench. There was a single, still moment in which Razor Ruiz, splattered with his boss's blood, looked up with wide eyes. He glanced down at Caqueta's body and to the ground behind the bench, where a tiny blade smoldered.

"Treachery!" he shouted. From within his trench coat he brought up a pistol-gripped Mossberg 590 12-gauge shotgun.

"Go!" Bolan told Burnett, drawing his Beretta.

All hell broke loose.

The unseen sniper cut loose with a rapid string of shots. Bolan spotted the gunman firing a scoped, match-barreled AR-15. He was on the roof of a nearby building. The Executioner pushed Burnett as the two men scrambled to the cover of a nearby tree. They threw themselves aside when several shots punched through the bark of the tree and into the asphalt path beyond. Burnett shouted a warning as they ran, the tree behind them catching fire from the inside out. Nearby civilians screamed and either dropped flat or ran. With no real way to counter the DU projectiles, Bolan and the detective could do only one thing. They fled.

Razor Ruiz ran after them, firing his shotgun blindly in the direction of the shooter. It was enough to foul the sniper's aim until the Caqueta Cartel man and his quarry were out of the sniper's line of sight.

Burnett was on his phone as they moved, calling in backup.

It was unlikely they'd arrive in time to take down the sniper. The shooter would undoubtedly be extracting by now. Still, Burnett had to try. When he was sure they were safely out of the gunner's killzone, Bolan put a hand on Burnett's shoulder and gestured to a recently tilled-over flower garden near the asphalt path. It had two-foot brick walls surrounding it. Bolan and Burnett crouched behind the bricks and waited.

"We need him alive, if we can get him," Bolan told the detective.

"No problem," Burnett said. "He's a law-abiding citizen. I'll just arrest him."

In a moment, Ruiz came running down the path, still carrying the shotgun.

"Ruiz!" Burnett shouted. "Stop right there!"

Ruiz yelled something incoherent, jacked a shell into his shotgun's chamber and punched a 12-gauge slug into the brick near Burnett's face. The cop jerked his head back, his fingers clawing at his eyes, screaming.

Bolan rolled away and surged to his feet, coming around the low wall and diving at Ruiz. He tackled the gaunt man and took him down roughly. The two rolled into the muddy grass near the path.

Ruiz was stronger than he looked. The two men grappled furiously, Ruiz screaming curses in Spanish the entire time. The cartel thug managed to get on top of Bolan as the soldier put his legs up in guard. Bolan did not want to shoot Ruiz, but the thug spotted the holstered weapon in his adversary's waistband and grabbed for it.

Slapping his right hand deep onto the tang of the Beretta in its holster, Bolan caught Ruiz's hand and forearm in the crook of his own arm. He tightened his arm, trapping Ruiz before the wiry man could pull the weapon free. Shoving with all his might, Bolan got his knees up in front of Ruiz, levering the man up. Then he fired a savage kick into his stomach. The cartel man rolled off Bolan, gagging and retching.

Bolan scrambled to his feet and he kicked Ruiz hard in the head. The man dropped to his belly on the ground and was still.

The Executioner drew his Beretta, glancing left and right—

And found himself staring into the barrel of a Glock.

Burnett was silent. Bolan glanced in the detective's direction and found him prone near the flower garden, unmoving.

"Move an inch in my direction and I'll shoot you in the head," the man with the Glock told him. He had Bolan covered from behind. From what he could see, looking over his shoulder, the Executioner couldn't identify the newcomer.

"Who are you?" Bolan asked.

"I could ask you the same thing," the man said. "Place the gun on the ground very slowly." He was just under six feet tall, solidly built, wearing cargo pants and a denim shirt under a tan photographer's vest. Bolan noted his footwear, which weren't work boots at all, but tan combat boots with tanker straps. On his face the man wore wraparound smoked shooting glasses. His prematurely gray hair was cropped close to his skull in military fashion.

Bolan glanced to Burnett again as he placed the Beretta carefully on the walking trail. There was no one close by; it was unlikely anyone would see what was happening and call for help. The gunman gestured Bolan back and then picked up the Beretta, his Glock never wavering. He tucked the Beretta into his waistband behind his back.

"He'll live," the man told him, jerking his head at Burnett. "Answer my questions and you might, too."

Bolan just looked at him.

"I want your name and the agency you're working for," the man said. He stood carefully out of Bolan's reach.

"You seem to have misplaced your rifle," Bolan said. He didn't know for a fact that this man was the sniper, but the look on the gunman's face told him he'd guessed correctly.

"This weapon," he said, his eyes flickering to the Glock,

"will punch through a dozen of you single-file. The caliber's different, but the ammo's the same. Now, answer my question."

Bolan eyed him hard. He was considering the lunge needed to reach the man when Razor Ruiz suddenly pushed up and attacked, screaming, a knife blade flashing in his fist.

The Glock went off. The gunman yelled in pain as Ruiz slashed deeply into the wrist of his gun hand, kicked him low in the shin and followed him down with the blade, stabbing again and again with sewing-machine strokes.

Bolan grabbed Ruiz by the head and peeled him off, twisting and hurling him sideways. Ruiz shook it off and wheeled on the soldier, his bloody knife held before him.

"Now, you bastard," Ruiz hissed, "now I carve off a piece of you!"

Bolan drew his SOG Pentagon knife left-handed. Ruiz narrowed his eyes as he took in the double serrated blade. The soldier crouched low, the knife reversed in his hand. "You don't have to do this," he told Ruiz. "That man—" he nodded to the fallen gunman "—is the shooter who killed your boss."

"I know!" Ruiz spit. "And I have taken revenge for him!"

"You have," Bolan said evenly. "You've even done me a favor."

"And now," Ruiz said, advancing with his blade before him, "I shall kill you and then the policeman, for luring us into this ambush."

"I don't know how they knew to take out Caqueta," Bolan said, slowly circling as Ruiz rounded on him, "or who they were protecting to do it. You can help."

"Help?" Ruiz laughed. In the distance, the first sirens wailed. "Why would I help you?"

"Your boss was going to help us find the source of the DU rounds," Bolan told him. "He knew it was in his best interests."

"He was wrong!" Ruiz lunged with the knife. Bolan sidestepped and slashed, scoring Ruiz lightly on the arm. The cartel killer snarled and backed off a couple of paces. "He never should have trusted the police. You see where it got him!"

Bolan could see the first uniformed officers closing on them through the park. He was running out of time. Ruiz glanced back and then to Bolan again. "They will take me," he said, "but not before I take you!"

When the thrust came, Bolan was ready. He slapped Ruiz's wrist with his right hand while drawing the Pentagon's blade over the top of the man's forearm, slicing deeply through the arm. Ruiz howled as Bolan followed up, slapping and trapping to the outside, moving to his opponent's right outside his weapon. With a stomp he broke the killer's ankle under the heel of his combat boot. Ruiz folded, wailing.

"Don't move! Drop the knife!" The uniformed officers were closing in, guns drawn.

For the second time in as many days, Bolan slowly raised his hands and did as he was instructed.

5

Mack Bolan sat on the bed in his hotel room, lacing up his combat boots. He wore his combat blacksuit, which to the casual observer would look like a black mock turtleneck and black pants tucked into his boots. The slit pockets of the blacksuit bore some of his gear, leaving room for much more. On the floor before him was a large shipping crate, delivered by special courier from Stony Man Farm early that morning. The Executioner was in the process of unpacking the crate when his secure phone vibrated.

"Striker," he said.

"Good morning, big guy," Barbara Price said brightly. "I take it you got Cowboy's special delivery?"

"Unwrapping it now," Bolan told her. "Did Bear and his crew have any luck with the photos I sent?"

"Transmitting now," Price confirmed. "The shooter in West's apartment was Basil Price, forty-eight. British, with a sheet that goes back a ways. A veteran merc with two years in Rhodesia, SAS, to his credit."

"Just the sort of person a private security firm might employ?" Bolan said.

"Possibly," Price said. We've queried NLI and their contractor, Blackjack Group. If they've got anything in their files, it's squirreled away where Bear can't crack it. Officially, Blackjack never heard of the man."

"Not surprising," Bolan said.

"It gets more interesting," Price said. "Your other body is John Paul Reynolds, thirty-six. Gulf War veteran, Marines, with some contract security work after that."

"And?"

"The work was with Blackjack Group," Price told him, "and it was while he was in Blackjack's employ that he died on the job, supposedly, a year ago in Baghdad."

"So he's been off the books for a year, playing dead, most likely doing black ops for Blackjack."

"Seems so," Price said.

"Then NLI is involved up to its board members' necks," Bolan concluded. "They're actively trying to sever links leading back to them, using Blackjack as muscle."

"Striker, if they took out West and sent someone else to destroy his records, then somehow keyed into your meet with Caqueta, they've got the city wired or they've got someone inside, maybe both."

"The thought occurred to me," Bolan said grimly. "Any luck with the hard drive I got from West's apartment?"

"Not much yet," Price said. "Bear has Akira working on it, but he says it's in pretty sorry shape."

"Have him keep at it," Bolan said. "It's the only lead I've got after Ruiz, who isn't going to talk on his own. Listen, Barb, I need you to contact Hal for me and let him know it's going to get heavier. I'll need him to run interference for me so I can do this my way. I'm done playing it subtle. I've got to put a stop to this. It's going to get a lot bloodier before it gets better."

"I'll tell him. And, Striker?"

"Yeah?"

"Watch your back."

"I will." He closed the connection.

From the closet where he'd left his windbreaker the previous evening, Bolan took his long, charcoal-colored canvas duster. The lightweight overcoat was perfect for the autumn temperatures, so he wouldn't be too conspicuous. More importantly, the long coat would hide a multitude of sins, as the saying went. Draping the coat over the hotel-room chair, he turned back to the crate Stony Man's couriers had dropped off.

The Farm's armorer had outdone himself. Cowboy Kissinger had sent Bolan's usual equipment with a few bonuses. Bolan first removed the big Desert Eagle .44 Magnum pistol from the box. Kissinger had sent a tactical thigh holster, which Bolan strapped to his right leg. It bore pouches for several spare magazines. He loaded them from the boxes provided and tucked it into place.

In addition to his Beretta 92-F Bolan now had his familiar Beretta 93-R machine pistol. Kissinger had included a custom leather pistol rig that would accommodate the 93-R with its attached suppressor vertically under his left arm. The 92-F he placed inside his waistband in its holster, which he repositioned for a reverse left-hand draw behind his left hip. He moved the SOG Pentagon knife closer to the midpoint of his back, where the knife could be drawn with either hand. He also distributed several loaded magazines for the Berettas in the pockets of his blacksuit. Finally, he clipped the SureFire tactical light in place in a left-hand pocket and clipped the Cold Steel Gunsite Folding Knife to the right. The sturdy, chisel-ground, Tanto blade combat folder had been sent at Bolan's specific request.

From the crate Bolan took Kissinger's final gift. Unfolding the stock, he admired the businesslike lines of the chopped and tuned Ultimax 100 MK4 as he brought it to his shoulder.

A machine gun made in Singapore, the Ultimax was a lightweight, gas-operated, select-fire weapon with a standard cyclic rate of 600 rounds per minute. A simple, robust design firing the 5.56 mm cartridge, easily fieldstripped with all pins captive, the Ultimax had a forward pistol grip mounted under a thirteen-inch barrel. A red-dot scope had been mounted on top of the receiver. Kissinger had included a shoulder strap compatible with Bolan's

93-R rig, so he could sling the weapon under his right arm. The Ultimax was fitted with an adapter that made it compatible with standard AR-15/M-16 magazines. The armorer had also sent several impressive 100-round drum magazines, the rears of the magazines made of clear Lexan to allow for instant assessment of the rounds remaining.

Bolan packed spare M-16 magazines and Ultimax drums in his canvas messenger bag, hanging the war bag across his body on his left side. Then he put on the duster, checking the concealment of his weapons in the full-size hotel mirror on the closet door. Satisfied, he left the room, stalking down the hotel corridors and making his way through the lobby and out the front door.

New York foot traffic bustled past him in both directions. Joining the stream, he allowed himself to be carried along by it. He had gone perhaps two blocks when, in the reflection of the glass front of an office building, he caught sight of the tail.

He had expected to be followed. Everything that had gone down so far indicated that NLI and Blackjack—if those were indeed the forces pulling the strings and triggers—were monitoring him and knew he was a threat. That was why they'd tried to take him out in Bryant Park. Bolan was through reacting, letting the other side dictate the terms. It was time to take the initiative and take the war to the enemy.

The Executioner walked until he found a suitable dark alley. He ducked into it quickly, as if trying to dodge the tail, but not so quickly that he was in danger of actually losing his pursuer. Once out of sight in the shadowy, trash-filled alleyway, he ran heavily to the midpoint of the alley and threw himself to the side, taking cover in the lee of an overfilled garbage bin. Seconds later, he heard footsteps at the mouth of the alley. There were at least two people following Bolan.

To their credit, they didn't waste time conferring with each other or calling out to him, telling him to give it up. They just moved down the alley, presumably with guns drawn. The Executioner waited until they encroached on his position. Then he struck.

There were three men, not two, all big, buzz-cut paramilitary types in casual civilian clothes. Bolan unclipped the combat light from his pocket as he rose, clenching the little aluminum flashlight, beam-down, in his fist. The first man had time to turn and claw for a weapon as Bolan hammer-fisted the light into the man's temple. As he dropped, Bolan snapped a soccer kick into the ankle of the second pursuer, then drove the flashlight up under the man's jaw.

The third man had drawn a silenced Glock. Bolan sidestepped, playing the bright beam of the light across the gunner's eyes to little effect. A pair of shots slapped at the concrete face of the building behind Bolan. He was already drawing the Beretta 93-R as he let the combat light fall from his grasp. A 3-shot burst spit from the custom suppressor, taking the gunner in the throat. He fell back, his head cracking on the filthy asphalt.

Bolan snatched up his fallen light and swiveled to cover the other two pursuers. In the stark beam of the light he could see the first man was still out, his head cocked at an odd angle. The second man was holding his broken ankle with one shaking hand, while groping for something under his jacket. Bolan put the beam of light on the man's face and covered him with his machine pistol.

"I need you alive," Bolan told him, "but to be honest, I only need *one* of you."

The man, his face twisted with pain, looked up at the Executioner.

"Take your hand out of your jacket very slowly," Bolan ordered.

The shots, when they came, echoed in the alleyway.

Bolan threw himself aside, seeking the shelter of the garbage bin. Full-auto fire came from a Ruger MP-9 in the hands of the

first downed man, who sprayed the alleyway. His target was not
Bolan, but the second man. The rounds burned through the victim and chewed into the opposite wall of the alley, igniting
small, hungry fires directly in the brick and mortar.

Bolan turned his machine pistol on the first man.

The gunman brought the Ruger MP-9 up under his own chin
and pulled the trigger. The blast sprayed the top of his head
across the alleyway in a rain of DU ammunition that broke up
the wall behind him.

Bolan, 93-R in hand, scanned the alleyway behind him. When
he saw no other threats, he bent quickly to search the corpses.
He found nothing but spare magazines for the firearms used.
There was no identification on any of the bodies.

"Down here!" someone called out. Bolan glanced toward the
mouth of the alley. The gunfire had been heard by someone, and
curious onlookers were milling about. He moved quickly in the
opposite direction, putting distance between himself and the
carnage. He had too much to do and could not afford to get em-
broiled in yet another analysis of his actions. The New York authorities were already strained to the breaking point where it
came to the mysterious government operative, Matt Cooper. He
couldn't take the chance that they'd let him go on about his business after finding yet more bodies in his wake.

As he walked briskly out of the alley and joined the stream
of foot traffic moving down the block, Bolan considered the
situation. He knew that hired guns, most likely NLI Blackjack
operatives, were tailing him personally. The hit on Luis Caqueta
could have been a coincidence and still could be; clearly Caqueta
had information that the DU ammunition's suppliers had wanted
concealed at any cost. It was unlikely that Bolan and Burnett had
been specifically targeted at Jonathan West's apartment, but the
timing of Basil Price's break-in was suspect. West had been
killed some time previously, apparently to keep him silent. He
either talked before he died, or he left behind equivalent infor-

mation, but the men who'd murdered him had deemed Bolan a sufficient threat to them that they'd bothered to come after him in force.

Bolan briefly wondered if perhaps more than one group was in play, but that didn't feel right. Reynolds and Price—one a much younger American former soldier, the other a hard-bitten British career mercenary—had nothing in common, at first glance, except for their skills. Both men were precisely the sort of employees likely to be hired by a security contractor like Blackjack Group. The Executioner would continue to assume that Blackjack and NLI were behind the scores of professional boots on the ground in New York. There was no overt legal action Brognola or his Justice Department could take in the meantime—not without proof. The Executioner didn't need to meet the same standards of evidence before he could take action, but a direct assault on NLI's assets, or on Blackjack Group, would have to wait.

If those working to cover up the DU ammunition source had decided to move on Bolan directly, he figured it was likely they'd target Burnett, as well.

The Executioner flagged down the first available taxi. The cabdriver nodded when Bolan gave him the hospital name, pulling smoothly into the never-ending stream of Manhattan traffic. Bolan leaned to the side until, through his window, he could see the taxi's passenger-side mirror. He watched for a time until he was satisfied that he was not being followed.

Fifteen minutes later, Bolan was walking down the corridor to Burnett's room. He had almost reached the detective when he heard loud voices. Then he heard a man scream.

The soldier broke into a sprint. His combat boots left black streaks on the waxed floor as he rounded the corner, the Beretta 93-R in his hand.

A body lay half in and half out of the doorway to Burnett's room. Bolan noted the expensive tactical boots on the prone form's feet. As he neared the doorway, a shot rang out. Bolan threw himself to the side of the door.

"Burnett!" he called.

"Cooper?"

"Cooper. Hold your fire!" Bolan shouted.

He waited for a moment before chancing a one-eyed look around the edge of the doorway. Burnett, wearing only a hospital gown, sat up in his bed, one foot on the floor. He held a stainless-steel Smith & Wesson .38 snubnose revolver in one hand, aimed at the door.

"Don't shoot, I'm coming in," Bolan warned.

"Please do," Burnett said.

Bolan stepped over the fallen man in the doorway, who looked to be dead. He was wearing a white medical smock and lying in a spreading pool of blood. The handle of what could only be a fork protruded from his neck.

"Hospital food," Burnett said as Bolan shot him a quizzical look. "You've got to draw the line somewhere."

Bolan took in the tableau before him. On the floor near the bed, a tray and a broken plate were overturned in a puddle of soup. The wall and floor were sprayed with blood. Burnett had hit the artery. Near the corpse was a syringe, still loaded with an unknown liquid.

"What tipped you off?" Bolan asked, checking the corridor with a backward glance.

"The boots," Burnett said. "That, and the fact that he was too polite. They don't waste any time on bedside manner around here. He brought my dinner and then fumbled the needle. I didn't give him another chance to stick me."

"How's the eye?" Bolan asked.

"Going to be okay." Burnett gestured to his right eye, which was covered by a circular bandage and some gauze. "I won't be using it for several days, though. The brick fragments scratched the cornea." Burnett's other eye was very red but apparently not injured as badly. The detective paused to snap open the cylinder of his .38, extract the spent round by hand and load a replacement from a speed strip on the bed next to him. "I'm going to stop keeping my gun under my pillow and start sleeping with it on me."

"You'd better get dressed," Bolan warned. "There may be more of them waiting to see if this one makes it out of the hospital to report." He bent over the corpse and took a shot with his phone camera. He'd transmit it to the Farm later. His guess was that little useful information would be turned up. NLI and Blackjack seemed to have deep pockets when it came to personnel—personnel with plausible deniability, at that.

"I have a car in the parking garage below the hospital," Burnett told him as they left the room and made for the stairs. Burnett had tried first to head for the elevators, but Bolan had stopped him. There was no need to trap themselves; Blackjack's operatives, assuming that's who they were, had no need of gift-wrapped targets. They were dangerous enough operating on an even playing field.

They made the garage without incident and took Burnett's Crown Victoria to the detention center. There, they were stopped in the screening area, where a uniformed officer checked Burnett's revolver and the Glock he'd retrieved from a lockbox in the trunk of his unmarked car. Bolan flashed the Justice credentials Brognola had provided him.

"I'm sorry, Mr. Cooper," the blond officer told him, gesturing to the tray connecting the foyer of the screening room to her booth, "but you're going to have to check your weapons. Firearms are not permitted past this point." Bolan hesitated. There were plenty of times he had relinquished his weapons when the need arose, but given the bold and ruthless tactics Blackjack had employed to this point, he didn't think it wise to give up his guns.

Burnett sensed the soldier's hesitation, though Bolan didn't know just how much hardware the detective realized Bolan was carrying. "Listen," he told the Executioner, his uncovered eye blinking rapidly as he squinted in the bright lighting of the foyer, "let me go in and speak to Ruiz. Maybe I can get something. Maybe I won't. You said yourself on the way here you didn't think he'd cooperate. Hang out for a bit and if I think you can get more, or if I need help, I'll call for you."

Bolan nodded. He'd seen the cop work and knew he was no amateur. It was a reasonable proposition. "You feel up to it?" he asked.

"I don't need both eyes to talk to this joker." Burnett smiled. "Though I think I'll keep my fingers away from his mouth. He's got a real rabid dog look to him."

"Good luck."

"Thanks," Burnett said. He waited while the young female officer buzzed him through, stepped through the security doors and disappeared down the hallway.

Waiting in the foyer, Bolan took a seat on one of the benches provided, his duster spilling over it and concealing the Ultimax and his other gear. His messenger bag thumped heavily on the wooden bench, but there was no one to notice. Except for the officer in her booth, Bolan was alone, save perhaps for the surveillance cameras that would be monitoring anyone sitting in the little room.

The soldier took a moment to key on his secure phone and transmit the photo of the hospital killer. Almost immediately, the phone began to vibrate with an incoming call.

"Cooper," he said, holding the phone to his ear.

"It's me," Barbara Price said.

The Executioner could picture the Farm's stunning mission controller seated at her desk. "What have you got?" he asked.

"Akira's turned up a lead on that hard drive," Price told him. "He's still working on it to see what else we can mine. Indications are that there's a lot of data someone tried to delete. That would be easy to recover if not for the damage to the drive itself."

"I figured," Bolan said, nodding, even though she could not see him.

"What we've got may help, though. Akira turned up a fragment of a spreadsheet program that includes payments made through a private mailbox at one of those shipping storefronts. We traced the shipper's records—Bear tells me their security wasn't terribly impressive—and the box is owned by a nonexistent limited liability corporation registered out of state. Some more digging turned up an address for the corporation, tied to yet another drop box, tied in turn to an address in Swedesboro, New Jersey."

"That's pretty thin," Bolan commented.

"It's all we've got so far," Price said.

"Send me the file. I'll visit as time allows. How far is Swedesboro from here?"

"You should be able to make it in a couple of hours, give or take. Why don't you let us send a team of blacksuits to check it? It will save you time."

"All right," Bolan said. He paused. "You gave my message to Hal?"

"Yes, and he's still buried, doing damage control. What the hell is going on there, Striker?"

"Things have gotten hotter than even I thought they would," Bolan said. "I came expecting drug gangs and I've spent most of my time fighting trained paramilitary troops. They don't care who gets in the way and they're highly motivated to stay out of our hands. They're audacious, ruthless and armed with the DU ammunition."

"We're untangling the bulletins and the complaints on this end, routing through and back to Hal's office," Price informed him. "Striker, if it gets much worse the governor's going to call out the National Guard. The mayor is burning up the phone lines between New York and Washington. Hal even got a phone call from the vice president about half an hour ago."

"I can't say I'm surprised," Bolan said grimly. "I'm not going to have much fighting room left. What about Justice intervention?"

"Hal is working the NLI front," Price said, "but they're stonewalling. Blackjack's reps won't speak with anyone. They've pulled up the drawbridges. Unless we can get some leverage on them, there's little to be done."

"I'll deal with them in turn, then," Bolan promised.

"Good hunting, Striker."

"Thanks, Barb." Bolan hung up.

As he secured his phone in a pocket of his blacksuit under his duster, three men entered the detention-center foyer. One, a slight man with thinning hair and round-framed spectacles, wearing a three-piece suit and carrying a briefcase, was obviously a lawyer. The second was a thickset Hispanic man wearing wraparound shades and a sport jacket that didn't hide the bulge of the gun under his left arm. He was obviously hired muscle, probably a bodyguard. Between the lawyer and the larger man was someone Bolan recognized from the intelligence files the Farm had transmitted.

Carlos "Eye" Almarone, Luis Caqueta's half brother, had been Caqueta's most brutal enforcer in Colombia. His record, Bolan knew from studying the intel, was no less distinguished. Multiple murders of men, women and even children were speculatively associated with him. Almarone was particularly fond, said the files, of the Colombian Necktie, cutting his victims' throats and leaving their tongues to hang from the slit. Almarone had a lazy eye, the obvious source of his nickname.

Almarone bristled when he saw Bolan. He was a head shorter than the Executioner, slim and tanned, wearing a beige, double-breasted designer suit. His craggy face was outlined by a thin jawline beard and carefully trimmed mustache. His dark eyes flashed behind half-tinted glasses as he glared at the soldier.

"You, *cabron*," he said. "I know you. You are as Razor described you."

"And I know you, Almarone," Bolan told him.

"I should kill you right here, *pendejo,*" Almarone said, taking a step forward. The Executioner looked down at him, relaxed but ready.

"Make your play, Almarone," he said without emotion.

There was a tense moment as Almarone almost took the bait. Then he backed off, slapping the back of his hand against his bodyguard's large chest. "This little *puto,* he thinks to goad me," he said as if sharing a private joke with the man. The bodyguard stared at Bolan, face frozen, clearly not amused. Almarone forced a laugh and pushed his lawyer forward into Bolan's path. "Here, *pendejo,*" he said. "My lawyer, he will fight my battles this day. We are here for Razor Ruiz. You will give him to us."

"That's not likely," Bolan told him.

"I'm afraid we don't have a choice," Burnett said as the officer in the booth buzzed him through the secure doors. He brought Bolan a stack of paperwork. "These were faxed over half an hour ago. Ruiz had them. He's being released, charges dropped. Lack of evidence."

"What?" Bolan demanded. He glanced at the papers and then back to the smug Almarone, who was whispering something to the lawyer. "Lack of evidence? The man stabbed Reynolds to death right in front of me."

"Self-defense," Almarone said. "Clearly, the powers that be understand that a man cannot be held accountable for what he does in the heat of the moment, in defense of his own life."

"The fix is in, Cooper," Burnett said through clenched teeth. "Someone upstairs has pulled strings."

"You will excuse us," Almarone said, ushering the lawyer toward the doors. "We are going to escort my family's trusted friend. I will be seeing you, *cabron.* I will be seeing you very soon."

6

"Do you really think anything will pan out?" Burnett asked, sitting in the passenger seat of the parked Crown Victoria. He had the directional microphone pointed out the window, where he leaned his elbow on the door. A half-empty coffee cup was cradled in his free hand.

From the driver's seat, Bolan swallowed the last of his hamburger, watching through the high-powered monocular he usually kept in his war bag. From their vantage point in the parking lot, hidden in plain sight among the rows of other cars, they could see Carlos Almarone, Razor Ruiz and two bodyguards seating themselves in the chain restaurant just off the Garden State Parkway. Fortunately, they chose a smoking-section booth near a window, making it easy to pick up their speech.

"I want Ruiz," Bolan said. "If we let him go to ground, there's no telling how long it will take to pick him up again. Caqueta was ready to tell us something, something useful. He knew this goes farther than West. Ruiz is the most direct route."

"We're obviously dealing with a lot of power in high places," Burnett countered.

"A predator is a predator," Bolan said simply. "I don't give a damn how many connections Almarone or his organization might have. I want Ruiz, and I intend to take down Almarone in the process. They're a means to an end."

Burnett looked at him, then back across the parking lot to the restaurant. "You're just lucky I had the surveillance equipment in the car. This morning I was lying in the hospital talking to a pretty nurse. I didn't figure I'd be on stakeout a few hours later."

It had been a fast ride from the city to just inside New Jersey, Bolan using all his wheelman experience to stay with the drug lord's Mercedes while remaining undetected. Burnett, with one eye bandaged, had been happy to let the soldier drive. Once Almarone and his men had chosen a place to stop, Burnett had gone on foot to a neighboring fast-food place and returned with lunch.

They'd picked up Almarone fairly easily. That, too, had been Burnett's idea. They'd merely tailed the man from the detention center's parking garage, Bolan being careful to use the heavy traffic to camouflage them. The Executioner had worried initially that Almarone would be looking for a tail, but his arrogance had apparently left him complacent. During the drive out of the city and into the neighboring Garden State, there had been no indication the drug dealer or his bodyguards suspected they were being followed.

Bolan took one of the two earbuds snaking from the directional microphone and placed it in his ear. Burnett did likewise. There was a lot of background noise and radio-frequency interference, but they could easily separate the target conversation from the rest.

"You realize what this means?" Ruiz was saying angrily. "Luis is dead, Carlos! Your own blood decorates the streets of New York! Taveras will be looking to take us down while we are weak!"

"What would you have us do?" Almarone said dismissively. "Go to war, now? Burn Taveras's home? Kill his family? Torture his pets, perhaps?"

"Damn you, I am serious," Ruiz said. "We are at war already! We have been killing El Cráneo soldiers for weeks. They have been killing our men. Now Luis has been murdered. Do you wish to appear weak?"

"I am serious, as well," Almarone said, his tone softening. "Do you not think I want to avenge my brother's death?"

"Now he is your brother," Ruiz said bitterly. "Yet when he

was alive, he was but the half brother you tolerated for the sake of business."

"You give me too little credit," Almarone said. "Blood is blood. I would hardly have gone to so much trouble, called in so many favors, if I did not care for family. Are you any less my family? Luis was no kin to you, after all. Do not forget that I got you out of custody."

"Then what are we waiting for?" Ruiz demanded. "We know where to strike. We must kill Stevens and any he has helping him. We must choke off the flow of arms before El Cráneo's advantage cannot be overcome! Do you want to lose this war?"

In the Crown Victoria, Bolan turned to Burnett. "Do you know a Stevens?"

Burnett shook his head. "No idea."

"Then it's a lead," Bolan said. He took out his secure phone and tapped out a quick text message to Stony Man Farm. *Check STEVENS. DU ammo source?*

"You," Almarone told Ruiz, his voice transmitted clearly enough through Burnett's directional microphone, "are going to the safe house. As am I. If we move now, mark my words, Razor—we *will* lose. I have contacted our people back home. We need reinforcements, heavy weapons. Our own supplies are dwindling and El Cráneo has too great an advantage if we cannot meet them with the same."

"How do you propose to smuggle these reinforcements into the country?" Ruiz asked.

"You leave that to me," Almarone said. "Until they arrive, until we are ready, we are staying the hell out of New York. Let Taveras believe he has won, for now. Let him think the death of Luis has forced us to flee the city."

"Hasn't it?" Ruiz said scornfully.

"Keep your head, damn you," Almarone hissed. "If it were up to you, we would let foolish pride lead us to our deaths! Would you not rather *win?*"

Ruiz had nothing to say to that, apparently. Bolan and Burnett listened as the men ate, talking business and revenge in vague terms. Eventually they prepared to leave. Bolan and Burnett packed up the surveillance equipment quickly and pulled out of the parking lot before Almarone and his men left the restaurant.

The Executioner gambled that the safe house of which Almarone spoke would be farther along the parkway. He floored the accelerator and took the vehicle two miles down the road until he found a suitable off-ramp. Then he took the on-ramp again, positioning himself on the shoulder so that he and Burnett could monitor traffic but remain relatively hidden by the slope of the ramp.

"Eyes open," Bolan said unnecessarily.

Burnett laughed. His attention did not waver, but he shook his head. "Eye open," he corrected.

It was only a few minutes later that the metallic-beige Mercedes cruised past them. Bolan waited before pulling into traffic behind a merging SUV, using the large truck to screen the Crown Victoria. Then he fell into the same pattern he'd used to follow Almarone from New York, always staying several cars back, being careful not to change lanes too often or mirror Almarone's driver as he moved in and out of traffic.

A short drive later, Almarone, Ruiz and the two bodyguards arrived in a suburban housing development in a nondescript neighborhood, within a nameless section of sprawl that looked like countless other square miles of the surrounding area. Bolan parked the Crown Victoria well short of the actual house, leaving Burnett to watch the car and monitor the radio. His weapons concealed under his long duster, the Executioner did his best to look casual as he surveyed the nearby houses. Next door to Almarone's safe house, there was no car in the short driveway. No activity was evident through the windows. Careful to stay out of sight of anyone peering out a window in the safe house,

Bolan approached the adjacent house from the narrow side lawn between it and the next structure in the row. When he got close enough to see the small front porch, he saw a pair of newspapers, still rolled and banded, waiting to be open and read.

Bolan circled around to the back of the house, monitoring the next house to make sure he wasn't spotted and called in by the local Neighborhood Watch or a busybody. At the rear of the house, he found a UPS package left by a driver, dated the previous day. It seemed very likely nobody was home. Quietly, Bolan removed the small pistol-grip lockpick given to him by Stony Man's Gadgets Schwarz. He jimmied the rear door lock with little trouble and eased the door open as quietly as possible.

Once inside, Bolan quickly checked the house. This was no time to discover a homeowner napping. Once he was satisfied that no one was home, he concentrated on what he could see of the safe house from the widows facing that side. As houses in suburban developments like this one often were, the neighboring home was identical in structure to the safe house next to it. That meant Bolan had the perfect vantage point to monitor movement in the house next door, without fear of discovery as he moved from room to room.

It took him twenty minutes to assess the situation. Almarone had wasted no time going upstairs. He hadn't moved since and was probably taking a nap, as the room in which he'd stopped corresponded to the bedroom where Bolan stood. The Executioner took in the pink wallpaper and posters for teenage boy bands that decorated this room. The bed was rumpled but made, covered in stuffed animals. He paused to pick up one of them, a life-size plush penguin, and placed it back precisely as he had found it. If all went as planned, the girl who slept there would come back from vacation with her family, or wherever she was, never knowing that the shadow of death had passed over her house.

The two bodyguards were posted at the front and back of the

ground floor—one in the family room, one in the kitchen. The Mercedes was parked in the single-car garage. There were no other personnel in evidence and no other vehicles had arrived. Bolan knew that could change at any time, especially if Almarone was planning to conduct business from this location. He could have any number of people arriving, from drug-running contacts to more guards to the reinforcements he was bringing in to fight his war with El Cráneo. If Bolan's plan had a chance of working, he had to move fast.

The problem was Ruiz. He was the wild card, pacing nervously from room to room, on the move constantly. He had stayed on the first floor. Twice in twenty minutes he'd gone out back to have a cigarette. He could as easily have smoked inside, but Bolan suspected the walls were closing in on him in there. The smokes were probably an excuse to get out into the air as much as they were a means to feed his habit.

Moving quickly around the back of the house, keeping low, Bolan vaulted the waist-high picket fence and made a beeline for the small rear porch. Throwing himself flat on the ground, he rolled up against the bottom of the porch at the side, the Ultimax digging uncomfortably into his ribs under his coat. Then he drew the Beretta 93-R and started rapping the butt of the gun in a slow rhythm on the wooden slats enclosing the porch.

The bodyguard in the kitchen responded almost instantly, nosing out onto the porch to see what could be the source of the noise. Bolan kept his raps slow and spaced like a heartbeat. The bodyguard's face, his expression more curious than suspicious, suddenly appeared over the edge of the porch.

Bolan shoved the butt of the machine pistol hard into the bodyguard's face, rolling away from the edge of the porch as he did so. The thick-necked man slumped over the rail.

The Executioner hurried up the steps of the back porch and into the kitchen. It was clear for the moment, but he could hear movement from the front of the house. Razor Ruiz, carrying a bottle of beer in his hand, walked into the kitchen through the attached dining room and straight into Bolan.

"Wha—" Ruiz's jaw dropped.

Bolan fired a left-handed palm heel up under Ruiz's jaw. The blow snapped the Caqueta Cartel killer's head backward, his teeth clicking as his mouth slammed close. The back of Ruiz's head left a dent in the drywall as the man ricocheted off the peeling wallpaper near the kitchen doorway. He stayed down.

"Razor?" the bodyguard called from the family room. "Hey! Razor!"

Bolan waited, unmoving, until the man came to investigate. He dropped him with a single blow to the temple. He fell without a word.

The Executioner secured all three men with strong plastic riot cuffs from a pocket of his blacksuit. On the kitchen table, a cheap card table covered in beer bottles, he saw a set of keys bearing the three-point Mercedes star on the fob. He pocketed them and then took the stairs, wincing as his combat boots made the carpeted steps creak under his weight. On the second floor, he checked the first bedroom, then the second, but Almarone was not in either of them. Bolan found him asleep in a large four-poster in the master bedroom. He holstered the Beretta, knowing that the next step of his plan called for more intimidation.

"Almarone," he said.

When Almarone didn't wake, Bolan kicked the bed, hard. The drug lord opened his eyes groggily, wiping a hand down his face before he realized what was happening. He made a grab for a weapon under his pillow.

"Don't," Bolan warned. Almarone stopped where he was. He was staring into the barrel of the Executioner's massive .44 Magnum Desert Eagle.

"So, *pendejo*," Almarone said, "I see you sooner than I predicted, it would seem."

"So it would," Bolan said. "Do you know why I'm here?"

"You are here to kill me, of course," Almarone said. "You are not the sort of *puto* who shoots a sleeping man. I give you credit for that, at least."

"I've put plenty of men just like you in the ground," Bolan said frankly. "But that's not why I'm here today. I need what you know. Luis Caqueta knew enough to try to make a deal. I'd have gunned him down like the rabid dog he was without a second thought, but not before doing just what he was hoping Burnett could do for him. I want to stop the flow of DU ammunition to El Cráneo."

"Luis was a fool," Almarone said. "What did his deal get him but a trip straight to hell?"

"You said yourself that blood is blood," Bolan said.

Almarone's eyes widened. "What do you want?"

"I want the information that Ruiz has," Bolan said. "The same information Caqueta had. I want everything you know about the source, about how you made your purchases, and about this Stevens."

"You know much already." Almarone nodded. "You do not need me."

"Then I'll kill you." Bolan gestured with the Desert Eagle, the barrel never leaving its target.

"Then you will kill me." Almarone shrugged.

"Carlos!" Ruiz shouted from the bottom of the stairs. "Carlos, he is here!"

Bolan backed off from the bed, still covering Almarone with the Desert Eagle. With his left hand he carefully drew the Beretta, covering the stairs. Ruiz, his eyes glassy, was inching his way up the steps like a worm, his feet bound at the ankles and his hands secured behind his back. What he thought he could do like that Bolan didn't know, but he had to give the cartel thug credit for loyalty.

"Tell him nothing!" Ruiz shouted.

Bolan waited for Ruiz to crawl up the stairs and down the

hallway to the bedroom. Almarone rolled his eyes as if he found the whole affair ridiculous. Finally, Ruiz managed to struggle into the room, snarling, pulling at the plastic tie that was biting into his wrists.

The Executioner walked over to him and kicked him in the head. Ruiz lost consciousness and was still on the rug.

"That was not necessary," Almarone said. "You will not shoot a sleeping man, but you will kick one who is tied and helpless."

"He doesn't play well with others," Bolan said. "Now. Let's talk about what Caqueta wanted to say."

"Where is your friend, Detective Burnett?" Almarone asked.

"He's not your concern right at the moment," Bolan said. "Now. You have no choice and you're acting in your own best interests, even if you don't want to admit it. Tell me what you know."

"Very well." Almarone sighed. "The man you want, the man behind Jonathan West, is Donald Stevens." The drug lord shrugged. "West was his man in NLI. Luis hired some investigators to look into both men once we learned that he was acting as representative for Stevens."

"How did you learn that?"

Almarone smiled. "Every man has his weaknesses, does he not? West was very weak indeed. He was clumsy, so clumsy that his attempts to sell Stevens's product brought him several times to the attention of the authorities. Did he not?"

Bolan didn't answer.

"I will take that as a yes," Almarone said. "West liked women. When he first contacted us and we arranged to purchase the special bullets, he was quick to tell us that El Cráneo was buying, too. He had limited supplies, he claimed, and how should he divide them, he wished to know. He said he could be persuaded to sell us more than he sold to our enemies. All it would take would be some…fringe benefits."

"You sent him hookers," Bolan said.

"Escorts. We run more than one such agency. West very much liked to talk. He spoke often of Donald Stevens, whom he resented. While West took the risks, Stevens sat safe in his factory here in New Jersey, he said. Stevens was West's boss in NLI, and it seems he never lost the taste for telling him what to do. West was becoming very anxious. Stevens had promised him much money for coming to work for him, for making enemies of NLI and their hired soldiers. West was very unhappy. He was not seeing the payment for which he had lusted for so long."

"So your people learned what NLI has been trying to hide," Bolan said. "The link between West and Stevens, and the fact that the problem goes deeper than a single rogue employee."

"More or less," Almarone said. "West had ceased to be useful to us. He was making excuses, selling us no more of the bullets, telling us there were no more to sell and that we would have to be patient. My spies within El Cráneo warned me that Taveras was stockpiling more than ever, planning to run us—us!—out of New York for good. It was clear West was lying. So I had him killed."

"You killed West? Not NLI?"

"What have I told you?" Almarone said angrily. "I had him killed thinking this would draw Stevens out of hiding. I had hoped he would have to start representing himself, at least in dealing with Taveras. As I say, we have people on the inside. Once we identified him we could kill him, too, or perhaps capture him and persuade him to help us instead of Taveras. I do not know why he chose sides in our little war. I would think the most money to be made is made by selling to both, no?"

Bolan said nothing. Almarone was making sense. West was killed, if the timeline was correct, just before Bolan was to meet him in Bryant Park. Perhaps West was acting on Stevens's orders and trying to find a new market to sell his product. Perhaps West was acting on his own, trying to score a payday on the side without Stevens's knowledge. Either way, he'd been killed before he could meet with Bolan.

"When you killed West, did your people search his home? His computer?"

"We did," Almarone admitted, "but West was good at some things. His computer we could not crack. He was very bad at other things, however. He left himself a note, telling of a meeting with a new client."

"In Bryant Park."

"Yes," Almarone said. "We discussed this, Luis and I," Almarone admitted, "but we could see no profit in meeting more potential enemies. It was thought perhaps Stevens would come out of hiding to meet with this new buyer, but we dared not make a move then and there."

"Why not?"

"The Caquetas have one war to fight already. Were we to blunder into the deal and shoot it out with these new people whom West had been courting, we'd have to fight on two fronts. The Caquetas are not weak, but we have our limits. Our fight is with El Cráneo."

"In other words," Bolan translated, "you're already losing to Taveras and you don't have the resources to take on another hostile group, the dimensions of which you didn't yet know."

"As you say," Almarone said through gritted teeth.

Bolan thought over what he'd just learned. He had assumed that NLI had found out about West and killed him to keep him quiet, then followed up on the meet to kill whomever might have had contact with West. That made sense; it closed the trail leading back to NLI, a corporation whose motives Bolan understood well enough. If the Caquetas had found West, however, how did NLI get the information? How had they known of the Bryant Park meet—and how did the timing of Basil Price's break-in fit?

"You now have everything Luis, Razor and I knew of this Stevens and his organization," Almarone said. "If telling you is in our best interests, prove it to me. Leave now."

Bolan looked down at the drug lord. "I think you misunderstand," he said evenly. "You and your men are responsible for a lot of innocent deaths. I'm here to put a stop to that."

"You said you wished to stop Stevens from selling his ammunition!"

"Yes, I do," Bolan said, the Desert Eagle rock solid in his fist as he extended his arm toward Almarone. "But you're not going to do any more killing, Almarone."

Almarone jerked his hand toward the pillow, clawing for his hidden weapon.

Bolan's finger tightened on the trigger of the Desert Eagle.

Suddenly, a smoking grenade canister punched through the bedroom's window and bounced across the carpeted floor.

7

Bolan caught a whiff of the tear gas as the stinging smoke filled the room. Almarone found the .45 automatic pistol he'd been reaching for, snapping off a pair of shots in Bolan's direction. The Executioner pumped the four-poster full of .44 Magnum slugs as he retreated from the bedroom, stepping over Ruiz as he did so.

As he took the steps two at a time, Bolan heard tear-gas canisters being fired into the windows of the ground floor. The house soon began to fill with acrid, white smoke. No stranger to the effects of such gas, Bolan was not troubled by it, though his eyes did water considerably. He reloaded and holstered the Desert Eagle before bringing up the Ultimax on its shoulder strap. He took a moment to swap out the M-16 magazine for a 100-round drum from his bag.

When the first operatives broke through the front door, Bolan was ready for them.

Wearing full black combat gear and load-bearing vests, the gunmen opened fire as soon as the front door was down. Bolan was convinced that these were mercenaries. Their equipment, their tactics and their demeanor all pointed to it. He returned fire, the Ultimax spitting 62-grain steel-core bullets, cutting the doorway at an angle and chopping down the gunners before they could bring their AR-15s to bear on him. Swiveling, Bolan sent a blast back the other way, knowing the operatives would enter from both sides to catch him in the cross fire. The Executioner heard someone scream above the gunfire as he held the Ultimax by its pistol grips, hosing first the kitchen, then the front doorway through the family room. Then he broke through the knot of fallen men in the kitchen and shouldered his way through the side door leading to the attached garage.

Almarone's Mercedes-Benz S550 squatted on its tires like a well-fed beast of prey. Bolan let the Ultimax fall to its sling and under his coat as he fished the car keys from his pocket. He let himself in and fired up the car's engine. Three hundred and eighty-two horses rumbled back at him from under the hood. He shifted the automatic transmission into Drive and crushed the accelerator under his steel-shank combat boot. The rear wheels bit and the car hurtled forward.

When the Mercedes crashed through the lightweight garage door, it caught two of the mercenaries. They were standing in the driveway, covering the house as more of their team poured from a pair of black cargo vans parked in front, when Bolan's commandeered vehicle smashed into them. There was a sickening crunch as one of the men was caught under the front wheels. The other was brutally shoved to the driveway after the vehicle's front fender plowed into him, breaking the headlight on that side.

Bolan had no time to hunt for window controls. As he whipped around the two parked vans, the hired guns on the front lawn and in the vehicles began snapping shots at him. He yanked the Desert Eagle from its holster and brought it up, aiming through his own passenger window. The blast from the hand cannon was deafening within the car. Bolan punched shots through the window and into the flanks of the vans, taking out two tires on one but failing to score a disabling hit on the other. Then he was rocketing down the suburban street, hearing 5.56 mm bullets tear into the trunk and spiderweb the rear window as the heavy Mercedes' engine pushed it to sixty miles per hour in under six seconds. The high-tech speedometer kept climbing as the Executioner sped away.

Then he heard the chopper.

Bolan caught sight of the OH-6A "Little Bird" helicopter as it rose high above the houses to his left. The chopper, battle-proved and agile, bore two M-134 miniguns, one of the six-barreled guns on either side. The 7.62 mm rounds would chop up his borrowed luxury car with little difficulty. He pressed the accelerator to the floor with all his weight.

The pilot brought the aircraft around in a tight arc that put Bolan's car in position for a quick kill. The soldier wrenched the steering wheel as the guns opened up, tearing up the road behind the Mercedes as it shot around a corner and down a side street. Bolan was grateful for the relatively light traffic. He could not afford to draw the chopper into noncombatants.

The Executioner found what he was looking for, dodging back and forth across the road as the Little Bird tried to pin him with its guns. The profusion of telephone poles and the tightly spaced houses worked in his favor as he tore erratically through the neighborhood. The chopper's pilot couldn't get a clear shot at him and was, for the moment, reluctant to start firing through houses or civilian cars.

Bolan knew from too much recent experience that the pilot would grow desperate and start using less caution. The soldier sped toward the overpass of the ramp to the Garden State Parkway. Estimating the distance, he slammed on the brakes, skidding the Mercedes to a stop under the shelter of the overpass, as close to its center as he could. He threw open his door and brought up the Ultimax.

The pilot brought the chopper in fast, both miniguns burning, walking the 7.62 mm NATO rounds in under the overpass to rip the Mercedes to shreds. He was a skilled pilot, but he lacked patience. Bolan had seen such target fixation before. The parked car was not the threat. The target, and the real threat, was the man who'd been driving. The Executioner, from the other side of the underpass, opened fire with the Ultimax.

From his vantage point flanking the hovering chopper, Bolan

targeted the tail rotor through his mounted red-dot scope. He fired through the rest of the 100-round drum as the Ultimax vibrated in his hands. The Little Bird started to turn to bring its guns to bear on him.

It kept turning, as the damaged tail rotor gave, sending the chopper into a spin. The pilot tried to put the wounded bird down but overcompensated, tilting wildly to one side. The main rotor dug into the asphalt and broke apart, whipping the helicopter under the overpass like a skipping stone. It came to rest in a crumpled heap on the other side before exploding, raining the area with scraps of metal.

The van Bolan had failed to damage was closing in. The side door was open, and a gunner with an AR-15 was shooting. Bolan made for the shelter of the underpass, bracing himself against the concrete wall. He drew the Desert Eagle again and punched hole after hole in the windshield of the oncoming van, fouling the driver's vision or hitting him outright. The van swerved, hesitated and then accelerated, as if deadweight pinned the gas pedal. Finally, the vehicle rammed nose-first into the concrete wall of the overpass opposite Bolan.

The Executioner reloaded his Desert Eagle and advanced on the wrecked van, the big pistol in both fists. A mercenary stumbled out the side door, holding a Colt .45 in his left hand. Bolan tracked him with the Desert Eagle.

"Drop it!" he ordered.

The man brought the .45 up and on target. Bolan triggered a single shot that drilled him through the chest, dumping him on the road. As he got closer, he saw movement within the van. Another survivor began spraying unaimed fire through the open side door.

Bolan emptied the Desert Eagle into the cargo compartment, moving laterally as he did so. He holstered the big handgun and drew the Beretta 93-R in one fluid motion, unclipping his combat light and holding it in his support hand as he swept the doorway of the vehicle. Nothing moved inside. At his feet, the man with the .45 was clearly dead, staring up from a puddle of blood.

"Hey!" someone shouted.

Bolan felt the kick coming and rotated with it, absorbing most of the powerful roundhouse. The Beretta was knocked from his hand. He came back with a hammer fist to his adversary's temple. The man ducked and backed off a pace, adopting some sort of martial-arts stance as he drew a knife from his web gear.

Bolan kept his distance, his hands open and low near his body. The mercenary who'd been hiding behind the van was young, with dirty blond hair and a desperate look. He was bleeding from a nasty scalp wound. He couldn't be much more than nineteen or twenty, the Executioner decided—full of ideas about seeing the world and having adventures, probably. It might just be possible to talk him out of this.

"Look," Bolan said, careful to keep himself positioned to evade or counter as the young man made tentative slashing motions with his knife, "you can walk away from this."

"In handcuffs, maybe," the kid growled, poking the air with his knife in Bolan's general direction.

"Don't," Bolan warned. "You aren't going to win."

"I have orders," the young man insisted. "Take you down and don't get caught, no alternatives. If I get caught, I die."

"What sort of hold do they have over you?" Bolan asked.

"Man, you have no idea," the kid said. He lunged with the knife.

Bolan slapped and checked the knife arm, moving to the inside and driving his elbow into the kid's throat. The young man went down gagging, losing his knife in the process. Bolan dropped a boot on his stomach, careful not to do it too hard. The kid doubled up, turning white. He rolled over and retched.

Bolan spotted his Beretta and scooped it up. He stood over the kid, aiming the machine pistol.

"Get up," he ordered. "Do it slowly. You can live through this. You don't have to die for Blackjack."

"Yeah," the kid said, curled into a ball with his back to Bolan. "Yeah, I do."

He rolled over suddenly, and Bolan saw the glint of metal in his hand. The Beretta spit flame once. The young mercenary was still.

The soldier leaned over the dead man and checked the body. There was nothing in his pockets, of course, and certainly no identifying materials of any kind. In his hand he clutched a tiny 5-shot, .22-caliber North American Arms minirevolver. Bolan took it, pulled the cylinder pin and checked the loads. Then he reloaded the tiny gun, set the single-action hammer on one of the safety notches between chambers and dropped the little gun in his pocket.

He looked back at the dead man. He was young to have chosen the life that had gotten him killed—but he was old enough to have chosen wrong over right. He had paid the price accordingly.

When the Crown Victoria came roaring up, Bolan brought the 93-R up to cover it before he realized it was Burnett behind the wheel.

"Hey, Cooper. Need a lift?" Burnett asked.

"How did you find me?"

"Are you kidding?" The detective jerked his chin in the direction of the wrecked helicopter. Heavy black smoke was rising from the mangled craft. "You leave a trail a blind man could follow. Well, a half-blind man."

"You okay to drive?" the Executioner asked as he got in on the passenger side.

"Sure," Burnett said. "I just can't take any turns to that side." He pointed to his bandaged eye. "You know what they say. 'Two wrongs don't make a right, but three lefts do.'"

Bolan looked at him incredulously.

"Sorry." Burnett's lopsided grin said he wasn't sorry at all.

Burnett's mood sobered as they neared the safe house. The building was not on fire, but white smoke or tear gas wafted from the windows and the building was badly damaged by gunfire. The garage door lay in pieces on the driveway, where a local police car was parked. There were no dead men littering the lawn or driveway; it was likely the mercenaries had taken any casualties with them. Two police officers were speaking to a crowd of civilians, who could only be neighbors giving their statements. The cops eyed Burnett and Bolan suspiciously as they drove up.

"Let me handle this," Burnett said. "I speak the language."

Bolan waited in the car as Burnett conferred with the cops. He scanned the area, feeling uncomfortably vulnerable in the parked car. The cargo van he had damaged was nowhere to be seen. It was likely the mercenaries had simply driven it away on the rims. Men motivated enough to kill themselves—and each other—rather than risk capture and interrogation would think little of damaging a vehicle to effect their getaway.

The Executioner had no doubt that running ID checks on the dead men in the van under the overpass would turn up individuals with backgrounds similar to those of Reynolds and Price—career soldiers of fortune with no direct ties to Blackjack Group and Norris Labs International. The helicopter might be more promising, as a check on its serial numbers might turn up a link to an owner who could eventually be traced to Blackjack. It was unlikely to be anything definitive, however, nor could Bolan see the information coming through in time to be of any real help.

Burnett gestured for Bolan, the two cops leaving the detective to return to questioning the witnesses.

Bolan climbed carefully out of the Crown Victoria, making sure the Ultimax and his other hardware remained concealed. There was no need to get the police on-site any more nervous than they already were, with the evidence of open war smoking in the midst of a previously quiet neighborhood.

"They don't like it," Burnett said as Bolan walked up, "but they're buying my authority for now. We can check out the house, for all the good that will do."

Bolan nodded. The two men walked up the heavily damaged front porch and stepped inside. The interior still reeked of tear gas, making Burnett cough and wheeze.

"Why don't you step outside?" Bolan suggested. "It won't take both of us to look."

Burnett nodded and made himself scarce. Bolan went room by room, searching for any sign of Ruiz or Almarone.

He found Ruiz on the kitchen floor. The walls and floors were red with blood. Ruiz was clutching a kitchen knife in one dead hand, something he'd obviously grabbed from the countertop. His eyes were open and his face twisted in a look of shock and disbelief. There was no way to count the number of wounds he'd suffered. To Bolan he looked as if he couldn't quite accept that hell had come for him at last.

Almarone had never made it downstairs. Bolan followed a trail of blood smeared on the carpet, leading from the master bedroom to another of the bedrooms down the hall. The drug lord was slumped in a corner. One hand still clutched at a neck wound, while the other was wrapped around the pistol with which he'd tried to kill Bolan. The slide of the .45 was locked open.

There was an entry wound in Almarone's forehead. The mercenaries had clipped him as he fired back, then let him drag himself down the hall before following him and finishing him.

There was little else for the Executioner to do.

He found Burnett out front, conferring with the officers.

"They've got it under control now," Burnett told him as they walked back to the Crown Victoria. "The local boys will be crawling over this before the other agencies get into the act. They'll be arguing who did what for months if not years. I downplayed your involvement."

"I appreciate that," Bolan said as he got in. "I'll drive."

"Works for me. Where are we driving to?"

Bolan considered that for a moment. There was the address in Swedesboro, but there was no telling if that would turn up anything and he was reluctant to move that far away from the city on so little possibility of payoff. Given that the heads had just been cut off the Caqueta Cartel nest of serpents, with more possibly headed into town, he wanted to get back to New York to see what shook loose.

"The Caquetas have reinforcements headed into New York," Bolan said, "but there'll be no one left to run the show when they get here. That right?"

"As far as I can tell," Burnett said. "Caqueta, Almarone and Ruiz were the top dogs of the cartel, in that order. Without them, you've got the drug-running equivalent of middle management, but nobody the troops would rally around. I mean, for all intents and purposes, the muscle might as well pack up and go home."

"These troops wouldn't include someone who could take charge? Someone from Colombia who'd be quick to take the reins?"

"To be honest, no," Burnett said, "Luis Caqueta kept pretty tight control. Everyone back in Colombia is a handpicked functionary, people he figured would be loyal to him. He didn't want anybody to get the idea they could go without him. That's why he didn't have more than Almarone and Ruiz in positions of power here."

"So the Caquetas are out of the picture?"

"I'd say so," Burnett said, sounding cheerful. "Couldn't have happened to a nicer bunch."

"At least I got what there was to get," Bolan said.

"You did?" Burnett said, surprised.

"Yes," Bolan confirmed. "Almarone admitted that the Caquetas killed West. He also gave me some dirt on West and outlined the relationship with one Donald Stevens, who is apparently the NLI employee who's gone rogue."

"Then how did NLI know about your meet in Bryant Park?" Burnett asked.

"There's no way to be sure," Bolan said. "They may have gotten it from West's computer before Price was sent back to destroy the evidence. But that doesn't make a lot of sense. Why send Price days later to destroy the computer and toss the place when they could have done that at the time they got the information? They must have had some other source. Sending Basil Price to West's apartment was an attempt to cover tracks after the fact."

"So that's a dead end."

Bolan looked at Burnett. "More importantly, how did Blackjack's operatives find us here?"

"What do you mean? They knew to take Caqueta in New York at our meeting."

"Yeah, they did," Bolan said, nodding, "but there are any number of holes they could have punched in Caqueta's security. They could have had Caqueta's place wired for sound. They could have an informant in the department itself. They could have been following Caqueta from the time he left for the meet."

"I doubt Caqueta's got any friends on the force." Burnett chuckled. "Still, you're right. So why not here?"

"We tailed Almarone here. We weren't followed in turn. I'd have noticed. So how did they know to show up here?"

"Maybe the safe house was a known quantity." Burnett shrugged. "Maybe they knew ahead of time he might run here, so they just showed up. Maybe they bugged his car. Like you said, there are any number of holes."

"I don't like it," Bolan said. "Something about it just doesn't feel right."

"We're back to square one, anyway," Burnett said. "What do you say we start from the other end?"

"Meaning, Taveras?"

"Meaning, Taveras." Burnett nodded. "If Caqueta is down for

the count, El Cráneo is sitting on a stockpile of DU ammunition in the middle of a sudden power vacuum. They've got ambition and now the only force that was keeping them in check is gone. Say you're a power-mad drug lord whose biggest rivals have just lost their leadership. They're in chaos. You might, I don't know, mop up a few of their operatives, maybe hit their businesses or homes to prove a point—show the rest of the community of criminals that you're not to be fucked with, as they say. But then what?"

"You know them," Bolan said. "What would they focus on? What does Taveras want?"

"He's the typical egomaniacal power-mad, would-be crime lord," Burnett said with a grin. "He lives for the day when the city is his and his alone. He wants dominance. He wants to be the man. That's what all the heavy hardware was for, after all—to sweep Caqueta aside and clear the way for his rise to power, as he saw it."

"A rise to power that NLI and Blackjack have helped make happen."

"Maybe," Burnett said. "The way I see it, it just makes it easier for jerks like me. I don't have to split my time between both groups anymore. And think of how tidy a New York crime scene run by just Taveras would be. There's something to be said for dictatorship. A lot of the infighting, a lot of the collateral damage, is minimized."

"A fine idea," Bolan said, his voice cold. "It's been done. They called it the Mob. I remember some collateral damage."

Burnett had nothing to say to that. Finally, he offered, "There's a club, a strip joint, on Thirty-third. Taveras owns it. He spends a lot of downtime there, sampling the girls and entertaining his foot soldiers. It's as likely a place to roust as any."

"All right," Bolan agreed.

"I don't know about you, but I could use a nap and a decent meal, not necessarily in that order," Burnett said. "Why don't you stop at your hotel. I'll take the car, get back to my place, have dinner. You can do…whatever it is you do when you're not shooting people. We'll converge on Taveras's club tonight after dark, when the action is."

"Fair enough," Bolan said.

8

Percival Leister stood amid the bullet-riddled debris in the center of the hotel room. He looked at the blood-splattered carpet, at the scorch marks on the walls left by the small fires that had erupted. Only the fast action of his men, the training they had received at Leister's behest, had saved them. He had lost far too many good men nonetheless. It galled him. It shamed him. It infuriated him.

Leister had seen real combat. He had walked the war-torn fields of Rhodesia. He had commanded men in battles so ruthless that the word *atrocity* put a positive spin on the acts he'd seen committed—and had committed himself. He was a veteran in every sense of the word, experienced in war, experienced in death, experienced in the taking of lives and the meting out of destruction.

That he should come to this, in an industrialized nation, appalled him. True, he was amid the Yanks in the United States, not home in his native England, but still. The colonists weren't the savages of Africa, for pity's sake. The operation should never have been so difficult. Hell, he should have been able to mop up long ago, silencing Stevens and leaving the Big Apple far behind.

Instead, he was surrounded by destruction and reminders of good men lost, a victim of his own attempt to be clever.

One of his men, Thompson, brought him the full report, assessing their losses and listing the various bribe money that had been spread around to cover up the events. One of Leister's field men was arranging for new quarters in another location.

Leister's attempt had failed. Now, to the list of men they'd lost in the skirmishes so far, he had to add several more bodies to a count that already included Reynolds and Price.

He would not miss Reynolds. The man was a capable field commander and had a military record that was impressive enough in its own right, but Leister had seen the type before. Reynolds was a hothead, a man who didn't learn from his mistakes. Caught off guard, Reynolds would put himself in the same situation over and over, hoping to intercept the ambush before it came. He'd had something to prove and walked around with a chip on his shoulder. Reynolds, unlike Price, had never realized that waging wars, fighting others' battles for them, was a business proposition. It had no honor and nobody kept score, save to tally the pay distributed at the end of each campaign.

Reynolds's behavior in Bryant Park simply bore out Leister's worst fears. The man had no sense of proportion, no sense of containment. Leister himself was not above staging operations on that scale, of course, but to then take the battle down a congested city street? Absurd. Better to let the quarry escape, regroup your own forces and find a new way to approach the problem, rather than to dig your own hole deeper, risking capture and exposure. Chasing after the big man who'd shot up their forces at Bryant Park would have fit with Reynolds's sense of personal honor, however. He'd lost men, and that meant that the man who'd killed them had to pay. Calculating his next step, using cunning rather than brute force, never entered into Reynolds's mind.

Most of Blackjack's employees were ex-military or would-be military men. While some were cynical—they stayed in line as long as the pay was good—many were still clinging to movie notions of what being a soldier of fortune was supposed to be like. Leister knew few men ever made their fortunes carrying rifles for others. There simply wasn't that much money in it. Even

Leister, who had risen through the ranks and weathered the storms to find himself in charge of Blackjack's combat operations, didn't have much money squirreled away. He had saved enough to provide for his own retirement, if he lived that long, and as the years went by he was starting to think he might actually make it after all. But he would never be a rich man.

He wondered sometimes at these fools who thought an honest day's work in an office, a field, or a factory was somehow less worthy than carrying a rifle and shooting men with whom they had no direct quarrel. Leister had lived in field camps, in foxholes, in leaking tents and in freezing temperatures. He had seen men die for lack of medical supplies to treat them. He had watched men grow gaunt, their eyes hollowing out, for lack of enough food to feed them. He had seen battles turn to fixed bayonets and knives because neither side had enough ammunition for an extended firefight.

He had seen many, many friends die.

He would miss Basil Price. The man had been a faithful friend, a good soldier, fighting many campaigns by his side. Basil had been the man on whom Leister could always depend, someone whose judgment Leister never needed to second-guess. No doubt someone like Reynolds would have sworn holy vengeance and gone looking for whomever had taken Basil's life. Leister, on the other hand, knew that it was just business. Basil had played the game and, unfortunately, he'd let someone get the drop on him. It was a very clean equation, one in which emotions need not figure. The transaction had been fair. Basil's bill had come due.

Still, as many times as he had seen death, losing a friend always saddened him deeply. At one time he had thought he'd spend his golden years surrounded by fellow wartime comrades, trading stories and telling lies. Now he wondered if anyone with whom he'd worked and warred would be alive, when that time came. He'd allowed himself to think Basil would make it, that he'd have at least one old friend by his side when the time finally came to hang up his guns and live a life of quiet leisure. He had looked forward to the idea of spending his days playing chess with Basil, or simply sitting and drinking coffee on the veranda of a small home in a tropical climate, purchased with the money he'd so painstakingly scraped together over the years.

Curse his luck. Curse his bloody, rotten luck. And curse Basil, too—poor, loyal Basil—for letting himself be killed by enemies who were even now vexing Leister. Such a pity. Such a waste.

Leister pushed thoughts of retirement from his mind. He was old and getting tired, but he still had a job to do. He had directed his lieutenants to prepare for a counterstrike, to hit back hard. Unlike Reynolds's notions of why such an attack should be mounted, Leister's own opinions on the matter were far more pragmatic. He simply had to see to it that Blackjack remained a force to be reckoned with, one that was not taken lightly—nor attacked casually. A properly planned, properly coordinated military operation would take care of that with, Leister hoped, a minimum of casualties among his dwindling resources in New York.

The further complication to this sordid affair was the big, dark-haired man.

With a heavy sigh, Leister returned to the task of sifting through the debris in the hotel room, salvaging what he could and identifying those items that would have to be destroyed before he and his men could relocate.

There was much to do, yet, and an attack to wage.

Blackjack Group was going hunting.

9

Stony Man Farm transmitted a text file to Bolan's secure phone outlining the career highlights and background information of Donald Stevens. It was useful context, but none of it provided the Executioner with more insight than did Almarone's brief commentary. Stevens, forty-six, had been recruited directly from a prestigious university and had worked for Norris Labs International ever since. For reasons the company would not disclose, he was let go at the end of the previous year. There were no records of his activities since then. He had not applied to other jobs, nor did he hold a permanent address anywhere in the United States. He had, for all intents and purposes, disappeared.

The personality profile Stony Man had managed to work up wasn't terribly helpful, either. Stevens was extremely intelligent. He had no family and no living relatives. He had no connections to anyone at all—which painted the psychological portrait of a genius loner, someone whose work occupied the sum total of his waking hours. His work was highly classified, but Stony Man's sources, as well as government contractors knew enough about NLI to know that it was generally related to arms manufacture. It was likely that Stevens was either involved in the development of the DU small-arms production, or understood it well enough to go into business selling it himself.

Everyone involved had assumed West was the culprit, but what little information there was on West pointed to Stevens, his boss. West had the technical knowledge, according to his résumé and work history. But he had never really risen to a position of power or influence. He had the mark of a follower, not a leader. Stevens was the likely source, the ringleader, as detailed by Almarone.

Somewhere, Stevens was sitting on a stockpile of DU rounds. He had either cached them after misappropriating them from NLI, or he knew enough and had resources enough to manufacture them himself. Bolan's money was on the latter. If NLI and Blackjack were willing to engage in open war to silence any ties back to them—including killing their own to prevent their capture and interrogation—the whole affair was larger than simply stealing a trailer's worth of rounds that would eventually be used up and off the market. If NLI saw Stevens's operation as an ongoing threat, one large enough to warrant the type of operation they'd mounted to this point, Bolan could conclude only that Stevens had a factory somewhere.

The report from the Farm had included photos from the blacksuits' raid on what turned out to be a small house in the suburbs. The Swedesboro, New Jersey, home was empty. There had been nothing to find. Bolan was glad he hadn't left the city to make the trip out there.

While Bolan and Burnett had been tailing Almarone, things were already starting to heat up in Manhattan. El Cráneo had staged two small raids on what Burnett believed were Caqueta holdings. One of these was a hotel in Manhattan, which had been largely burned to the ground. The other was an auto repair and detailing shop just outside the city. The hotel had produced nearly a dozen casualties, while the auto yard had been almost as messy. At the auto yard, the Caquetas had been hit in their cars. The rival gang had shot through the vehicles with DU ammunition, wiping out what remained of their competition. Also during that shooting, bullets had passed through a Caqueta vehicle and penetrated an adjacent storefront, setting fire to that building in the process. Two civilians, customers in the store, had been killed. The fire got out of control and gutted most of the building and another adjoining address.

The mayor was screaming to the governor for the National Guard, Burnett had informed the Executioner. The possibility of martial law loomed. Bolan wasn't opposed to the idea if it helped lock down El Cráneo but knew it might make it more difficult for him to track down Stevens. Until Stevens and his pipeline of ammunition was shut down, any solution reached—no matter how bloody—was a temporary move at best. All Stevens had to do was wait until he could find other customers. He might pull up stakes and find an entirely new market, unleashing his hellish war by proxy on the streets of another city. Bolan was determined not to let that happen.

Someone knocked softly on the door to Bolan's hotel room.

The Executioner drew his Beretta 93-R and stood next to the door. "Who is it?" he asked.

"Just me," Burnett's voice came back. "I come bearing gifts."

Bolan opened the door. The detective glanced at the gun in Bolan's hand but didn't comment on it. He was carrying a fat vinyl case under one arm.

"What have you got there?" Bolan asked.

"Leadership has its privileges." Burnett winked. "You don't think I just drive around with a directional mike and a video camera in my car all the time, do you? Surveillance is the best tool my task force has in dealing with Taveras, Caqueta and their boys. If we can get them on video, on record, we have a better chance of nailing them down. I've had teams watching people from the Caqueta and Taveras organizations. I've also got Taveras's club, the cozy little place we're about to visit, wired for picture and sound—and don't ask me if it's legal, because I'm bending the rules."

"Bending them how hard?" Bolan asked.

"Let's just say I'm hoping the ends will justify the means so

I don't get fired." Burnett shrugged. "If I do this completely by the book, I'll never get anywhere. But then, you wouldn't know anything about that, would you?" The big detective grinned.

Bolan shook his head. He was more aware than anyone just how badly the system worked against those it was designed to protect. "So what is that?"

Burnett removed a portable DVD player and a couple of rewriteable DVDs from the case, inserting one of them into the folding machine and turning up the sound. "It turns out that last night, before today's fireworks," Burnett said, "Taveras had an extremely interesting meeting. The video's a little dark, but the sound's fine. The monitoring team brought this to me when I stopped in at the department."

"Who's on it?"

"Oh, you'll love it," Burnett promised. He took the small, flat remote control and pressed a button. The DVD loaded and began to play.

On the little screen, the picture at a strange angle thanks to the position of the hidden camera, nearly naked women could be seen gyrating on poles in the background. At a small, round table in the foreground, two men sat smoking cigarettes. A third was sitting on a reversed wooden chair, leaning on the backrest.

Bolan recognized the men from his intelligence files. The smaller, fatter of the three was Pierre Taveras, the leader of El Cráneo. He was a sweaty, squat man, his face covered in stubble. He was wearing an ill-fitting black suit. The collar of his blue shirt was open at the throat. He had small, beady eyes, a round, fat face and a giant hook of a nose.

To his right sat Julian "July" de la Rocha. De la Rocha was slim and good-looking, with a smile full of capped teeth, a chiseled jaw and perfectly styled black hair slicked into a small pompadour on his head. He, too, wore a tailored suit, but his fit properly. Gold medallions and chains decorated his neck and filled the gap at his chest where his shirt was open.

The man sulking on the chair nearby was Jesus Molina. Molina was a big, almost hulking man, with a sleeveless shirt struggling to cover his massive chest. He had the thickset features and protruding brow of a Neanderthal, but there was a glint of cunning in his dark eyes that was visible even on the grainy video. Bolan knew, from the Farm's report, that while de la Rocha was Taveras's field lieutenant and right-hand man, Molina was the muscle on whom Taveras depended to enforce his will as law within El Cráneo. No guns were visible, but it was a sure bet every one of the Skulls present was armed and dangerous.

A fourth man stood before the table. The top of his head was cut off in the picture, but his face was visible. He was of average height, with exaggerated posture and a long, waxed mustache framing a gaunt face. When he spoke, it was with the clipped and aristocratic tones of a refined, British accent.

"This character," Burnett said, pressing the Pause button and pointing to the British man, "is known to us. We've got a full workup on him. He's been keeping to the shadows because he's moderately famous. I knew I'd seen him somewhere, so I found the write-up. Turns out he gave an interview to a magazine a few years back, something I remembered reading when I bothered to keep up on all the gun rags and SWAT periodicals and such."

"Who is he?" Bolan asked.

"That," Burnett said proudly, "is one Percival Leister. He was a veteran of the counterinsurgency war in Zimbabwe— formerly Rhodesia. He was SAS in the Rhodesian armed forces. When things started to go bad for the mercs in Rhodesia, he even tried, unsuccessfully, to defect to the South African Defense Force with his unit and equipment."

"Let me guess," Bolan said. "He's involved with Blackjack Group."

"Rumor has it," Burnett said, "that he heads the show. I've got a friend in the State Department who's convinced of it, in fact. I'm willing to bet we haven't seen him up to now because he knows his famous face would be recognized. I guess he figured he'd be fine, hiding under the same rock as a cockroach like Taveras. But now we have the link you were looking for. Although—"

"This is another not-strictly-legal tap?" Bolan asked.

"Sort of."

"It won't matter," Bolan replied. "Let me get a copy of this to my people. It may be enough to shake something loose, higher up."

"You can have this DVD," Burnett told him. He pressed the play button and the video resumed, this time with dialogue.

Taveras squinted at Leister. "Who are you," he asked bluntly, "and what do you want here?"

"You don't know me, Mr. Taveras," Leister said calmly, "but my employers know you."

"You tell me nothing," Taveras said.

"Fair enough," Leister said. "I work for a security contractor. That contractor is in turn employed by a very large company with certain…interests. Among those interests is peace and prosperity."

"Peace," Taveras said disdainfully, drawing deeply on the cigarette he held between his index finger and thumb. "What do I care for peace?"

"Surely," Leister said in his proper British accent, "it is more profitable to be at peace than to find oneself at war."

"You might think that," Taveras said, nodding. "You would be wrong."

"I don't follow you, old chap," Leister said, confused.

"Mr.—"

"Leister," the mercenary leader said, introducing himself. "Percival Leister."

"Mr. Leister." Taveras nodded. "You are here to ask me for something. Why else would you come to me with your pretty words and your manners and your talk of peace? I do not ask for anything, Mr. Leister. I take what I want. El Cráneo knows no fear. We have no mercy. We ask no favors. We smash our enemies, and when our enemies are dead, we move in and we take. That is not peace. That is to conquer."

"I see." Leister sniffed. "And this great strength of yours…it does not, perhaps, come from special weapons sold to you by mere men? Men who are far from conquistadores, but simple merchants?"

Taveras's eyes narrowed dangerously. At their boss's obvious displeasure, Molina and de la Rocha shifted uncomfortably where they sat. Bolan watched as the giant Molina's hands began to flex.

"What do you know of this?" Taveras finally asked.

Leister smiled. "I know that your organization's recent victories in your ongoing war to *crush your enemies,* as you so colorfully put it, are due to the introduction of depleted uranium ammunition, which you are using to good effect in your street skirmishes."

"And?" Taveras demanded.

"And," Leister said, "I represent the business concern that is ultimately the source of that ammunition."

"Why did you not say so?" Taveras said. "We would have contacted—"

"No," Leister interrupted. "I do not represent Mr. Stevens."

"You do not?"

"Mr. Taveras," Leister said, "Donald Stevens previously worked for the concern that employs me. He is no longer affiliated with our conglomerate. He is, as you might say, a rogue element. He is dealing with you quite without our approval and without our support."

"So?"

"So," Leister said, "it will ultimately be the case that we find our wayward former employee and put an end to his unsanctioned business activities. That, as I understand it, might put a significant crimp in your own enterprises—at least insofar as you currently conduct them using the product misappropriated from us."

"So the bullets are stolen," Taveras said.

"In a manner of speaking," Leister offered. "Let us say that the formula for them and the means through which they are produced are a matter of proprietary information. Stealing them is tantamount to industrial espionage."

"So what do you want?" Taveras demanded. He stubbed out his cigarette angrily in the glass ashtray on the table before him.

"We would like to come to an understanding," Leister said, gritting his teeth as he spoke. "I am prepared to offer you certain considerations if you cooperate."

"What would those be, exactly?"

"It is only a matter of time," Leister insisted, "before we find Donald Stevens and put an end to his sales to men such as yourself. My employers understand only too readily that you may be resentful of this development."

"I just might be, yes," Taveras said coolly.

"Quite." Leister nodded. "We are, unfortunately, entirely inflexible on the point of the ammunition sales. That does not mean, however, that we are not open to extending to you certain other considerations."

"Make your offer, damn you," Taveras said.

"Indeed," Leister said. "Cooperate with me. Tell me what you know of Donald Stevens, his associate, Jonathan West, and your business deals with these men. In return for this disclosure and your assistance, my employers can make available to you a variety of conventional weapons that will assist you in your business endeavors."

"But not the special bullets."

"Not those, no," Leister said. "You must understand that these were not meant to see widespread market availability at this time. My employers would be deeply embarrassed to see their involvement with this sordid affair disclosed. We would ask for your continued silence on this matter. In return, we would make other weaponry available to you—weaponry not directly traceable to us that nonetheless will make your endeavors significantly easier."

"Automatic weapons?" Taveras asked.

"Certainly."

"Rockets? Missiles?"

"Possibly." Leister nodded. "We would need assurances as to your discretion."

"Of course," Taveras said thoughtfully. "And what if I refuse? What if I do not cooperate? What if I tell you to go to hell and continue to conduct my business my way, because I am a man who does not ask and does not give favors?"

"That would be unfortunate." Leister shook his head.

"And why would that be?"

"Because we would then have to proceed with our plans regardless," Leister said. "We would have to treat your organization as an obstacle to our goals. Should that happen, it would go badly for you."

Taveras blinked. He began to laugh, a low, mirthless chuckle rolling from his fat lips. "Badly for me? No, I think it would go badly for you. Look at you! You come here and make threats? You demand what you cannot afford to take by force? You insult me. What is more, you disgust me. You are weak. I am not impressed."

"That," the British mercenary said, "is a foolish assumption."

Leister took a fast step forward. As Bolan watched the video, the British mercenary slammed a palm heel into Molina, knocking him over. At the same time, the older man shot a vicious front kick at an angle to the table, catching de la Rocha in the shin. When the El Cráneo man recoiled, Leister bounced his head off the table. He slumped in his seat, dazed. Taveras was clawing for a weapon when Leister's hand came up with a Browning Hi-Power, the 9 mm weapon trained on the drug lord's face.

"I'd think again about that, old boy," Leister said. The weapon was cocked and his finger was on the trigger. Molina had recovered quickly and stood poised to tackle the mercenary, but Leister apparently saw him in his peripheral vision. "I wouldn't do it," he told the big man. "You may take me down, but not before I put a few holes in your boss, here."

"Sit," Taveras ordered Molina. His eyes never left Leister's pistol.

"Not so weak after all, eh?" Leister asked.

"No," Taveras admitted. "You do appear to have some balls, little man."

"Good," Leister said. "I'm glad we have that settled. Now," he announced as he began to back away from the table, "I am going to take my leave of you. I trust I've made a sufficient impression. My employers will be in touch regarding their offer. I'd like you to think about it. When you're done thinking about it, I would urge you to negotiate in good faith. This can, as I've said, end very badly. It might also end well for both of us."

"I should kill you," Taveras said.

"Mr. Taveras," Leister said, shaking his head slightly, his pistol never wavering, "I may have roughed up your guards, but I have been very careful to extend to you the respect and courtesy a man in your position deserves. I assure you, no insult is offered. Should you choose to accept my employers' terms, you will lose no face. You are, in fact, taking action to better your own position. That is the type of forward-thinking vision held by a true leader, the sort of man destined to greatness."

Taveras perked up visibly at that. Bolan had to hand it to Leister; he was very good. He'd walked into Taveras's lair and spit in the man's eye, but he was giving the prideful drug lord a way out that would not look like giving in.

"I will…consider your offer," Taveras said finally. "Leave quickly before I change my mind."

"Of course," Leister said. He backed out of the frame. Once

he was gone, Taveras slapped de la Rocha awake and then began cursing at him in Spanish.

Burnett switched off the DVD player. "You see?" he said. "It's not an ironclad link to Leister's employer, but it's a positive ID on Leister himself. Whatever links he has can be followed from him back to whatever proof you need. At least, that's what I was hoping."

"It may be enough." Bolan nodded. "It doesn't tell us much for certain, but it does tell us just how big this is. If NLI is willing to wheel and deal with someone like Taveras, there's a lot at stake."

"They've already proved they're willing to kill," Burnett said.

"And die," Bolan added. "But to people like this, life is cheap. If they're willing to trade, to deal, to come to some sort of agreement with an organization like El Cráneo, they're willing to sell their souls for an alliance that could hurt them down the road. By sending Leister, they're telling us that whatever's going on is large enough that they're willing to take that risk in order to cover their tracks in the short term."

Burnett nodded. "Do you think he'll take the deal?"

Bolan shook his head. "There's no way to know. If he's smart, greedy or both, he just might. There are certainly plenty of men in his position who'd care more about the money to be made, not to mention the long-term security of a pipeline to military-grade weapons, than they would about an insult to their honor. But I've met plenty of hard cases who'd only too gladly hurt themselves to get payback."

"So what do you think?" the detective asked.

"You're the expert on Taveras and his organization," Bolan said. "Just how violent is he? Just how vindictive is El Cráneo?"

"He doesn't have Caqueta's flair or his experience," Burnett said, "but he's certainly just as mean. He's also got expensive tastes, including women, cars and—the rumors go—his own product. It could go either way."

"It doesn't matter," Bolan said finally. "We're going to see to it that he doesn't get to decide."

"Ready to meet the man in person, then?" Burnett asked.

Bolan drew the Desert Eagle from the holster on his thigh and checked the massive weapon.

"Let's," he said.

10

The gaudy club bore a neon sign proclaiming its name "Busty's." Bolan grimaced as he and Burnett left the Crown Victoria illegally parked and closed on the front of the strip joint. The Executioner wore his duster and the full complement of his weapons, the pockets of his blacksuit full to capacity with lethal implements and emergency gear. Burnett held his shotgun low against his leg, doing his best to walk casually.

"You sure you're okay with that eye?" Bolan asked.

"Absolutely," Burnett said cheerfully. "What's the plan?"

"I'm going to go straight in," Bolan told him. "You circle around back, through that alley." The soldier gestured with a jut of his chin. "If I flush anything your way, make sure you stop them from getting out."

"Gotcha." Burnett nodded. He hustled off, still holding the shotgun near his body so it wouldn't be too obvious.

Bolan paused, feeling the weight of the hardware concealed on his person. Taking a mental inventory of the weapons and supplies at his disposal, he walked with long strides straight through the crowd of voyeurs, hookers and street trash milling about in front of Busty's. The doorman moved as if to stop him, took one look directly in Bolan's eyes and thought better of it. The Executioner swept past him and stalked through the entryway, pausing inside the door to let his eyes adjust to the dim interior lighting. Compared to the streetlights outside, it was almost pitch-black in the club.

The décor was familiar enough from Burnett's surveillance video. From his position, the soldier thought he could see the corner where Taveras's reserved table would be hidden. The dim, red lighting did not conceal the gyrating displays of female flesh on the raised platforms spread almost randomly throughout the floor space, but it did obscure the faces of those watching the women. Bolan moved carefully, penetrating deeper into the club, moving with the taut determination of a panther. He'd made it across a third of the floor when the first of Taveras's security people noticed him.

The security guards—members of El Cráneo, without doubt—wore street clothes rather than uniforms, but there was no mistaking the bulges of firearms under their shirts and jackets. There were three of them, all Hispanic males, and the one in the lead was reaching under his leather blazer as he closed on Bolan. "You! I don't know you," he said as he approached.

"I don't know you, either," Bolan said. When his hand came up from under his duster, the .44 Magnum Desert Eagle was clenched in his fist.

The El Cráneo man had time to clear leather, barely, with the Glock he held. Bolan's bullet chopped him down in his tracks, the shot plowing through his face and blowing a massive exit wound in the back of his skull. As the two guards behind the falling man took aim, Bolan brought his support hand up, bracing the Desert Eagle in a two-hand grip as he shot the first one, then the other of the men. They fell without returning a single shot, their blood splashed in gory streaks on the club floor behind them.

The cannon fire of Bolan's massive pistol sent the club goers and dancers into a frenzy. They were practically climbing over one another as they ran for the exits. Bolan ignored them, sweeping the crowd for new targets, alert to the threat of return fire from Taveras's men. He reached the rear of the main club floor and found a door near Taveras's table. It stood ajar.

Bolan took a moment to swap magazines in the Desert Eagle, seating a fully loaded one, before holstering the massive pistol and bringing up the Ultimax. The light machine gun had a 100-round drum in place already. The soldier planted one combat boot on the half-open door and sent it crashing inward as he ducked to the side of the doorway.

Two shotgun blasts echoed through the opening, punctuated by the sound of the weapon's action being pumped. Bolan shoved the Ultimax around the corner, pushing its shoulder sling to full extension, and sprayed the room. He heard the shotgunner cry out and drop the weapon to the floor. Before he moved from cover, he triggered another long burst to cover his entry into the room.

An El Cráneo gunner was spread limply across the floor, which was pocked with bullet holes. The Mossberg pump shotgun had taken a few rounds, too, one of which had left a deep gouge across the receiver. Bolan bent to check the shotgun, found it empty and tossed it aside. The little room was empty. Another wooden door bearing graffiti waited at the opposite end of the small space.

That was when Bolan heard the breaking glass.

The soldier whirled as, behind him, the broad and darkly tinted windows at the front of the club were smashed inward. Black-clad commandos bearing assault rifles and wearing load-bearing vests began streaming through the opening.

Blackjack Group had come calling.

The Executioner wasted no time. As the first of the mercenaries entered the club, he lowered his shoulder and rammed his way through the door leading in the opposite direction. No shots met him and no opposition presented itself as he swept the air before him with the muzzle of the Ultimax. He took for granted that more men would be entering through the rear of the building, in order to contain their targets. Bolan's first priority was to get out of the immediate line of fire. His only option, facing numbers so overwhelming, was to stage an immediate and brutal counterassault. He wondered if Burnett had been taken down by the Blackjack operatives, but if so, there was nothing he could do for the detective.

The soldier found himself in a hallway dotted with dressing-room doors and what were apparently storage closets. He saw no one. It was possible there were dancers hiding under tables or behind the doors, but they were not the immediate threat, nor were they in immediate danger. Gunfire from the front and back of the club was growing louder as the mercenaries closed in. The screams of the club's customers and staff were growing fewer, too.

Bolan found what he needed at the end of the hallway. The fire door was clearly marked with the silhouette of a stick figure walking on a stairway. He slammed into the crash bar and bounded up the concrete steps two at a time, his combat boots echoing in the stairwell.

As Bolan made the top of the stairwell, the fire door was pushed open again. He leaned over the railing from his landing and triggered a short burst from the Ultimax, forcing the pursuing mercenary to duck for cover. Then the Executioner was through the doorway on the second floor.

The soldier quickly surveyed the area as he glide-walked laterally away from the stair doors, the Ultimax trained on the door and ready to intercept any attackers. He was in an access corridor that most likely led to some sort of VIP or party room above the club. Burnett had told him as they drove to Busty's that Taveras maintained offices above the club. Those would not be far. If Taveras was there at all, it was likely he'd be holed up, armed to the teeth and ready to wait out the largest of the invasion forces.

The stairway door slammed open. As the first mercenaries

pushed through, their assault weapons leading, Bolan cut them down with a withering hail of fire from the Ultimax. The Executioner watched with grim satisfaction as three of the Blackjack operatives fell on top of one another in the doorway, dead before they knew what hit them. Bolan risked exposing himself only briefly as he pushed the bodies back one at a time with his booted foot. When the doorway was clear, he let the metal fire door slam shut. Then he took a small pocket roll of duct tape from a pocket of his blacksuit. From his war bag, he produced a fragmentation grenade.

Bolan left the grenade taped to the doorway with the pin pulled, the tape holding the spoon in place. He'd have to leave the door unguarded to continue his assault. The numbers were falling. With luck, his booby trap would give the next batch of hired guns something to think about if they decided to try another assault through the stairwell.

The soldier made his way through the VIP room, which was empty except for a low stage and a trio of stripper poles. The floor around the poles was dotted with a few threadbare easy chairs, but there was no other furniture to use for cover or concealment. Bolan moved cautiously past these, checking the shadows, and kicked open a hollow-core wooden door in the far wall.

The Executioner's kick was punctuated by the loud thump of his grenade exploding. He thought he heard a scream, close enough to be a victim of the blast. Strobe lights set in the ceiling of the office corridor in which he stood began to pulse as a deafening fire alarm started to bleat from small speakers next to the lights. He was running out of time.

There were three doors in the office corridor—left, right and dead ahead. The hallway was so narrow he could not extend his arms fully on either side. Allowing the Ultimax to fall to the end of its sling under his duster, Bolan drew the 93-R from its custom leather shoulder holster and flipped the selector switch to

3-round burst. He unclipped his combat light with his left hand and held it under the pistol, his thumb on the tailcap switch. Then he planted his foot just below the doorknob, firing a vicious front kick into the wood.

The room was empty. There were no lights on inside and only the nausea-inducing strobes of the fire lights in the hallway. Bolan used his light to sweep the space, making sure no one lurked there. The little room was a storage closet filled with boxes of file records. Several plastic trash cans of recyclable bottles and cans were stacked in one corner.

Bolan turned and stopped before the left-hand door. He checked the VIP room briefly from the hallway and could still hear gunfire downstairs. No more Blackjack operatives had ascended, however. He could only guess that Taveras's security on-site was keeping them busy, while his booby trap had made them leery of hurrying upstairs without sufficient backup. The Executioner had seen the mercenaries operate all too many times, however. They would not hesitate for long.

Beretta and flashlight at the ready, Bolan kicked open the left-hand door.

He was thrown back into the corridor wall as the wooden door rebounded with impossible force. He cracked his head painfully on the cracked plaster as he went down, losing the Beretta in the fall.

Jesus Molina loomed over him.

The hulking El Cráneo enforcer grabbed the Executioner by his coat lapels and lifted him bodily, slamming him into the wall with all the energy his swollen biceps could generate. Bolan cracked the back of his head again, an electric shock traveling down his spine. As the soldier reached for his weapons, Molina slammed his ham-size left fist into Bolan's gut. The punch was followed by an immediate right hook to Bolan's jaw that snapped his head painfully back. The Executioner hit the floor heavily, blackness crawling over his vision as he started to lose consciousness. Molina bent over him, his huge frame crushing the soldier beneath him as he wrapped his fingers around Bolan's throat.

It was not the first time Bolan had been on the receiving end of a beating, nor would it be the last. The Executioner was a ruthless, trained and combat-experienced operative, but he had learned long ago that he would never be the strongest, the fastest or the most skilled fighter. The numbers were simply against him.

But there would never be an enemy more motivated than Mack Bolan.

Fighting through the haze, knowing his life depended on his next act, the Executioner clawed for a weapon. His right arm was pinned. Molina, on top of him, held a knee over Bolan's right flank, pinning the Ultimax and blocking the soldier's access to the Desert Eagle. There was no way the soldier could draw a breath with Molina choking him. He had no options. Then he realized his left hand still gripped the combat light.

The aluminum body of the light came up in Bolan's fist as he drove the head of the flashlight into Molina's temple. The giant man's eyes went wide with the first blow. His grip on Bolan's throat slackened.

The Executioner struck him again, harder.

The little aluminum tube concentrated the force of Bolan's blow. Something in Molina's skull broke with a sickening crunch. The huge man's eyes rolled up into his head. Bolan pulled himself free, lashing out with a kick that felt as if he was stomping a boulder. He managed to put some distance between himself and Molina, though, drawing the Desert Eagle as he scrambled across the corridor floor on his back.

His vision still blurred, the Executioner was lining up a shot on the staggering Molina when a bullet tore through the giant's forehead and dug into the wooden door at the far end of the hallway. Molina fell forward and was still. Bolan had time to note the gaping exit wound above his face.

"A simple thank-you will do," Percival Leister said. He was dressed in black combat fatigues, though he didn't wear the load-bearing vest or other harnesses sported by his men. In his right fist was the Browning Hi-Power he'd used to end Molina's life.

"Can't leave anyone behind, don't you know," Leister said, sounding almost apologetic. "I don't pretend to know who you are, you cagey bastard, but I can guess. I suspect you'd like very much to speak with Taveras's crew. I can't allow that. My employers can't allow that."

"Your employers," Bolan started to say as he brought up the Desert Eagle.

"Stop!" Leister ordered. "Put it down. You can't make it, lad. Just put it down." The Hi-Power in Leister's hand was aimed at Bolan's chest. "I'll kill you."

"You'll kill me anyway," Bolan said.

"That may not be necessary," Leister said. Bolan still held the Desert Eagle, but he wasn't trying to aim it at the British mercenary. Leister, in turn, sounded almost conciliatory. "Hasn't there been enough bloodshed over this miserable business?" he asked.

"Your men didn't seem too concerned with bloodshed in Bryant Park," Bolan said.

"That was excessive." Leister nodded. The walkie-talkie on his belt chirped. Leister brought it to his mouth with his left hand, his Browning steady, his gaze never leaving Bolan. "Leister," he said.

"We've got the ground floor contained," the voice said. "The last of Taveras's men on-site are neutralized. Orders?"

"Stay where you are, for the moment."

"The cops are gonna be here any minute," the voice protested.

"Just do your bloody job," Leister said impatiently. "Get the teams mobilized, verify the floor is clear and get the hell gone."

"And you, sir?"

"I just have a loose end or two to tie up," Leister said. "Move!"

"Yes, sir."

"Now, then," Leister said to Bolan. "I don't suppose there's any chance we can come to some sort of agreement? I'd rather not make enemies of more government agencies than I must."

"I didn't say I worked for the government," Bolan said.

"Please." Leister grinned. "You obviously work for the Justice Department or some other federal agency. I'd rather not murder you if it is not necessary. Can't we deal?"

"The way you cut a deal with Taveras?" Bolan said. "Why proposition him if you were just going to take him down?"

Leister paused at that, obviously unsure how Bolan knew as much as he did. The feeling was mutual, as far as Bolan was concerned.

"Very well." Leister shrugged. "Yes, I did offer to cut a deal with Mr. Taveras, for reasons I'm certain you can guess."

"Then why raid his club and kill his men?" Bolan asked.

"What else could be done?" Leister said grimly. "I made an attempt to deal with Taveras in terms I thought his kind could understand. My employers are not mass murderers, after all. We're trying to *prevent* more problems."

"This is how you prevent problems?" Bolan asked.

"You know their type," Leister said. "One cannot afford to show weakness. Not long after I made Taveras my generous offer, El Cráneo hit the hotel from which we were operating. I lost good men."

Bolan digested that. "So Taveras has been busy, but not all the targets were surviving Caquetas."

"Indeed," Leister said. "What I'd truly like to know is how they knew where to find us. I suppose Taveras has his own informants. I tell you, this town is rotten. It's like a great tree that's been eaten inside by every bug imaginable. It will please me to leave it."

"What do you want?" Bolan asked him.

"Ever direct," Leister said. "That's what I like about you Yanks. It's this simple. Look the other way. Let my men do what we came here to do. The end result will be…well, let's say it will get the job done. You and I both know about the DU ammunition. Stay out of my way and I'll see to it the problem disappears."

"No matter who gets killed?" Bolan asked. "How many will die when you start supplying Taveras with arms in return for his cooperation?"

"I'd say that's not likely to happen now," Leister said. "We're going to have to eliminate him. Wouldn't you like to see that happen? Think of the time and effort we'd save you. Why, you're not even footing the bill. Your government pays well to have people like mine fight their wars, guard their convoys, safeguard their very important persons. Would it really be such a stretch?"

"Don't kid yourself," Bolan said. "You're not doing anything noble. You're being paid to erase a problem that will make your employers look bad—a problem so big they don't care how many people have to die to ensure the cover-up happens."

"True enough," Leister admitted. "But is there really such a big difference? The U.S. government does the same thing. It does it on even larger scales."

"But you're willing to wage open war on the streets of an American city," Bolan said.

"Now you're being hypocritical, don't you think?" Leister said. "Open war is not so rare on the streets of other cities through the world—cities about which the U.S.A. isn't exactly so timid when it comes to waging its wars."

"Innocent people are dying," Bolan said. "More will die for the sake of your cover-up."

"It can't be helped," Leister frowned. "Listen, I'm quite willing to be reasonable about this." The mercenary began to back away. "But don't push your luck. Cheerio." He backed out hastily the way he'd come, disappearing into the VIP room.

Bolan surged to his feet, fighting the wave of nausea caused by the sudden movement. His head throbbing, he charged after Leister. With the Desert Eagle in both hands, he cut the doorway wide and plunged into the VIP room.

Leister was already gone. Somewhere downstairs and just outside the club, police and fire sirens were wailing. The strobe lights of the fire-alarm system continued to blink as the alarm wailed on.

Bolan holstered the Desert Eagle. He went back for his Beretta, found the weapon and checked it before stowing it. Then he made a cursory check of the strip club's office. There was no one hiding there and nothing to find. Bolan was ready with the explanations he would have to offer when the first of the police officers reached the second floor of Busty's. Fortunately for Bolan, Burnett was with them. He had a first-aid kit cold pack on the back of his head.

"Cooper," he said. "No luck?"

"I had an interesting chat with our friend Leister." Bolan nodded.

"He got away?"

"Unfortunately."

Burnett looked grim. "That's too bad. I'm afraid I wasn't much help here, myself."

"You forget to duck for a low doorway?" Bolan asked.

Burnett shook his head. "Somebody clubbed me from behind. Probably one of Leister's men as they mounted their attack. I never would have figured they'd strike so soon."

"Leister told me he was hitting Taveras for attacking his men. Seems El Cráneo's official position on deals with Blackjack is an emphatic *no*."

"So it would seem," Burnett said. "Now what?"

"Sir!" One of the uniformed officers came running into the room with a cell phone open in his hand. "Sir, urgent call for you!" He handed it to the detective.

"Burnett," the big man said. He listened. His face grew pale as the voice on the other end spoke.

"What is it?" Bolan asked.

Burnett closed the phone without saying anything. He looked at Bolan. "El Cráneo is making its move. I've got a standoff in the middle of Times Square, for God's sake!"

11

Bolan made his way on foot up Forty-third Street, past throngs of curious New Yorkers, threading his way through the crowd until he reached the police barricades. The lights of Times Square mixed with the lights of passing automobiles and the blue-and-red bubbles atop the police vehicles. Manhattan was having a hard week, it seemed, and there was no doubt in the Executioner's mind that things were going to get a lot harder before the sun came up. He was stopped at the barricade but flashed his Justice credentials, which got him through and face-to-face with the officer in charge on-site.

"Cooper," he informed the man. "I radioed ahead."

"Pendergast," answered the big, bullet-headed officer in navy SWAT fatigues. He carried an AR-15 slung over one shoulder. "I confirmed with the department. You're cleared to go in, for all the good it will do."

"What's the story?"

"El Cráneo," he said. "They're looking to make a statement in a big way, we guess. They've got six vehicles, all big SUVs, forming a blockade of their own at the center of Times Square. Just drove in, circled the wagons and started shooting up the place. I've got civilians down, plus four officers. Shot through their vests *and* through their car. It isn't pretty."

Bolan's face darkened. "I'm heading in."

"The perimeter is a block up," Pendergast told him. "Halfway there you'll see the APC. We're gearing up, so if you think you're going to do anything, you'll have to be fast."

"Gearing up? For what?"

"We're taking the armored personnel carrier in. I don't know what you think you can do, but it's going to be over with pretty soon."

"You can't do that," Bolan told him. "They'll cut you apart."

"Look, Cooper," Pendergast said disdainfully, "you may have some high-powered backers in Washington, or whatever the hell, but we aren't exactly amateurs here. Stay out of my way. I don't have the authority to warn you off this site, but you don't have authority over me, either." He turned on his heel and walked away to confer with some of the officers nearby.

Bolan didn't waste time trying to argue. He made for the APC, a six-wheeled tanklike truck with no turret. Gun ports were placed strategically on the sides and in front. The rear loading doors were open. Bolan identified himself to the personnel there and waited while they conferred with Pendergast by radio.

"Sir," one of the officers told him, "please move out of range of the vehicle. We're about to move."

"Do you understand what you're driving into?" Bolan asked him. "This vehicle isn't going to protect you."

"They may have armor-piercing ammo, sir," the young officer said, climbing into the hatch, "but they don't have anything heavier than rifles. We're more than a match for them." As he spoke, several armed officers piled into the rear of the vehicle, securing the hatch doors behind them.

Bolan ran for it. He moved quickly in the direction of the barricades, looking for an opening. Behind him, the APC started up and began rolling toward the center of Times Square.

The Executioner reached the barricades, which were set well back from the circle of trucks in Times Square. Several officers were crouched behind shields, as well as the engine blocks of their police cruisers and support vehicles. The El Cráneo forces were crouched well out of sight behind the barricade formed by their trucks. All of the SUVs were black with deeply tinted windows. There was no way to see who might be inside them, or what they were doing. Some men were visible moving around behind trucks, but they were careful to stay as hidden as possible. There would be no way to get a clear shot at them, even for the police snipers who were doubtless watching from nearby rooftops.

Bolan took his secure phone from his blacksuit and dialed the number Burnett had given him.

"Burnett," the detective answered.

"You were right," Bolan confirmed. "They're already headed in, come hell or high water, and they don't want to hear that it's not going to work out."

"Told you," Burnett said. "What next?"

"I have a plan," Bolan said. "Are you in position?"

"Circulating through the crowd, just like you said," Burnett answered. "Just another asshole talking on his cell phone in a crowd of strangers. What do you want me to do?"

"There's no way El Cráneo would trap itself like this, just to send a message," Bolan told him. "They're going to have eyes and ears outside their barricade, someone coordinating things undercover. I need you to use your detective's eyes to spot whomever that might be."

"Eye," Burnett said.

"Whatever," Bolan told him. "You up to it?"

"Leave it to me," Burnett told him. "What are you going to be doing?"

"Making trouble," Bolan said. "It's going to get ugly when the police move in. Keep your head down."

"Will do."

Bolan snapped the phone shut and weighed his options. The APC was rolling inexorably toward the police barriers.

The Executioner made his decision, checked the drum in the

Ultimax and fell in behind the moving vehicle. As the myriad flashing, strobing, neon and high-intensity lights of Times Square blinked above him, the Executioner noted the shadows and observed his opposition. Beyond the police barricades, crowds of New Yorkers gawked, watching the scene unfold with no knowledge of just how dangerous the battleground was about to become. The APC rolled slowly onward. The police inside were similarly unprepared for the firestorm that awaited them.

When the signal came, the El Cráneo killers were waiting. As one they brought the barrels of their weapons around from the cover of the SUVs. Bolan caught the movement, a subtle change that would be hard to see from within the armored vehicle.

"You in the APC!" Bolan shouted at the top of his lungs. "Officers, this is Cooper, Justice Department! Turn back now! You are outgunned! I repeat, you are outgunned!"

Whether the men in the vehicle heard Bolan and ignored him, or never heard his warning, the Executioner would never know. A shot rang out—from behind his position, somewhere within the crowd. The DU bullet burned into the back of the APC just over Bolan's shoulder.

Hell erupted.

Bolan threw himself flat on the ground. Streams of DU ammunition poured from the El Cráneo shooters within the circle of SUVs. The focused fire poured over the APC, punching and burning through the vehicle as if its armor wasn't there. From his position only feet from it, Bolan could hear fragments ricochet within the armored vehicle as its occupants were at once torn apart and roasted alive. The screams of the dying men drowned out the shouts and cries for help from among the suddenly terrified throngs of spectators.

The cross fire grew more intense. Bolan realized the rear of the APC had taken more fire. He did the only thing he could do. He began rolling to the side, trying to move his body away from the APC. Burning DU rounds ripped the air above him and tore into the pavement where he'd been.

Bolan's only chance was to avoid being hit. There was no body armor and no obstacle he could put between him and the El Cráneo guns that would save him if he took a round somewhere critical. Even a relatively survivable wound would be much worse if made by one of the DU bullets. With no way to defend and no place to hide, he had one choice.

He attacked.

From his back, Bolan brought up the Ultimax and sighted between his feet. There, beyond the nearest of the police barricades, he saw them—the El Cráneo gunners who had to have been posing as spectators. They were armed with submachine guns and were still spraying the APC, fixated on the larger target. Knowing he would have only seconds at most, the soldier carefully lined up his shots. The angle would send his 5.56 mm rounds into the concrete facade of building beyond. He could afford no misses if he was to minimize the risk to innocent New Yorkers beyond his targets.

Battle-callused fingers tightened on the grip of the Ultimax. Bolan pressed the trigger again and again. The red-dot scope picked out the silhouette of each shooter's head against the lights of Times Square. The El Cráneo gunners fell one after another.

The APC began to burn like a pyre. Flames licked the sky, bright enough to rival the frenetic electronic billboards. From the circle of SUVs, the gunners began to track secondary targets. The police returned fire from their barricades. Several were shot through their cruisers as the El Cráneo gunners sprayed the vehicles. The merciless DU rounds did their work only too well.

With the threat from behind neutralized, Bolan rolled back into the dubious shelter of the burning APC. Using the lee of the vehicle as both cover and concealment, the Executioner crouched and scrambled away from the killzone. When he reached the dead men behind the police barrier, he began searching quickly through the bodies.

Several of the men had 9 mm machine pistols, while one had a MAC-10 chambered in .45. One of them, however, had wielded a short-barreled M-16. Bolan appropriated the dead man's loaded magazines, the cartridges bearing unusual red and silver tips. He tossed several magazines of 9 mm DU ammunition into his war bag, as well. Then he swapped out the drum magazine in the Ultimax, praising Cowboy Kissinger's custom magazine adapter as he slapped the M-16 magazine into place.

The night was bright with tracer fire against the city lights. The cops were firing back but taking a pounding from their positions. Bolan lost count of the number of officers he saw go down, cut to pieces behind their cruisers or shot through concrete barriers that should have protected them. The tracer rounds fired by the police marksmen were ineffective against the circle of trucks. Taveras's vehicles were armored. Most of their tires were now flat, but the vehicles themselves were intact. The men behind them continued to rain merciless DU fire over Times Square.

Bolan retraced his steps, again using the burning APC to cover his approach. Taveras's plan had been bold and smart. Men hidden in the crowd had helped him create a deadly cross fire and would have provided him with an escape route, given him a means to punch through the police line when his men were ready to leave. The cops nearby had been gunned down with the first salvo. Pendergast and his men were now fighting for their lives and pinned down where they fought. The tactician in Bolan could admire the way the operation was supposed to work, even as he fought to dismantle it.

The burning APC and the dead El Cráneo men beyond formed the only safe channel where Bolan could operate without being targeted by the police, too. While Pendergast—if he was still alive—had met Bolan and presumably knew not to shoot him, there were too many other officers on-site who wouldn't know Bolan from the gang members. That was a risk the Executioner had assumed by crashing the party. He was more than used to watching his own back for friendly fire.

Bolan took a shooter's crouch on one knee, bracing the Ultimax on its folding stock against his shoulder. The heat was almost too much to bear. Sweat poured down the Executioner's face and stung his eyes as he put the red-dot scope over the engine block of the nearest SUV.

The soldier's practiced eye caught movement behind the truck. He fired. The Ultimax vibrated under his hands, its low recoil allowing him to keep his deadly shots on target one after another.

The DU rounds bored through the armor-plated SUV, sparking and flaming, taking out the man behind. Bolan quickly engaged the next target at the rear of the same vehicle, tracking the shadows of feet visible beneath the trucks. He saturated the rear of the SUV with DU rounds and was rewarded with another kill.

The front of one and the rear of a second SUV were within Bolan's field of fire. He dropped his first spent M-16 magazine and slapped home another. Walking the shots in, following the bursts of flame that erupted whenever one of the rounds scored a hit on the pavement or the trucks, Bolan ventilated the ends of both vehicles and the men who believed themselves safe behind their armor. It was fitting, the Executioner thought, that these men should die from behind and within the false shelter of their vehicles, as had so many of their victims.

The rest of the El Cráneo gunners had caught on to what was happening and were moving. Bolan broke from his position and headed straight for them, taking the fight to the enemy. The sudden onslaught put them off balance. Bolan followed his DU bullets in, spraying down the trucks and burning through them. With nowhere to go except into the crosshairs of the waiting police, they froze. The Executioner burned down each of them in turn.

The SUVs began to smoke and flame as brightly as the APC. Bolan shut out the stench of burning flesh as he stalked among the bodies, checking each one carefully. The police began to advance on his position, covering each other in groups of four, led by Pendergast. The stocky man held an MP-5 in his hands and looked around at the carnage with wonder. The blazing, dancing firelight turned Bolan's face demonic as shadows danced across it.

"Are you all right?" Pendergast asked finally.

Bolan nodded at the hulk of the APC. "Better than they are," he said grimly. "Take a long, hard look around, Pendergast. If you can't accept the reality of what you face, this is the result."

Pendergast said nothing.

Bolan left the man standing amid the smoking ruins of the El Cráneo vehicles. He checked the bodies, looking for Taveras, but saw no one he recognized. In the pocket of his blacksuit, his phone began to vibrate.

"Cooper," he answered.

"It's me," Burnett said. "I'm at Seventh and Forty-first. I think I've got what you wanted."

Bolan rushed toward the detective, dodging the ever present New York City crowds. Media vehicles were pressing through the thick traffic, followed by still more police cruisers, with some beleaguered ambulance crews switching their sirens on and off trapped in the bumper-to-bumper mess. The Times Square conflagration, while not the equal of terrorist attacks the city had seen, would not stand alone in the eyes of the authorities or the city's residents. Taken in total with the other high-profile shootings, Bolan knew it would be the last straw. He did not relish the phone call he was likely to get from Hal Brognola in response to this latest incident, but deep down he knew the big Fed would understand. At least the Executioner had managed to minimize the damage and stop the massacre before it could encompass more civilians.

He found Burnett waiting with a pair of uniformed officers outside the entrance to a chain seafood restaurant.

"Here?" he asked.

"You should try their cheese-garlic biscuits," Burnett said without smiling. "Here's the deal, Cooper. Officers Hickey and Messina." He gestured to each of the cops in turn. "I grabbed them as we were leaving the barricades. Two more, DiFlorio and Sober, are watching the back. Our man's inside."

"Our man?"

"It's July de la Rocha." Burnett nodded. "You were right. While everyone was watching the action, I scoped out the crowd like you said. De la Rocha was circulating through the spectators with a cell phone. When the sleepers in the crowd cut loose, I'm pretty sure it was de la Rocha who gave the word."

"How did he end up here?" Bolan asked.

"When it started to go badly for El Cráneo, he faded fast," Burnett said. "This guy is smooth, too. He didn't act like there was the slightest thing wrong. Just snapped his phone shut and walked out of there, as casual as you please. I followed him, got backup and had Sober and DiFlorio take the back after he went in here."

"Did he see you before he went in?" Bolan asked.

"He could have," Burnett admitted. "There wasn't time to be real sneaky about it."

"All right," Bolan said. "You men take the door. You saw the target?" Both officers nodded. "Good. He doesn't come out. Make sure your friends in back know it, as well."

He looked at Burnett. "Let's go."

Inside the restaurant, Burnett briefly conferred with the hostess. She directed the two men to the establishment's kitchen. De la Rocha, or someone matching his description, was apparently a regular visitor to the place, for reasons unknown to the young woman.

"I'll bet good money this place is owned by Taveras, or a company we can tie to Taveras," Burnett said.

"It wouldn't surprise me," Bolan said. "El Cráneo probably

maintains a network of safe houses and bought-out locations where their people can disappear."

They found the kitchen and Burnett cornered the first cook he saw, describing de la Rocha. The man—a young Hispanic in a dirty white apron and equally soiled white shirt—jerked a thumb toward the cooler. "Yeah, he comes and goes. We call him the Phantom. The manager said not to worry about it."

Bolan drew the Beretta 93-R. The cook's eyes went wide and he backed away. Burnett drew his Glock and covered the cooler door as Bolan pulled it open, covering the opening with his machine pistol.

Cold air wafted out. The shelves inside bore the usual restaurant items. A bucket of lettuce soaking in water sat undisturbed just inside the doorway. Plates of plastic-wrap-covered desserts waited in their racks.

"Shit," Burnett said.

Bolan, suspicious, moved inside the walk-in cooler. He scanned the walls and then fixed on the back of the space, which was blocked by a rolling cart full of covered plates on racks. He reached out and moved the cart away.

"Burnett," he said. "Cover me."

A solid shove against the far wall of the cooler was all it took to move it away. It swung on squeaking hinges, revealing a concrete-walled access chamber. Crumbling concrete steps led into a low-ceilinged utility tunnel lighted fitfully with battery-powered stick-on dome lamps.

"Jackpot," Burnett said.

"Call your men," Bolan told him. "There's no point guarding the back or the front. De la Rocha will be long gone. We'll want to search the tunnel."

A cursory inspection of the access chamber revealed nothing useful. Burnett detailed DiFlorio and Messina to follow the tunnel to its end. They radioed back when they emerged in an alley a block away. De la Rocha was long gone.

"Shit," Burnett said again. "Come on, Cooper. Let's get out of this icebox. I want to find the manager. He might know something."

A shot suddenly rang out, blowing apart a crock of salad dressing on the shelf nearest the detective. He flinched and ducked. Bolan punched the Beretta in the direction of the threat and triggered a single shot as his arm hit full extension. A short, dark-haired man with a revolver fell forward on the floor of the kitchen, blood welling from his center of mass. Kitchen staff stood frozen and staring, unable to process what they'd just seen.

"Let me guess," Burnett said, standing again and looking to Bolan. "That's the manager."

Bolan said nothing.

12

As the first gray-yellow streaks of dawn greeted Camden, New Jersey's residents, one of them regarded the sunrise through a grime-streaked window overlooking the crumbling waterfront district.

Donald Stevens sat behind a cheap particleboard desk laden with computer equipment. Three flat-screen monitors stared back at him, their displays covered in three-dimensional rotating drawings of various weapons and cartridges. A small window in the corner of one monitor showed the status of the warehouse's elaborate security systems, each one armed and ready. Before him, on the only space on the desk not cluttered with printouts, reference books or other pieces of machinery, was a Colt Gold Cup .45 automatic pistol. It had a brushed chrome finish and was loaded with his latest and most powerful explosive-tipped depleted uranium rounds.

It annoyed Stevens no end to have to contemplate taking up arms himself. Theoretically he was not opposed to it, of course. He could hardly be North America's preeminent arms designer if he suffered from an irrational fear of or disdain for weapons. He was not, however, a hands-on person. The dirty work was for those who did not, who simply *could* not, aspire to higher goals.

Still, there was self-preservation to consider.

Stevens had no trouble acknowledging his own brilliance. Recruited by Norris Labs straight out of college, he had always known he was destined for great things. He was a born engineer with a penchant for designing implements of destruction. He built his first primitive but potentially lethal catapult, albeit on a small scale, at the age of ten. By his teens, he was experimenting with rockets and homemade explosives. Before he graduated high school, he had used the equipment in the school's auto shop to manufacture his first crude—and quite illegal—handgun. No one ever knew of that. He had that weapon to this day, locked in his safe with his more secret designs.

In college he had excelled in chemistry, physics and mechanical design, focusing all his projects on weapons theory and warfare. One of his professors, a man retired from Norris Labs himself, spotted Stevens's talent early on. He watched the young student until he was sure, then contacted NLI. The company's recruiters made Stevens an offer that seemed impossible to refuse, at the time. As he reflected on those early, eager days, his memories were bitter.

At first, it all seemed to be going as he'd hoped. He was Norris Labs' prodigy, the favored son of NLI's board of directors. Immediately after his arrival, he developed a streamlined manufacturing process that saved NLI millions of dollars per year in processing its conventional rifle ammunition on contract for the U.S. military. Stevens had followed that success by redesigning the specifications for the rifle rounds NLI was contracted to produce—specifications that were in turn adopted by the military as preferable to those they'd been using.

Those projects were nothing, however, compared to the secret "black bag" specifications to which Stevens was designing. He knew, from the beginning, that some of the materials he was asked to work with and some of the designs he was asked to provide, were minor or major violations of international treaties or domestic laws. Norris Labs was offered considerable leeway under license to the U.S. government, but there were limits. Stevens's employers asked him to cross those lines. He did so gladly. The challenge, the inner drive he'd always had to create something better, more efficient, more powerful, something eminently more lethal, were all the motivation he needed. As he broke more and more laws, foreign and domestic, he grew to love new challenges. His employers goaded him on, always asking for more, always asking for better. He did not care why they were so cavalier with the law, why they courted so much danger.

Stevens, now an older man, knew only too well why any group of businessmen would break the law or traffic in war. There was money in it. Conventional arms were profitable, but cutting edge, ever more deadly and often illegal arms were obscenely profitable. As more and more fringe groups, banana republics, rogue nations and garden-variety terrorists and criminals cropped up, the markets for NLI's less-than-legal munitions grew.

The company's lawyers worked hard to keep it out of trouble, to establish for it the plausible deniability that kept such a juggernaut in business. The company's security contractors worked just as hard assassinating anyone who threatened NLI's empire. This included more than a few of Norris Labs' own employees—not to mention their families—when leverage was needed and messages had to be sent. The price for endangering the company was clear enough. Most of those who'd sold their souls to the devil that was NLI knew that death was preferable to incurring the company's displeasure.

Stevens toiled for years as a dutiful employee of NLI. Despite the company's illicit activities, many of his designs were deemed too dangerous politically to see the light of day. He might not have minded that so much, despite the disappointment at seeing his worked shelved indefinitely, if there had been some compensation for his efforts. As the years rolled past, however, Stevens realized something. When it occurred to him, finally, it was far worse than any problem he'd previously considered. It was worse than a technical problem, worse than the threat of being caught helping to develop and manufacture illegal arms, worse than the moral implications of whatever violations he might have committed at home or internationally.

Donald Stevens was being taken for granted.

He had an ironclad contract, had signed countless nondisclosure agreements and was bound by simple fear of prison in many cases. He had no legal recourse. Norris Labs, as his employer, was legally entitled to any and all profit and outcome of his brilliance. His designs were NLI's designs. His very thoughts belonged to them. Anything he even considered developing while working with NLI's resources became the property of the company. He had even, in his foolishness, signed various noncompete agreements in his youth. For all intents and purposes, Norris Labs International owned Donald Stevens's soul. The company was only too aware of what it possessed.

Stevens received a bonus each year, to be sure. His employers and the obsequious fools on the board were only too happy to invite him to their parties, bestow on him their meaningless awards, flatter him with their insincere thanks and pay lip service to his opinions. At the end of every day, however, Stevens was *human capital,* a resource to be used until it was no longer profitable. At that point, according to the terms of his contract, Stevens was legally obligated not to work in the arms-development field for a period of no less than five years. That was, as far as he was concerned, simply adding insult to injury.

Norris Labs took what he designed. It paid him far too little, in his opinion, to compensate him. While his processes and devices, from chemical-manufacturing methods to guidance systems for cruise missiles, earned the company billions worldwide, Stevens was lucky to see a six-figure salary. It galled him to be used in that way, to be treated by NLI as if the company were doing him a favor in shortchanging him. When his best work was sealed away in dark vaults, never to be seen again, when his would-be masters on the board told him he was not to pursue a particular line of development, it bothered him more each time. The last straw had been the depleted uranium small-arms ammunition.

It was such a simple concept, Stevens was amazed no one had invested in it before him. The battlefields of the day were the domain of depleted uranium rounds in heavy weaponry. Why not small arms, as well? In a day and age when fighters were increasingly armored at the individual level, why not develop the counteragent to that armor and do so preemptively? Stevens had also capitalized on the pyrophoric properties of the materials he was using, adding the accelerant tip to turn the rounds into truly explosive individual firebombs that were also amazing penetrators.

Then NLI had slammed the door in his face.

They treated him worse than they'd ever treated him before. They hadn't just taken him for granted, they'd acted like he'd done something wrong. They had paid him for years to develop lethal armament. Then, overnight, they'd decided he'd gone too far. The rounds were a liability to the corporation, they said. There was too much backlash concerning depleted uranium rounds in heavy weaponry already, they complained. Turn the rounds smaller and make them man-portable and you'd unleash a firestorm of negative public sentiment, worse than the campaigns to ban land mines or the torture of enemy combatants, they whined. The company was already on the receiving end of investigations into its weapons trading overseas, they said, and Blackjack Group was becoming similarly high-profile in its war contracting. Norris Labs couldn't afford the liability the DU rounds represented, they finally concluded. Hide the design, suppress the technology and make the whole thing go away, they ordered.

No more.

Stevens realized at that moment that he'd had enough. He was done being used. He was done toiling in relative poverty. It was time to take what he'd created and truly benefit from it. Along the way, he'd see to it that NLI paid for their arrogance, for their misuse of his genius.

Donald Stevens discovered that there was real money to be made in the arms market.

He'd started small, but not that small. He diverted to international buyers whole shipments of conventional arms, using Jonathan West's computer skills to make it happen. West had, in fact, been integral to his plan. Stevens was an idea man, after all. He did what he did at the highest levels of thinking. It was West who had the practical know-how to put the plan into action. The two had worked together for long enough to become something approximating friends, which was rare for both of them. West was also young enough and money-hungry enough to jump at the chance Stevens offered. Theirs was purely a business relationship, but one that had worked. West had set up the practical side of the operation, helped him build their initial capital. Now he was dead.

Stevens sighed and picked up the handgun, racking the slide and engaging the frame safety. He had known, abstractly, just how dangerous to NLI was the production of DU ammunition. The paper trail led back to Norris Labs, after all. The initial proceeds from arms shipments to terrorist groups and rogue nations had ended up in an offshore account Stevens used to purchase equipment—and to purchase silence. He'd set up shop in Camden, buying the warehouse space, hiring security people, bribing local officials and getting his machinery up and running. He'd greased wheels with the local organized-crime groups. He'd spread around so much money, in fact, that West's crude attempts to find markets for the DU ammunition had met with reasonable success, despite some missteps.

The scope of what he was doing to NLI had not truly occurred to him, however, until they started sending their Blackjack operatives to kill him.

West's death was shocking enough, but the rampage of Blackjack mercenaries through New York City had shocked Stevens to his core. It was then that he realized just how dangerous his operation was to the company. If his link to NLI was discovered, the fact that he was acting on his own would not matter. He and NLI, and with them Blackjack Group, would be seen as a single enterprise, committing what were essentially war crimes on American soil. The public-relations nightmare would be matched only by the legal ramifications. Powerful men ran Norris Labs—and powerful men had few compunctions about who they silenced to keep that power. Stevens had not truly appreciated just how far such men would go. It was beyond murder. It was open war. Donald Stevens had declared war on NLI, and NLI had met his challenge with vicious, brutal zeal.

The real irony was that NLI had met Stevens's tactics on the same terms. He had spread the depleted uranium ammunition they had tried to suppress and to hide. He had struck back at them, making vast sums of money in the process. So they had come for him, and they had done so with the same DU rounds. Blackjack had always believed in fighting fire with fire. Now, with the genie out of the bottle, they were going to lay waste to the entire landscape before sweeping all of the pieces under the rug. It made a sort of ruthless sense.

Stevens was not without his own resources, of course. The vast sums of money he'd made in the arms market allowed him the best in automated security and antipersonnel devices for the factory. He also had his own security people—contractors from a rival company whose owner had no love for Blackjack. Armed security guards stood their posts within and outside the Camden factory.

Stevens, perhaps because he was so comfortable with academics, with theory, had made what now seemed a prescient decision. He had paid his contractors not just for armed muscle, but for intelligence. Security contractors were only too eager to play CIA on someone else's dollar, it seemed, and Stevens was happy to indulge them. Among the services provided for him by his contractors were surveillance and intelligence gathering locally. His men watched his assets and ran down any potential threats to his well-being. Stevens, in turn, threw money at them. Everybody was happy, and Stevens stayed reasonably safe. He had to admit to himself, however, that he had never really expected them to turn up anything.

He was, therefore, taken by surprise when one of his field men called to relay the bad news.

They'd called just that morning—the two men Stevens paid to monitor the Swedesboro house. He was proud of that house and what it represented, though West had helped him with the working details. Starting with the assumption that paper trails always led somewhere, they'd deliberately arranged for the trail to end at the address in Swedesboro—an unremarkable tract home in a sea of similar homes in an unremarkable development in New Jersey. From a nearby home, Stevens's security men monitored the house day and night. If someone came knocking, they could follow up and ascertain to what extent those visiting had penetrated Stevens's operation. They had done so now, not once, but twice.

The first time, men whom Stevens could only assume were law enforcement or government personnel had raided the house. They hadn't stayed long—just poked around long enough to reassure themselves there was nothing there. This meant Stevens's defenses were working as they should. Someone had investigated and found West but, thanks to West's arrogance and Stevens's cunning, they'd found only the younger man. Stevens was confident he remained in the shadows, undetected, free to continue his work.

That morning, however, the security men had called to say the house had been raided a second time. Stevens had immediately recognized the leader of the raid in the digital video e-mailed to him by his men. Percival Leister was the man behind Blackjack Group. Stevens had encountered him more than once at Norris Labs, even using his men to field-test various munitions and weapons. If Leister was attending to things personally, things were dire indeed. Stevens knew Leister preferred to remain the man behind the curtain, much as Stevens himself did.

Stevens's men had earned their pay by following Leister. The Blackjack mercenaries had spent considerable time tearing apart the Swedesboro house, but eventually they'd left. Stevens's men had tailed them quietly and found the location from which they were now working. Several teams were holed up in a motel just outside Swedesboro. If the reports Stevens had watched on television overnight were any indication, he'd lost countless men in the cross fires of what had to be gang wars and police intervention. It was possible that the men at the motel were all of Leister's reserves. Stevens wondered how long it would be before NLI decided Leister and his people represented a link back to them. Who would they get to eliminate that threat?

Then again, given the rumors he'd heard and the things he'd actually seen, it was possible that NLI had every confidence in Blackjack Group's discretion. Men who were so afraid for what might happen to friends, family and relatives that they would rather die than fail or be captured—that was the Blackjack way, as Stevens understood it—could hardly be expected to roll over on the employer.

It seemed likely that the market for Stevens's product was played out in New York City. He would have to shift his focus until things calmed down in Manhattan. It would be some time before the criminal elements of New York could reassert themselves. That was all right. He could find buyers in other cities and in other states. He would have to adjust his pricing to take shipping into account, if he was to branch out farther. That, too, he could handle. But if Blackjack had gotten far enough in its investigation to find the house in Swedesboro, he had a decision to make.

Stevens had expected the authorities to find the house eventually. That was what it was there for. He knew that Blackjack employed private investigators and had government contacts of its own, but he had counted on the contractors being unable to dig as deeply as their government counterparts. If that was not the case, it was conceivable that Stevens and West had not buried their tracks deeply enough. If Blackjack could find the house in Swedesboro, Blackjack and the U.S. government could find the warehouse. West's death introduced a further complication, for Stevens had no idea just how much evidence his late partner had left behind. It could not have been too much, as it had taken this long for the enemy to come knocking on Stevens's New Jersey door, but still… The risk was real and it was there.

Stevens was not about to take on the full power and might of the U.S. government, but then, he didn't really have to. All he had to do was stay a step ahead of the authorities. It would be a terrible bother to move the Camden factory to another location, taking time and money to do it properly and with the needed secrecy. It could be done, however. He would take that step if it was absolutely necessary.

He had enough men to take on Leister's people. At least, he thought he did. They would be dangerous and difficult to defeat, but he believed his own forces were equal to the task. He might not have another opportunity to face so depleted a force, if the report he'd been given was accurate as to numbers. To make the attack was to take a grave risk, however. He would have to commit most of his men to the act and pay them a handsome fee to convince them to undertake the project in the first place. If he lost them, he'd lose his security force and be helpless. Well, he had to admit, perhaps *helpless* wasn't the word, given the other security measures he had taken. But he was not comfortable without a human component to guard his investments.

He was mulling over all of this when his phone rang again. Placing the pistol back on the desk in front of him, he put the receiver to his ear without saying anything.

"Stevens?" It was Taveras.

"Yes," Stevens answered.

"I trust your operations continue?" he said. "You have had no problems?"

Taveras had never before inquired as to his welfare, and the drug lord did not strike Stevens as a humanitarian. The only ex- planation was that Taveras and his people needed more of what Stevens had so ably provided.

"I am well," Stevens told him, "though I admit I have had my concerns. Are you calling to arrange another shipment?"

"We can discuss that," Taveras said. "But I have another mo- tive, *amigo*. I have recently been visited by an enemy of yours. Someone who wants very much to find you. Someone who thought he could trick me and insult me, get me to help him find you and kill you."

"Is that so?"

"Yes," Taveras said, "that is so. But you do not have to worry. I gave this man a message. He was not quick to take my mean- ing, and now I owe him all the more. But I will see to it he learns."

"Why are you telling me this?"

"We have enemies in common, *amigo*. The better prepared I am to deal with them, the better able I am to show them what it means to trifle with El Cráneo."

"I see," Stevens said. "You want a discount."

"Surely you can see the benefit to both of us?"

"Tell me," Stevens said, suddenly putting it together. "Your visitor, the man who insulted you and whom you wish to teach a lesson—was he British?"

"Yes," Taveras said through clenched teeth. "Yes, he was."

"I see," Stevens said again. "Mr. Taveras, I believe we can indeed help each other. Tell me, would it be terribly useful to you to know exactly where you could find this man?"

There was a pause. "Yes," Taveras said, sounding surprised and pleased. "Yes, I would very much like to know that."

"Then consider your next shipment half off, to cover the expense of the favor you are about to do me," Stevens suggested.

"I am listening."

"The man you want," Stevens began, "can be found in a motel in Swedesboro, New Jersey."

13

Bolan stood in the small shower stall in his hotel room, letting the hot water sluice away the aches and pains he'd accumulated in the previous days' combat. He'd been awake before dawn, only to be greeted by another text message briefing from the Farm. While Stony Man had no new intelligence to offer, Brognola had briefed Price on the political situation in New York. The jaws had snapped shut.

Martial law had been declared and the National Guard was on the streets, called out by the governor at the request of New York's near-hysterical mayor. A dawn-to-dusk curfew was in effect, temporarily. Armed soldiers roamed the streets. The various authorities involved, embarrassed and even shamed by their inability to contain the threat offered by New York's warring gangs and the mercenary operatives, were hoping a show of force would put things right. Bolan had no particular faith in barring the gate after the horse had left, but he suspected the situation in Manhattan would indeed improve.

It was a simple matter of attrition coupled with the pressure exerted by the National Guard. Taveras had suffered heavy losses in his ongoing war with Caqueta. He had taken a real bloody nose in Times Square, too. The fact that he'd felt it necessary to send a very public message about who ruled the streets told the Executioner a lot. It told him that the raid on Busty's had made Taveras feel weak and at a disadvantage—so much so that he was willing to engage in public terrorism to put El Cráneo back on top.

Given his losses and the difficulty he would have staging any operations or pursuing his usual drug trade with martial law in effect, Taveras was essentially neutralized. Bolan did not know what El Cráneo's next move would be. He could not see what that move *could* be. He was unsure what his own next step should be, for that matter, but that did not worry him. The Executioner was an old hand at playing the operation by ear to see what would shake loose. He would either hit the streets on his own, doing his best to stay out of the National Guard's way while trying to ferret out a new lead on Taveras or Blackjack, or Burnett would come up with something.

As resourceful as the detective had proved to be, Bolan was not terribly surprised when he showed up at the hotel, grinning like a Cheshire cat.

"It's a good morning to visit the Garden State," he said without preamble.

"What?" Bolan said, closing the door behind the lanky detective.

Burnett folded his large frame into one of the hotel chairs, steepling his fingers as he looked up at Bolan. "I told you, I'm connected—and being the task force leader has real advantages. I've got us another tip."

"How definite?"

"Oh, pretty definite," Burnett said. "Only the precise location of Percival Leister."

Bolan raised an eyebrow. "How did you get that?"

"Another of my very useful taps." Burnett smiled. "At this moment, Leister and his Blackjack boys are holed up in the less-than-two-diamonds Starbrite Motel, a Triple-A unapproved establishment just outside Swedesboro, New Jersey."

"Swedesboro," Bolan repeated.

"Yes," Burnett said. "Why, ring a bell?" He grinned again.

AFTER TAKING TIME to gear up, Bolan drove and Burnett rode shotgun as they traveled to Swedesboro. It was late afternoon by the time Bolan pulled the Crown Victoria to the side of the road, off the exit ramp and well down the street from the Starbrite Motel. The soldier checked his magazines and the function of his Ultimax before nodding to Burnett.

"Ready?"

"Absolutely," the big cop said, jacking a shell into the chamber of his Remington 870.

"You sure you want to do this?" Bolan asked. "There won't be any backup."

"Hell, you don't have to tell me twice," Burnett said. "I doubt we could convince the locals of the need to lend us manpower for a lead generated by an illegal wiretap. And you'd have quite a job getting anyone released from my department with New York practically under razor-wire and occupation."

"Just making sure," Bolan said.

"Yeah, I know." Burnett grinned. "You don't want my messy corpse on your conscience. Trust me, I know what I'm getting into. And I've seen you work."

Bolan nodded.

"According to my source," Burnett said, "our boys are in units 17, 18, 19 and 20. I'm guessing those black Suburbans parked at the end of the row belong to the Blackjack boys."

Bolan and Burnett approached the motel parking lot, careful to stay at an extreme angle to avoid being seen from the front windows. They took cover behind the boarded-up facade of a defunct gas station next to the motel. "Let's keep this simple," Bolan said. "Circle around the back of the building. Don't get spotted. Cover the structure from the opposite side, but stay parallel to the front for as long as possible. You don't want to tip them off or catch a bullet."

"Sure thing," Burnett said. He started to go.

"Burnett," Bolan called quietly after him.

"Yeah?"

"Stay away from the trucks."

"Gotcha."

Bolan waited patiently for Burnett to get into position. He did his best to stay out of sight, lurking behind some low and neglected shrubs in the adjacent lot. Once he was certain the detective was out of his direct line of fire, he brought up the Ultimax and braced its folding stock against his shoulder. With a magazine of captured DU ammunition in place, he put the red-dot scope over the first SUV in the row.

The weapon rumbled in his hands.

The explosive penetrators ripped through the gas tank of the first SUV. The rear of the vehicle exploded in a fireball that rocked the front of the motel. With the Ultimax at his shoulder, Bolan moved forward, sweeping the killzone in front of him. As he closed in, he tracked the second and third SUVs, sweeping them with DU rounds and watching in satisfaction as they, too, burst into flame.

The Executioner was careful to position himself at an angle that kept his rounds punching into and past the rooms at the end of the row, away from the adjacent units and thus not in the direction of any innocents who might be staying in the motel. With any luck, they'd keep their heads down and resist the urge to run outside to see what was happening in the parking lot.

Circling clockwise, the soldier cut wide around the burning vehicles, covering the target doorways of the motel. He dug into his canvas messenger bag and changed magazines as he went, replacing the DU rounds with conventional 62-grain steel-tipped cartridges in his last 100-round drum. When no one emerged, he triggered several short bursts into the doors.

The sound of a shotgun blast to his left brought him up short. Burnett was running his way, triggering another round behind him as he cradled his shotgun. "Move, move, move!" he shouted. "They're right on my tail!"

Bolan realized what was happening and turned away from

Burnett, aiming for the far right corner of the building. The first of Leister's mercenaries rounded the motel, match-barreled AR-15s braced against their shoulders, and opened fire. Bolan had time to throw himself backward, the Ultimax still held before him.

A DU round burned through the receiver of the weapon and cored past his chest.

He rolled, his duster suddenly aflame where the round had passed across his chest. He shed the coat, rolling out of it and pulling the quick-release strap for the Ultimax harness, leaving the shattered light machine gun on the ground behind him. Then he was up, drawing the Beretta 92-F with his left hand and the 93-R machine pistol with his right. As bullets streaked past him, he gunned down the nearest mercenaries with precisely placed 9 mm hollowpoint rounds.

To get out of the line of fire, Bolan lowered his shoulder and crashed into the nearest motel-room door. He briefly noted debris consistent with Leister's men—take-out food containers on a table, black paramilitary clothing piled on one of the two beds, a nylon war bag open on the floor full of cleaning supplies and boxes of cartridges. He plowed past this to the bathroom. As he'd suspected, a large, translucent window in the bathroom was open. Leister's men had gone out the back and circled around, rather than charge stupidly from the front to certain death.

The soldier kept going, climbing out the window and landing heavily on his feet on the littered ground behind the motel. Mercenaries at either end of the building, watching around the corners, realized he was there as he extended both pistols in their directions. Firing to the left and to the right, Bolan ran up the small hill leading away from the back of the motel, seeking higher ground and a tactical advantage. He tagged two more of Leister's surviving team as he went.

The shooting stopped.

Bolan paused, both weapons still extended before him, covering the rear of the building. He saw a face in a window to his right, a civilian peering out from behind the curtains. Bolan shook his head sternly at the face and it disappeared. He waited a moment, but the gunfire did not resume.

A car door slammed, and a vehicle tore out of the parking lot at the front of the motel.

Bolan ran. He charged down the hill and around the corner, rolling as he did so to avoid any ambush fire that might be intended for him. None came. He saw a small car with Delaware plates fleeing the lot. When he drew down on the retreating vehicle and triggered a 9 mm round through its rear window, the little car swerved before fishtailing around toward him.

The Executioner could see Leister behind the wheel. Face twisted with determination and anger, the British mercenary abandoned any hope of escape and came straight for Bolan, pushing the car's feeble four-cylinder engine for every horsepower he could squeeze from it. Bolan stood his ground, emptying the magazines in both Berettas, hammering at the engine before placing one of his shots in the windshield directly in front of Leister.

The car slowed, but only slightly, before it clipped the rear of one of the burning SUVs and smashed to a halt. It hit one of the rooms vacated by Leister's men. Bolan quickly changed magazines in both Berettas, holstered the 92-F and closed on Leister with the 93-R before him.

Cursing, the mercenary struggled to kick open the bent and damaged driver's door.

"Leister!" Bolan shouted. "Put your hands behind your head! It's over!"

"Dear boy," Leister said weakly, climbing painfully out of the vehicle, "you can take that hands-behind-the-head rot and shove it up your arse. I'm too old to play that game." He swayed on his feet as he faced the Executioner, his Browning Hi-Power held loosely in his hand. Blood streamed down the side of his head and stained his abdomen. He'd taken a round to the left shoulder. Blood soaked his left arm, which hung limply at his side.

"Drop the gun," Bolan ordered.

"No," Leister said. He made no move to bring the weapon up, however.

"I said, do it!" Bolan barked.

"Would you calm yourself, damn you?" Leister shook his head. "We both know how the game is played, don't we?" He staggered away from the car, put his back to the motel wall and allowed himself to slide to the sidewalk in front of the building. The Hi-Power fell from numbed fingers and scraped on the paving. Leister sighed heavily and reached inside his black fatigue jacket.

"Don't!" Bolan took a step forward, the 93-R covering the man's movements.

"Jesus and Mary, you're spun up tightly." Leister almost laughed. He took his hand slowly from inside the jacket. It was holding a pack of cigarettes. "If I promise these don't contain poisoned darts or sleep gas, will you allow me one last fag?"

Bolan said nothing. Leister took that as assent, fished a disposable butane lighter from the pack and lit a cigarette. He coughed badly as he drew the smoke into his lungs, but took a second drag as soon as he'd recovered.

"You seem to be having trouble," Leister told him, "accepting the fact that you've won."

As Bolan watched the mercenary, mindful that the cagey and experienced operative might try some last-ditch means to kill Bolan or simply escape, he checked his peripheral vision for any sign of Burnett. The detective's handiwork was evident not far from where Leister sat. Three men, all with fatal shotgun wounds, were strewed about the lot. Burnett himself had disappeared.

There wasn't much time before he'd have to leave or face another tie-up with the authorities. Bolan knew he'd have only a few more moments before the local police arrived.

"This," Leister said, gesturing to the Hi-Power on the sidewalk nearby, "is the part where I bravely take my own life, to prevent you from interrogating me. You magnificent bastard." He chuckled around his cigarette. "I should have known from the first, from that day at the park. With whom have you served? Don't try to tell me you don't have a list of campaigns under your belt that would put Patton to shame."

Bolan said nothing.

"Of course." Leister nodded. "Of course you can't tell me. But dead men tell no tales, eh? What will it matter?"

"There's not much time," Bolan told him.

"Oh, don't I know it," Leister said, "but perhaps more than you think. We took the time to grease the local wheels. I think you'll find local response time inhibited, somewhat. We have a moment, purchased at a steep price in a seller's market."

"Tell me what you know about Stevens."

"There's not much to tell, old chap." Leister sucked at his cigarette. "The tale gets a bit sordid, however. My employers—"

"Blackjack Group, contracted by NLI."

"Yes," Leister confirmed. "I don't suppose they'll be able to hide behind their lawyers and their damned plausible deniability much longer. Damned murderous bastards."

"Murderous?"

"You don't think hired fighting men are exactly eager to shoot themselves, do you?" Leister said. "I've had to be ruthless at the helm, Colonel." He laughed. "Or is it General? Don't tell me you were rank and file."

Bolan said nothing.

"You've got to understand how Norris Labs works. They have more money than God. They made it very clear that there was no end to how much they would throw at me—for a price. For a heavy price, indeed."

"Go on."

"All I had to do to earn my extravagant pay," Leister said, "was ensure the absolute, total loyalty of my men. They had to be willing to die before they'd reveal any secrets. I had to run a very tight ship indeed. Of course I made it my habit to employ only those men on whom I could get the proper leverage. Families, lovers, relatives of some sort—all cataloged, all easily located. Kill a few to set an example, make it clear you're not above raping a man's wife and children and showing him the videotape before you put a bullet in his brain, and the others learn quickly. Our cohesion was what made Blackjack so formidable. Norris Labs' damned board of directors could certainly appreciate that. Ours has been a long and profitable relationship." Leister coughed again. He stared down at the blood in his palm. "Shit. I feared as much. Something inside me is very much broken."

"Why tell me now?" Bolan asked.

"Because I'm damned tired," Leister said. "Tired of them. Tired of owing my soul to the company store, as they say. Just tired."

"Stevens," Bolan prompted.

"If I knew where to find him," Leister said, "I'd tell you. The damned board has had us killing left and right to stop the bastard from manufacturing and selling more of those depleted uranium rounds, but it's worse than that. He was working on another design before he was let go, or quit or however it worked out. You've heard of *dirty bombs,* I imagine?"

Bolan nodded.

"Stevens was designing a sort of uranium microshell based on the same technology. Fire a magazine of his little devils at a target, and you'd leave behind measurable, harmful radiation. It's a vile weapon, Colonel. Something that can take any place at any time and turn it into a radioactive hot zone. Knowing Stevens and how in love he is with his own designs, it's only a matter of time before he finds a ready market for the evil stuff. Can you imagine? My employers were, of course, terrified that he'd get that far before he and his bullets were finally traced back to them. It was bigger than a public-relations disaster. They were looking at multiple lifetimes behind bars if it got out just how many illegal pies they were shoving their filthy fingers into."

"You don't have any idea where I can find Stevens?" Bolan asked.

"Well, hell, old boy." Leister coughed again, weakly. "He's here somewhere. I don't think he'll be far. Somewhere in this godforsaken state. The Garden State, for pity's sake! What a joke."

"What else do you know?"

"Nothing that would be of much help, I'm afraid," Leister admitted. "At least, nothing more that I'm willing to tell you."

"I could make you talk."

"Not likely," Leister said. "Unless you're good with short deadlines. My bribes won't hold the constabulary at bay forever. But then, I don't have much more time, anyway." He stared at his bloody palm. "Stupid, thinking I could run down an armed man in that little cracker box."

Leister leaned back, resting his head against the motel wall. The he opened his eyes again, staring into the barrel of Bolan's machine pistol as if looking far past it. "Oh, damn," he said.

Percival Leister's eyes turned glassy. The Executioner watched the light fade from them. He holstered the Beretta 93-R and placed his fingers against Leister's neck, checking for a pulse. He found none.

Bolan nodded once at the dead man and turned away. There was much more work to be done.

The Crown Victoria rolled up. Bolan spotted Burnett behind the wheel and walked up to meet the vehicle.

"It's about time," he said mildly. "What happened to you?"

Then he saw the look on Burnett's face.

The detective looked stricken. Bolan had just enough time to put his hand on the butt of his Desert Eagle when the barbs of the Taser shot out and speared his chest. As he convulsed under the voltage that coursed through the wires, he had a hazy picture of July de la Rocha crouched in the backseat of the vehicle, a gun pointed at Burnett's back behind the seat.

Struggling through the pain and muscle spasms, Bolan managed to draw the Desert Eagle and trigger a .44 Magnum round through the chest of the man crouched next to de la Rocha. The El Cráneo thug's blood splattered across de la Rocha's face, but Taveras's lieutenant was already moving. He leaped over the dead man. Bolan triggered another round, but it went wide as he fought the Taser's effects. De la Rocha lashed out with a collapsible baton, catching the Executioner across the wrist hard enough to make him drop the big pistol. Then de la Rocha was on top of him, striking repeatedly with the baton.

Bolan managed to grab the handle of his knife and slash out with it, once. He felt resistance and warm blood as de la Rocha screamed but kept beating him. The blows about his head and neck hammered him down into darkness.

His last thought was that Percival Leister would have company that night, wherever he was going.

14

The relentless pounding inside Bolan's skull woke him some-time in the night.

He avoided making any sudden movements. If he was truly injured, there was risk involved in pushing too hard, too soon. If he wasn't, he didn't want to telegraph to any waiting enemy that he was awake and fit for action. With his eyes closed, he slowly took stock of his condition, quietly flexing and testing his limbs while mentally noting his aches and pains.

Satisfied, he finally opened his eyes, squinting against the light from the bare bulb in the socket above him.

Bolan looked around cautiously. He was seated in a wooden chair, his arms tied behind his back and secured to the chair, his legs similarly tied to the front chair legs. His blacksuit had been cut away above the waist. His prison was a damp basement room with a rough concrete floor, perhaps twenty by twenty feet. A metal pole a few feet from him supported the ceiling overhead, which consisted of wooden rafters and molding yellow insula-tion. Except for his chair and a light metal folding chair a few feet from him, the room was empty. Water pooled in a corner from a crack in the foundation. A small window set high on the wall behind him contained a single pane of glass, too small to crawl through, spray-painted black. A sturdy and very old-looking wooden door was set in the wall in front of him. It had a rusted metal knob. He could not see any light beneath it from whatever was beyond.

His belt had been taken from him, as had his boots. The pockets of the blacksuit pants he wore were empty. He was barefoot, shirtless, bound, alone.

Despite the throbbing in his head and the bruises on his face and chest, Bolan was pleased.

The enemy had made a fatal mistake. They hadn't killed him.

Held in this way, it was likely his captors had interrogation in mind. That didn't worry him. While Taveras and El Cráneo had a reputation for brutality, it would take more than the threat of a Colombian necktie or a long chat with a car battery and some jumper cables to make him worry about what would come next.

In Bolan's experience, most of the would-be interrogators on the criminal scene were amateurs. They were long on talk and short on guts, relatively weak sadists who had no stomach for getting truly bloody when working over their victims. The true professionals, the master torturers, were in a class of their own and generally quite easy to spot. Bolan had seen all too many people reduced to what the Italian Mob had called "turkeys" by the skilled hands and keen blades of the Mafia's professional interrogators. Neither Taveras, nor anyone he employed, was likely to rival such monsters.

Granted, they could kill him. A relative amateur like de la Rocha was likely to do just that unintentionally. All it would take would be someone a little too eager to beat on him or disfigure him, someone who didn't know well enough the fine line between pain and death. If that happened, there was little the soldier could do about it. He was not inclined to consider the possibility, either, given just how often he'd found himself in similar situations.

The fact was, where a man like Bolan was concerned, the only realistic choices were to kill him immediately, or do to him such devastating damage that he would be unable to move, barely able to speak, until his captors were finished with him. They hadn't done either of those things. Bolan would show them just how foolish a choice that was.

He tested the ropes. They were simple clothesline. That, too, was an amateur mistake, one Bolan wouldn't have thought Taveras or his people would make. He began working against the line, pulling and stretching, to give himself enough slack to work his way free.

The heavy door rattled as someone from the outside turned a key in its rusted metal lock. The door creaked open to reveal July de la Rocha. He wore a silk shirt and a pair of slacks that might once have been part of a designer suit. The sleeve of his left arm was rolled back, revealing a white bandage around his forearm. De la Rocha carried Bolan's own knife, the serrated blade unsheathed and gleaming dully in the unfiltered light from above. Jutting from his front left pocket was the nozzle of a portable butane torch.

"I did not think you would be out for long," de la Rocha said. "I have this—" he gestured with the knife "—and you, to thank for my arm. Very soon, my own pain will be as nothing, while you will be begging me to kill you."

"Is that so?"

De la Rocha paused and looked at Bolan suspiciously. "Will you be so brave when I cut out your eyes and feed them to you?" he said. "Perhaps when I do the same with your fingers? And with your own knife. I wonder just how strong you are."

"Stronger than you," Bolan said, holding de la Rocha's glare.

De la Rocha, confident that his prisoner was helpless, smiled and pulled the metal chair to him. He reversed it and sat astride it, leaning on the backrest with Bolan's knife still in one hand. He toyed with the blade idly, moving it slowly back and forth in the air as he spoke.

"You killed the Brit."

Bolan was silent.

"You do not seem to understand what you are meddling in," de la Rocha said, his eyes narrowing. "The Brit was ours. The right to kill him belonged to El Cráneo. You have insulted us, as he insulted us. Just as he was to die for that, you will die for it. But not right away. Not quickly. Not without great pain."

"He's dead," Bolan said. "You wanted him dead. What does it matter who killed him?"

"Do you have no understanding of honor?" De la Rocha sounded indignant. "He dared to speak to us as children. He expected El Cráneo to bow and scrape for him, to take what he allowed us rather than taking what we wanted. We taught his people a lesson—and then he dared to strike at us on our own territory! He was marked for death from that moment."

"Like I said—" Bolan shook his head "—he's dead."

"He is dead because you killed him, not because justice was done!" de la Rocha shouted. "And you. You are a mystery. El Cráneo will avenge its honor on you. But not before I learn who you are and why you are here."

"I'd say El Cráneo won't be doing much avenging of anything," Bolan said. "Where are we right now? My guess is a safe house somewhere. You're hiding. Leister and his men did you real damage. The war with Caqueta took its toll, as well. I'm willing to bet you don't have much left in the way of resources."

"Lies!" de la Rocha said. He leaned closer to Bolan. "We have more power than you can imagine."

"And what will you do with all that power?"

"We will do what we are destined to do," de la Rocha said proudly. "We will rule the streets of New York."

"That's right," Bolan said. "Taveras is destined to be lord and master of a criminal empire, is that it?"

"Who better?" de la Rocha said. "Pierre is a strong leader. He will do what others could not. He will unify New York under El Cráneo. You cops will be helpless against us."

Bolan let that go. He was no cop, but de la Rocha didn't need to know that. "You're kidding yourself. It's never going to happen that way. Better men than you, with organizations larger and more powerful than El Cráneo, have tried."

"What would you know of it?"

"Stevens and his ammunition won't last forever," the soldier ventured. "Your manpower isn't inexhaustible, either. The National Guard's on the streets of New York. I don't care how dangerous your weapons might be—are there enough of you to take on a whole army? That's what you'll be up against if you show your faces in Manhattan anytime soon."

De la Rocha growled low in his throat. "Why are you here? Why did you kill the Brit? Who are you?"

"I'm the man who took down your men in Times Square," Bolan said. "Didn't you get a good look at me while you were busy running for your life?"

De la Rocha's eyes widened. "You? You are *him?*"

"I am." Bolan nodded. "Oh, I almost forgot. I also killed Molina." It was not strictly true—Leister had dealt the *coup de grâce*—but it had the desired effect.

"*You* murdered Jesus? Not the Brit?"

"I wouldn't call it murder," Bolan said. "It was more like a mercy killing."

Roaring, de la Rocha lunged for Bolan. The Executioner yanked his hands free of the stretched clothesline and got his arms up in front of him, deflecting de la Rocha's knife arm as he drove the edge of his hand up under the man's jaw into his neck. The El Cráneo killer fell backward as Bolan's charge took him onto his bound feet, toppling chair and all over de la Rocha. The soldier heard his opponent gasp for air as Bolan's full weight dropped on his chest. Pinning de la Rocha's knife arm with one hand, Bolan dropped a savage hammer fist onto de la Rocha's face.

The smaller man stopped moving.

Bolan grabbed the knife and, sliding himself awkwardly off

de la Rocha's chest, slit the man's throat with the serrated blade. He used the bloody blade to cut the rope from his legs, stepping free and flattening himself against the wall next to the door. He waited, the numbers ticking by, until he was sure no one had heard the scuffle and was coming to investigate.

When he was certain, Bolan allowed himself a deep breath.

He bent to search the body. De la Rocha was carrying a stainless-steel Taurus PT-92. It was loaded with conventional 9 mm ammo. Sticking the weapon in his waistband, Bolan searched further but found only a small packet of white powder that was probably de la Rocha's personal stash of cocaine. There was nothing else of use.

Bolan gripped the knife in his left hand and drew the Taurus with his right. The door was unlocked. De la Rocha had been so overconfident that he hadn't felt it necessary to secure the room while inside with his prisoner. Bolan eased the door open as slowly as possible, minimizing the squeaking of its rusted hinges. It made some noise, but not a great deal. He was hopeful no one would notice it. It was possible any noise would be dismissed as de la Rocha returning from whatever was beyond the basement door, but Bolan couldn't count on that. There was no way to know what arrangements the El Cráneo lieutenant might have made, or how much backup he might have. If de la Rocha's attitude was any gauge, however, he wouldn't have done much. In the dead man's mind, the future had already been written and the prisoner was already dead.

He crept up the rickety wooden stairs beyond the door, the Taurus low against his flank in a retention position. There was another door at the top of the steps. Bolan used his knife hand to turn the knob, awkwardly juggling the knife, easing the door open as quietly as he could.

He emerged in a Spartan kitchen. There was a table with a pair of folding chairs, a small refrigerator humming in one corner and a broken oven with its front door hanging by a single hinge. White paint was peeling from the cupboards. A short, bald Hispanic man with soft features was seated at the table eating a bowl of cereal. When he saw Bolan, he fumbled for his sidearm.

Bolan shot first.

The bullet went slightly low, into the man's open mouth and out the back of his head. Even at close range it was clear the fixed sights on the Taurus weren't adjusted quite right. Bolan noted it mentally. He crouched and covered the door leading from the kitchen.

Two El Cráneo hardmen came running at the sound of the shot, one on top of the other. Both were dressed in sloppy sweats and carrying handguns. Bolan met them with gunfire, taking them both down. The Taurus was not fully loaded and locked open as he did so. With no spare magazines to load, the Executioner tossed aside the useless pistol and scooped up the nearest weapon. He press-checked the Glock 17, double-checking the magazine, as well. Then he continued on.

The empty dining room of the safehouse emptied into a living room containing a couple of couches and a battered television. Pizza boxes and beer cans were strewed about the room. The television was on and tuned to a Spanish-language variety show. The front door of the house, at the opposite end of the living room, finished its arc as it swung inward.

Bolan shoved the Glock into his belt and ran.

A fourth El Cráneo man was running for his life from the house. Bolan absently registered the residential neighborhood beneath a moonless night sky, sidewalks illuminated in fits and starts by yellow-white streetlights above. It would have been an easy shot, but he didn't want to risk it. There was a chance the gunfire from within the house would go unnoticed, but shots on the street would bring police and he wasn't ready for their intervention yet. Instead, he ran after the gang member, his legs pumping, his feet stinging on the pavement of the quiet street. Despite the pain of his recent injuries and bruises, he caught the

winded man easily, diving and tackling him. The smell of cigarette smoke clung to the man's baggy clothes.

"Get off me, *pendejo*," the man whined. "Get off!"

Bolan fired a right hook into the man's jaw. His head snapped
back and he started groaning, holding his face. The soldier
grabbed him by the back of his shirt and dragged him to his feet,
hooking the knife around his neck. The gang member froze at
the sight of the blade and stopped resisting, effectively cowed.
He let the soldier drag him back into the safehouse, past the dead
men and into the kitchen. There Bolan pushed him into the one
of the chairs.

"Now," Bolan said, jamming the knife blade-first into the
wooden table to make a point, "I'm going to ask the questions
and you're going to respond truthfully. Cooperate and you might
live long enough to see the inside of a prison. Refuse and I'll
just kill you where you stand."

The sullen gang member looked up at him from his seat. "You
will not kill me. You are a cop."

Bolan yanked the Glock from his waistband and pointed it at
the man's head, his arm at full extension. "I'm not a cop," he
said. "I don't have a lot of time, either. Tell me what I want to
know or I'm getting out of here. Don't think I'm leaving you
behind alive, either. Now. What's your name?"

"Javier."

"Fine, Javier," Bolan said. "I don't have your late boss's flair
for the dramatic, so let's cut to the chase."

"What do you want to know?"

"Where's the cop who was with me? The big man. Your boss
was driving his car when I last saw him."

"I don't know what you're talking about."

Bolan gestured with the Glock. "This weapon has a fairly
light trigger pull. I'm taking up the slack now."

"No, wait!" Javier grew frantic. "I really do not know! There
was no other man. July brought you and just you! If there was

another man, he is not here. I don't know where he might be! Please!"

Bolan considered that. It was possible that Burnett had escaped, or even that he was released. It was equally possible that he'd been killed.

"Where can I find Taveras?"

"He is not here. He did not come with July. We came by ourselves. July said he had business to conduct. He said he would join us later, if he could."

"So you're in hiding."

"We are. We are very few. July was talking about recruiting, about purchasing more arms. I do not think there are many of us left, just a few with the boss. El Cráneo is finished, I think."

"Let's hope," Bolan said.

"You said you would take me to the authorities," Javier said. "You may do so now. I will be out on bail soon enough. We still have lawyers. I will make no trouble—"

Even as he spoke, the man lunged, producing a small one-handed folding knife from somewhere inside his waistband.

Bolan checked the killer's knife arm with his free hand and shot Javier in the head. The thug fell like a sack of potatoes and was still. The knife clattered on the floor.

The Executioner made a complete search of the safe house. There were two bedrooms upstairs. One contained duffel bags full of the El Cráneo members' clothing. Bolan found a clean black T-shirt and put it on. He also found his Liger belt and threaded it back through the loops of his blacksuit pants. His combat boots had been tossed aside in a corner of the kitchen, it turned out, while his war bag with most of his spare magazines was with the duffel bags upstairs. The Beretta 92-F he'd carried as a backup was missing, but the little minirevolver he'd taken from the Blackjack mercenary was still in the bag. He counted himself lucky.

Bolan left the bloody knife behind after wiping it for prints.

The sheath was missing and he could not find a reasonable replacement, so toting it was more of a liability than an asset. He recovered his folding knife from the pocket of one of the dead men, however, and clipped it back in his own pants. It would fill the necessary role of combat knife.

His Beretta 93-R and the battle-scarred Desert Eagle .44 Magnum were in the war bag with their holsters. He strapped these back on after checking their loads and actions. Most importantly, his secure phone was in the war bag. Neither de la Rocha nor his men had thought it anything but a cell phone, apparently, though it was also password protected to prevent tampering. He switched it on, checked it and—with no other options—simply dialed Burnett's number.

The phone rang several times before someone answered.

"Burnett," the detective said.

"This is the ghost of Christmas past," Bolan said. "I'm glad you're not a ghost, yourself."

"Cooper? Holy shit! Where are you?"

"Hang on," Bolan told him. He went to the living room, opened the front door and took a quick look outside. Nobody was moving on the street, at least not that he could see. He could barely make out the street sign at the end of the block. He noted the numbers on the front of the house and read Burnett the address. "Offhand," he said, "I imagine that's a street address in Swedesboro or a neighboring town. I can't guarantee anything, and I won't know for sure until I've had a chance to look around."

"I'll send a car for you," Burnett said. "Hell, I'll pick you up myself if I have to check every town in the state."

"I'll wait, then," Bolan said. "What happened to you? How did you get away? How did they get you in the first place?"

"Wrong place, wrong time," Burnett asked. "When the Blackjack shooters came out of the woodwork, I admit it, I ran. I figured I'd get the car and bring us some mobile cover. I got there just as Taveras and his crew rolled up. They aren't stupid—they fingered me for a cop and figured I'd make a good distraction. Hell, Taveras ought to know me by now. I've been making his life difficult for quite a while. They recognized me as me, or they just knew what I was. Either way, they stuck a gun in my ribs and told me to cooperate."

"Why didn't they kill you?"

"I told you," Burnett said with a chuckle, "they're not stupid. Taveras doesn't have a lot of compunctions about killing cops, but he didn't need to kill me and make a bad situation worse for himself. He's got enough problems. After they took you down, they kicked me out of the car and drove away. I figured you were dead, man."

"More dangerous men have tried," Bolan said.

"I don't want to know," Burnett said. "Sit tight. I'm on my way."

Bolan snapped the phone shut and looked around him at a house full of dead men.

It was a start.

15

"Striker?" Barbara Price sounded worried. "Are you all right?"

"Don't worry, Barb," Bolan said, standing in his hotel room after a hot shower. "It was nothing I couldn't handle."

"That's good to hear," Price said, though she didn't sound very relieved. She listened as Bolan updated her, transmitting more photos and notes he'd taken and made with his phone.

"Manhattan is still battened down," Bolan concluded. "I'm sure things haven't gotten any less interesting for Hal."

"No," Price confirmed, "he's been in rare form."

"I don't doubt it. I have two loose ends here—Taveras, and whatever's left of his people, are one. The other is Donald Stevens and what Percival Leister told me is his munitions factory. The links to NLI and Blackjack are solid. Is there any chance Hal can move on them?"

"Not on the basis of Leister's testimony, no," Price said. "It won't constitute evidence, especially if NLI pulls in the drawbridge and calls out the lawyers. You'll need to find something more substantial before we can go after the companies themselves."

"I'll get to work on that, then," Bolan said.

"We can help with the next step," Price said. "Akira turned up a fragment from the hard drive you recovered. It turned out to be a shipping invoice for some chemicals and other equipment. We've traced the address. It's a waterfront location in Camden, New Jersey. I'm transmitting a map and details now."

"New Jersey," Bolan repeated. "I can't say I'm surprised. I'll get on it."

"I'll mobilize the appropriate teams," Price said. "I'd rather get them on-site and have them unneeded than wait. If Stevens's factory is truly there, it has to be locked down."

"Excellent. I'll call you when the op's done."

"Striker?"

"Yeah, Barb?"

"Try to be more careful this time."

"I will." Bolan closed the phone.

IT TOOK AN HOUR to finish preparing, cleaning and checking his weapons and loading the pockets of his fresh blacksuit. Burnett showed up, the bandage off his bloodshot eye, and the two of them conferred briefly over the material Bolan had—though the Executioner didn't tell the detective where he got his information or how. They spent an uneventful ride back to New Jersey yet again. After surveying the waterfront area, Bolan directed Burnett to park a few blocks away. They'd walk in, staying together to maximize their chances and see what defenses Stevens had to offer. Bolan did not kid himself. The warehouse would be heavily defended, if not by human opponents, then by whatever devices an arms designer like Stevens was capable of creating.

As Bolan and Burnett walked, the Executioner pondered the decrepit facades and boarded-up buildings they passed. Camden, New Jersey, was, according to some measures, the poorest city in the United States. It was also one of the most dangerous, rife with crime and violence.

The waterfront was a high point in Camden's bleak hit parade, featuring a popular aquarium and the battleship-museum USS *New Jersey*. Bolan and Burnett were not in town for sightseeing, however. The warehouse where Stevens was located occupied a particularly decrepit stretch of the waterfront district, far from anything of interest to even the most ardent tourist.

The warehouse occupied a block that was in turn enclosed by a tall fence topped by barbed wire. Bolan, his canvas messenger bag slung across his body, removed the light windbreaker he wore over his weapons and gear. There was no more need for concealment. It would be impossible to hide what he was about to do.

"Here's where we part company," he told the detective. "You know what to do?"

"It's not a complicated plan." Burnett shrugged. "You go in, shoot everyone. I wait out here to catch any stragglers and run interference when the cops show up. If they show."

"They'll show," Bolan said.

"Just follow the enormous explosions and clouds of black smoke, right?" Burnett said. He stuck out his hand. "You're all right, Cooper. Try not to get yourself killed in there."

Bolan returned the handshake firmly. "I'll do what I can."

The fence, the building's first line of defense, was not much of an obstacle. Bolan, windbreaker in hand, scaled it easily. At the top he folded the windbreaker on itself and placed it over the barbed-wire strands. Then he scrambled over the top and landed heavily on the other side.

"Find something to take cover behind," he told Burnett. Drawing the Beretta 93-R, he pulled the slide back far enough to verify that a round was chambered. Before him, the cracked and weed-dotted asphalt of a long-abandoned parking lot separated him from the warehouse.

As he walked, crouching slightly and scanning the building's boarded windows for some sign of danger, he half expected to take a sniper's bullet. It would not have been difficult for Stevens to station riflemen at strategic points throughout the building. He was mildly surprised when he encountered no resistance. After a quiet journey from the fence to the building, he moved along the warehouse perimeter. He passed a couple of doors that were sealed tight from the inside, possibly permanently secured. Finally, he found a metal access door that, while locked, rattled in its frame when he tried the handle.

Transferring the Beretta to his left hand, Bolan drew the Desert Eagle and backed off a few paces. The crack of the .44 Magnum shell echoed across the parking lot as the lock exploded. Bolan waited for a moment to see if the shot would draw Stevens's forces—if he had them—out of hiding, but nothing happened.

He pushed the door open.

The hallway within was dark and narrow, with a low ceiling. Bare two-by-fours supported plywood sheets that composed the walls and ceiling. Bolan secured the Desert Eagle and adopted his familiar supported grip with his combat light illuminating the gloom.

Bolan's boots made the floorboards squeak beneath him. He started down the hallway.

He almost stepped on the first of the mines.

The bright, white beam of the flashlight saved him. He was sweeping the floors, walls and ceiling in a methodical pattern as he moved slowly down the corridor, listening intently for any hint of enemy activity. As he played the beam across the floor in front of his feet, he caught the glint of metal about two feet in front of his left toe. Carefully, he crouched, resting his hands on his thighs as he peered at the object blocking his path.

The object was, in fact, one of twenty or thirty he could count in the beam of his flashlight, once he started looking for them. Arrayed on the rough wood floor before him, spread out in a hexagonal pattern, were countless small metal cylinders, about one inch high and two inches in diameter, each tipped with an inset metal disk that might have been a pressure switch—or might have been something else. Bolan backed off a few paces and removed the compact night-vision monocular from his war bag.

The Executioner preferred to sweep darkened areas with a portable light, rather than relying on light-gathering technology

like the monocular. With a firefight likely there was too much
chance of being blinded, even if only temporarily, by a bright
flash through the night scope. He also did not like to constrict
his peripheral vision in a combat scenario, preferring instead to
keep his wits about him and his vision unobstructed. The night
scope did have one advantage, however. Through it, he could easily make out light beams that would otherwise be invisible to the
eye.

He swept the corridor through the scope. He'd suspected
some kind of high-tech laser grid was tied to whatever the devices on the floor might be, but there was nothing. At least, there
was nothing he could see with the equipment available to him.
There was a high degree of risk in penetrating the fortified lair
of a man like Stevens, but it was a risk the Executioner was willing to take. Someone had to stop Stevens before the war he'd
touched off went any further—and before he could spread the
cancer of his weapons to other cities, touching off the flames of
similar conflagrations.

As he considered what to do, he dismissed the idea of trying
to remain unobserved. He assumed Stevens had passive security
and surveillance equipment in place and most likely knew the
warehouse had been invaded. Even if he did not, Bolan did not
intend to come and go quietly. He was there to stop Stevens and
demolish his factory. There was no way to maintain stealth. This
was not a soft probe, but the hardest of hard charges.

Bolan stowed the monocular and once again adopted a supported flashlight grip, this time with his Beretta 93-R. He
switched the machine pistol to single shot and backed up as far
as he could while keeping the objects in view. Then he aimed
carefully at the closest of them and fired.

The 9 mm hollowpoint bullet struck the top of the mine and
set it off. Instead of exploding, however, it erupted. A jet of
bright-orange molten metal shot up from the metal cylinder in
a shower of sparks. A wave of heat hit Bolan's face. He squinted

against the flare of light as the burning metal started to chew its way through the wood of the floor. Small tongues of flame licked at the edges of the hole created by the mine as it consumed itself. The jet had reached high enough to touch the ceiling and had left it scorched.

Bolan removed a bandanna from his war bag, took a small plastic squeeze bottle of water and sprayed the contents over the bandanna. He tied the moist cloth over his mouth and nose to act as a filter, screening out the worst of the smoke. The fumes weren't actually too bad, because the fires were rapidly putting themselves out.

The soldier moved forward cautiously, playing the beam of his light over the crater in the wood floor. By rights, the flaming booby trap should have set the entire hallway ablaze, taking the building with it. Clearly the wood of the walls, floor and ceiling had been treated with some sort of flame-retardant substance. That made perfect sense. Mines that took down an entire building wouldn't be of much use to those counting on them for perimeter security.

No audible alarms were initiated by the destruction, but it seemed likely Stevens would have the facility wired to inform him of a perimeter breach. That was fine. The Executioner was about to roll right over Donald Stevens and whoever might be there to protect him. It was inevitable.

Bolan started firing. He shot out several more of the floor mines in a loose pattern reaching to the far end of the corridor. Each one erupted, a few of them spraying enough molten metal to trigger adjacent mines. Bolan continued shooting until he had activated every mine he could see with the beam of his flashlight. The corridor blazed with light and became an oven. Sweating, the soldier waited for the fires to burn themselves out. Then he reloaded the Beretta and proceeded carefully down the hallway, stepping over the holes and checking every inch of the floor ahead with his flashlight. Each mine had created a pit in the wood roughly eight inches deep. The cross-section of each hole revealed that the wood planks forming the floor were reinforced with some sort of flame-resistant insulation beneath. Below that was steel plate.

At the end of the corridor, the path made a sharp right turn. Bolan cut it wide, stepping cautiously and carefully. The floor space before him stretched ahead into the darkness. He paused to use his monocular again to check for invisible beams, again finding nothing. The flashlight, however, picked out the slender silver thread of a trip wire at ankle level.

He considered cutting the wire but rejected the idea. Suddenly releasing the tension might trigger whatever device was connected to the wire. He used his flashlight to check the floor beyond, as well as the walls and ceiling, then stepped very carefully over the wire.

His combat boot came to rest on the floor beyond the wire. A square of flooring beneath his foot dropped half an inch as he put his weight on it.

Bolan threw himself down and forward without hesitation. He felt a blast of air on his neck as several projectiles flew over him. The heavy smacks of metal against wood sounded like a hydraulic log splitter.

The soldier waited, immobile, his Beretta held before him along the floor with his flashlight, but nothing else happened. Very carefully he got to his knees and then on his feet, stepping over the wire again and noting the camouflage pressure plate in the floor. The wood was the same material as the boards of the rest of the corridor floor, but it was obviously only a shell under which the trigger switch was hidden. He stepped lightly as he moved back to the corner he'd rounded earlier, playing his light over the wall that faced the trip wired hallway.

Half buried in the plywood of the wall were half a dozen metal disks the size of drink coasters. He pried one of them free and examined it. It resembled a circular saw blade, its edges cut with notches that turned its perimeter into a series of aerodynamic teeth. Images of ninja and *shuriken* flashed through his head. Stevens was either drawing his inspiration from the same, or he had reinvented this particularly sharp wheel. Regardless, it was likely the wall at the opposite end of the hallway concealed a launcher or launchers designed to hurl the saws when the switch was triggered. He pocketed the saw blade and turned back to the task at hand.

Bolan was not about to try to sneak through a darkened killing chute dotted with triggers for the blades. Instead, he simply took cover behind the corner of the hallway, aimed the Beretta 93-R around it and started shooting single shots. He spread his fire down the hall, sparing a few double- and triple-taps as he peered around the corner with one eye, targeting the trip wire closest to him.

It took a while and Bolan was forced to burn through several of his magazines. He was rewarded, however, with periodic bursts of saw blades as the bullets punched the triggers in the floor or severed trip wires farther down the hallway. Some of the blades nicked others already stuck in the wall, raising sparks as they ricocheted. Bolan was forced to dodge one that came winging his way after bouncing off another blade. The saw missed him.

It took him some more time to creep down the cleared corridor, careful to step on the triggered pressure plates whenever possible. Twice he thought he could see seams in the floor under the beam of his flashlight, triggers that his gunfire had not tripped. He avoided these and the two trip wires he'd also failed to snap.

At the end of the hallway, the corridor took a sharp right turn again. It was not lost on Bolan that the path he was following was falling back on itself again. There were a series of slits in the wall that were obviously the mouths of the launchers—spring-powered, air-powered or however they propelled their projectiles—that had fired the saw blades. There was no way to tell if he'd triggered them all, so he was extremely careful to avoid their lines of fire. At the opening of the third corridor, he checked once again for beams. This time his monocular picked up several of them crossing the available space. A series of small projectors was mounted on the walls, in the corners at the ceiling.

As he had before, he took cover behind the corner leading to this latest hallway. Then he aimed his Beretta at the lenses and started shooting. One by one they shattered. Bolan checked again with the monocular before replacing it in his bag. The corridor was clear as far as he could see. Nothing had happened when the beams ended, however.

He took a step forward, then another, checking the floor for more pressure points or wires. The beams might have been a decoy, or they might simply have been designed to alert someone to the fact that an intruder had gotten this far. Bolan did not suppose that made much difference, though if the light beams were a decoy, that meant some other threat was waiting for him.

When he reached the halfway point of the hallway, an alarm sounded. It was a distant but loud mechanical bell, like a school bell. A few seconds after it started, the wall at the end of the corridor opened. It split apart on both sides, the camouflaged double doors fronted with plywood but clearly steel underneath. Bolan raised the Beretta as the first of the security detail pushed through the doorway.

There were four of them, and they carried ballistic shields before their bodies. From what Bolan could see past the shields, they wore full body armor and face shields. He flicked the selector of the 93-R to 3-round burst and filled the air between him and the guards with 9 mm interference as he turned and ran back the way he'd come. The guards opened up with their weapons— bullpup-style, high-tech Steyr AUG assault rifles—just as Bolan rounded the corner. The 5.56 mm DU rounds tore through the wall behind the soldier, igniting small fires that smoldered fit-fully amid the treated lumber.

Bolan dropped the empty magazine in his Beretta and swapped it for one of the 20-round magazines he'd loaded that morning. He had marked the end with an X of white-out fluid. It and several more like it were full of DU rounds stripped from the submachine gun magazines he had recovered from the El Cráneo shooters in Times Square. Racking the slide of the gun as if he was trying to rip it free of the machine pistol, Bolan brought his weapon on target as the first of the armored guards rounded the corner.

The triple-bursts of DU penetrators punched through the man's ballistic shield as if it wasn't there. He screamed as the rounds found his body, boring flaming holes through his flak vest and chest cavity. The smell of burning flesh reached Bolan's nos-trils as the guard fell and began to writhe in agony. Bolan spared him a mercy round that chewed through his helmet without dif-ficulty, splashing Lexan and brain matter through the exit wound onto the floor.

Bolan backed off a few paces. It would take the others a mo-ment to decide what to do, with the tables turned on them as they'd been. The Executioner did not give them that time. He aimed at the corner of the wall, estimated the height and began triggering 3-round bursts through the wall itself.

The angle of Bolan's fire took his DU rounds through the cor-ner and into the hallway beyond. There were more screams and a burst of flickering light from the flames the rounds generated. Bolan swapped magazines for a fresh supply of depleted ura-nium slugs, then charged around the corner with the Beretta and his flashlight in his hands.

The scene that greeted him was something out of a horror film. A second armored trooper, convulsing in his death throes, was burning brightly on the floor. The other two were retreating, headed back for the double doors. As they lined up single file,

Bolan snapped the Beretta to head level and triggered another burst.

Three 9 mm rounds slammed into and through the helmet of the first guard. They continued into the back of the second man's head. Bolan saw sparks and a shower of blood as the man in front fell forward. The guard behind him landed on him, both of them dead before they hit the floor. The Executioner advanced, following them to the doors and stepping through. A heavy plastic curtain made of overlapping sheets of black Mylar waited beyond the doors. When he pushed through that, he blinked in the sudden bright light of multiple overhead fluorescents.

"Don't fucking move!" someone shouted.

Bolan froze where he stood. He was in a large room with two levels, the second level a railed catwalk that traveled around the perimeter. The paint was peeling and the railing of the catwalk was dotted with rust. A layer of dust coated the floor. There were doors at the far end of the room at the right and left sides, plus the double doors from which Bolan had emerged. A man in urban-camouflage fatigues stood on the railing aiming a .45 pistol at him. Four men with AR-15s stood loosely arranged around Bolan, their weapons trained on him and their faces grim.

"Don't move. Don't try anything. It's over," the man on the catwalk said.

"Place the weapons on the deck," one of the riflemen ordered. Bolan complied, removing the Desert Eagle and placing it next to the Beretta on the floor. He stood over his guns with his hands low near his sides. He was careful not to move.

"Good. Just like clockwork," the man with the .45 said. "I told Stevens that whole James Bond tunnel thing was ridiculous. I figured we'd get a few dead homeless guys in there and not much else. I can't believe it worked just like he said it would. His little funhouse kept you busy while we got into position to collect you. We watched on closed-circuit TV, you know. You were supposed to die in the third tunnel. I got to hand it to you. You're not bad."

"Who are you?" Bolan said calmly.

"I'm Rawl," said the man, "Jordan Rawl, Hills Protective. My people and I provide security for the facility you have just invaded. You are an armed and obviously dangerous intruder. You forfeit your life in your trespass of this facility."

"I'm with the Justice Department," Bolan told him. "You don't want to be on the wrong side of this."

"Tragically," Rawl said, extending his pistol and sighting on Bolan's head, "you will be killed before you can identify yourself. On the off chance that your body is ever discovered, my men can hardly be held liable for terminating an armed stranger breaching our defenses through hostile action."

"Shooting an intruder is one thing," Bolan said. "Dumping the body is another."

"I would do nothing of the kind," Rawl told him. "It seems my men, trying their best not to kill you, will only wound you, allowing you to limp away. It would seem you survived only long enough to meet your end while in hiding."

"Lots of men with bullets through the brain crawl off to die alone," Bolan said.

"You'd be amazed what a wad of money will do for the average medical examiner," Rawl said. His face turned deadly serious as he aimed the pistol. "All right, enough screwing around. So long, asshole."

16

Bolan dropped to one knee and hurled the object he'd quietly palmed from a pocket of his blacksuit. The sharp little saw blade spun through the air and sliced into Rawl's face. He jerked back, screaming, triggering several shots from the .45, but his aim was off and Bolan was already in motion. The Executioner dropped and spun, bracing himself on his hands as he whipped his right leg around in an arc that toppled two of the nearest riflemen and sent the third crashing into the fourth. One of the AR-15s fired, but Bolan ignored it, grabbing up the Beretta and the Desert Eagle and bringing them on target together.

The Desert Eagle boomed in the enclosed space. The first rifleman went down, a gaping hole where his head had been, his rifle falling from his grip. Even as he took the forward target, Bolan aimed the 93-R at a forty-five-degree angle, drilling a second guard with a 3-round burst of DU ammo to the chest. The man shrieked as he burned from within, until his brain finally got the message that he was mortally injured.

Rawl recovered and began firing methodically from the railing. One of his shots cratered the floor near Bolan's foot, so the soldier took a moment to throw a .44 Magnum round that way. The heavy bullet slammed into Rawl's face. He was dead before he fell over the railing, dropping to the floor below.

Bolan kept firing on the move. He emptied both guns as he whirled and dodged, lining up the other shooters as they tried desperately to fix on him. Just as he killed the third rifleman with a shot to the midsection, the fourth man emptied his magazine with a burst that went high and wide over Bolan's right shoulder. Bolan's own guns were also empty.

The rifleman heard the hollow, ominous click of an empty AR-15 and began clutching at the pouches on his web belt, struggling to produce another magazine. Bolan dropped his pistols, closing the distance between himself and the shooter, drawing and thumbing open the Cold Steel Gunsite knife in a single fluid motion. Just as the guard managed to bring a new magazine up to the well of his rifle, Bolan was on him, slashing him across the throat on the upstroke and then again on the backstroke as he took the man down to his right side, dropping him bleeding to the floor. He dropped an ax kick on the back of the fallen man's head, driving the heel of his combat boot into the doomed man's skull. The shooter twitched several times and was finally still.

Standing amid the corpses, bloody folding knife still in his hand, Bolan paused to catch his breath and survey the damage.

No one and nothing moved.

He wasted no time contemplating his work. Retrieving his pistols, he reloaded and holstered them. He took as many spare magazines of DU ammunition as he could find, searching the dead men. Lastly, he took one of the heavy-barreled AR-15s and examined it.

The weapon was a civilian AR-15 with a chromed match barrel and an obviously modified selector switch. The work done on the weapon was visible but not crude, displaying knowledge of the weapon that Cowboy Kissinger would probably have grudgingly acknowledged. This rifle had settings for single-shot and full-auto, rather than the 3-round burst found on later variant M-16s. The barrel guards had been removed and replaced with guards equipped with accessory rails. A vertical foregrip and Streamlight Tactical Light were mounted to the weapon.

Bolan tested the bright white light and then sighted across the room. He fired the weapon experimentally a few times, satisfying himself that it would hit where he aimed. The DU rounds left burning holes in the wall.

Planting his combat boot, Bolan kicked open the door to the left. The room beyond was full of boxes of paper and trash, roof shingles, pieces of drywall and other construction debris. He reversed course and tried the door on the right. It led to a stairwell, where the hastily erected pathways of plywood and two-by-fours gave way to the concrete-and-cinder-block construction he would have expected from an old warehouse of this type. He could see at least three or four landings above.

A metal fire door slammed somewhere high above him.

More of Stevens's security guards were coming and they weren't wasting time trying to be sneaky about it. Bolan watched them take the landing at the top of the building. He moved up half a flight, targeted through the stairwell and held down the trigger of his captured weapon.

The spray of 5.56 mm DU rounds caught two of the men. The explosive penetrators ripped through their legs and through one man's chest, dropping them both. The man with the chest wounds was killed immediately, while the other man lived long enough to take a second burst through the floor as Bolan finished the job.

The guards realized what Bolan was doing and turned the tactic against him, burning through the stairs and landings below with DU fire of their own. Bolan was forced to retreat back the way he'd come.

Changing magazines on the run, he clicked on the light mounted beneath the barrel and used it to guide him back through the corridors leading to the ambush room. In the hallway of the rotating saws, he triggered one of the remaining trip wires and was forced to throw himself aside to avoid taking a spinning blade in the back. It was only moments before he was back at the door he'd used to breach the building. He shouldered it open, emerging in the bright white light of the morning.

Bolan ran, trying to get into position as quickly as possible. Stevens and his men might be monitoring him through hidden cameras, but it wouldn't matter if his plan worked. He circled the building, chose a likely spot and crouched to steady the AR-15.

The big black rifle spit DU rounds in a long burst. Bolan emptied the magazine, firing in an arc to the left of his body, from low to high. He hit the magazine release, dropped the empty one and slapped home a fresh round, smacking the bolt release and chambering the first round of the new magazine. Then he emptied it, as well, changing magazines again as he surveyed his handiwork.

The explosive penetrators had chewed an arc through the wall of the building, leaving gaping, burning holes in a line that described an arched doorway. Bolan put his shoulder against the cinder blocks and pushed with all his might. The shattered wall gave, tumbling the cinder blocks over, creating a breach in the building that the soldier could scramble through. He climbed over the rubble with the AR-15 at the ready, the light's beam thickly visible in the concrete dust.

He found himself on a manufacturing floor. High ceilings above him ended in metal rafters that supported what appeared to be sophisticated chemical-fire suppression equipment. There were multiple machines on the floor, some of them chugging away. Bolan saw empty brass casings being loaded into one machine from a hopper. In another, a spinning drum was separating chemicals of some kind. In a third, red-tipped cartridges were being primed automatically, one after another, as they filed into the bowels of the machine on multiple single-file conveying trays.

A far wall dominated by large scrolling doors was the entrance to a loading dock. Crates upon crates that Bolan presumed were filled with completed DU ammunition sat waiting for loading. The warehouse floor was piled high with chemicals, explosives and other volatile materials that would make for more than sufficient means to raze the place.

The Executioner intended to leave nothing standing.

He saw no evidence of workers. The machines appeared to be designed to operate on their own with minimal interference, but all required that materials be loaded into them before they could commence their mechanical efforts. Bolan imagined that, if there was no other staff, Stevens might pay his security guards to do double duty feeding the machines. If that was the case, it would make his job easier. If there were factory workers, he could not guarantee they were not innocents pressed into service—illegal aliens, the homeless or any number of marginal- ized denizens of the area who might be too desperate for money to ask too many questions. He would see to it such workers got to safety before the warehouse came down, if there were any. With luck the only personnel on-site were Stevens and his hired guns.

Bolan moved from machine to machine. He inspected each and decided that there was no need for special plans. A few well- placed DU rounds into some of the stored chemicals would start a fire sufficient to detonate the rest of the explosives. He looked back at the gaping hole he had created and realized just how close he'd come to setting off the explosions already. His rounds, traveling at a slight upward angle, had missed the machinery and chemicals but sprayed an office area on an elevated platform above the manufacturing floor.

The metal mesh stairs leading to the office were intact. Bolan took these two at a time, covering the office as he did so. The large windows of the office, affording a commanding view of the manufacturing area, had been punched through in several spots but had not broken. They were apparently Lexan blast shields, which explained how they'd fared so well under the depleted uranium onslaught.

Inside, Bolan found two dead men on the floor. Both wore fatigues matching those of the security men he'd already taken down. Some papers scattered around the officer were burning, as was a computer terminal in one corner, but the blaze had not grown any larger.

The destruction of the computer was unfortunate. It looked to be a total loss, which meant there was no point in trying to pull the drive. Bolan searched through the debris in the office but could not find anything other than technical specs and programming notes for the machinery below. There was nothing to tie Stevens with Norris Labs International, which meant there was nothing he could pass on to Brognola to help take down the company behind it all. Stevens had gone rogue and committed crimes of his own, yes, but the research he was using belonged to NLI, and it was NLI that had tried so hard—and killed so many—to cover up the whole thing.

If he had to, the Executioner would bring his war to NLI's doorstep, doing with blades and bullets what legal resources could not accomplish through the system.

Another door led from the rear of the office area to an adjoining space on what would be, if Bolan correctly estimated the height of the warehouse floor's ceiling, the top floor of the structure. This was as likely a spot as any for Stevens's office. Judging from the size of the building and what he could see of the manufacturing floor, there wasn't room for much else in the structure besides the killing chute and ambush room he'd already visited. Stevens had done a thorough job of converting the available space to his purposes.

The door opened into a wide studio area divided by cloth cubicle walls. Bolan searched these with his light-equipped rifle poised for action. Each cubicle contained a workstation and several other pieces of equipment, including a digitizer tablet of the type used in computer-aided drafting. Bolan suspected that from these terminals, Stevens had designed, and run simulations for, the weapons to which he had devoted his life.

Every station had been destroyed.

The processors had been shot through with DU rounds, their cases shattered, their boards molten. Many were still smoking and a few still burned slightly. A few stations with external hard drives or disk drives had seen the attached hardware smashed with what might been the butt of a gun or knife. There would be no evidence worth gathering among these machines.

The destruction was recent. Bolan spotted the reinforced metal door beyond the cubicles. There was a surveillance camera mounted above it, the red LED beneath its lens blinking slowly. A speaker was set in the wall next to the camera. Bolan approached with the AR-15 pointed ahead, scanning the walls, floors and ceiling for more mechanical threats. There were no booby traps that he could see, but Stevens had proved extremely resourceful. He had no desire to take a tiny saw blade to the neck, or lose a foot in a shower of molten lead.

"My, you're a determined one, aren't you?" a voice said from the speaker.

"Stevens?" Bolan said.

"I am Donald Stevens," the voice said with resignation. "I suppose you're here to tell me that it's over, that I should surrender and that no one else has to die."

"Not really, no," Bolan said frankly. "Someone else does have to die. That someone is you."

There was a pause as Stevens digested that. "You can't mean simply to murder me."

"It's not murder," Bolan said. "It's simple justice. A lot of people have died because of you. They weren't just gang members, or operatives from Blackjack or your own goons. They were innocent civilians in New York. There were also police officers doing their jobs. Then there are the people who weren't killed, but who have had to live in fear because of the war you helped unleash on their city. You have a lot to answer for, Stevens. Too much, in fact, for any penalty but death to be just."

"Why would you tell me this?" asked the voice from the speaker.

"We both know it's true," Bolan told him. "I could try to negotiate with you. I could try to lie to you, tell you we can cut some sort of deal if you'll come quietly. But I'm not a police officer, Stevens. I'm a soldier fighting a war. You're an enemy combatant. You have to die."

"I could kill you. I could kill you before you get me," Stevens said.

"You could try," Bolan said. "You won't, though. You said it yourself. It *is* over. You just don't want to see it."

"I'll give you one chance to leave now, with your life," Stevens said. "I'll give you safe passage out of the building."

"You'll give me nothing," Bolan replied. He made certain the AR-15 had a full load and then stepped back from the door. "I'm coming through. Your own ammunition, the death you've been spreading around New York City, is going to help me do it. Your only option, Stevens, is to take your own life before I do it for you."

There was a pause. Bolan snapped the AR-15 up against his shoulder and prepared to fire.

"Wait," Stevens said.

The door opened, sliding aside on a track in the floor. It was extremely heavy steel and moved on well-maintained hydraulics. Bolan moved cautiously inside, the rifle aimed at the man within the office.

Donald Stevens sat backlit by the window, the view of the waterfront district contrasting sharply with the grim, sparsely furnished room. He was seated at his cluttered desk, a .45 automatic pistol held in his right hand. The barrel was placed against his own temple.

"Don't shoot," Stevens said. "You need to know something."

"No explanations you have to offer will change what I'm here to do," Bolan informed him.

"Not an explanation," Stevens said. As he spoke, his voice grew stronger, more determined. "I don't think you realize who you're dealing with, soldier," Stevens said mockingly. "I just might take my life, all right. But if I do, you and everyone within a half-mile radius are going to be having a very, very bad day."

Bolan said nothing. His finger tightened on the trigger of the AR-15.

"I said don't!" Stevens shrieked. He used his free hand to tear at the button-down white shirt he wore. As the shirt opened, it revealed a circular white bandage taped to his chest.

"What is that?" Bolan asked.

"Underneath this bandage is a small heart monitor," Stevens said. "My final insurance, let's say. The monitor is connected to a computer located somewhere in this building, hidden so a casual search will not turn it up. It is running software that I wrote, software that monitors my heart rate."

"And?"

"And I'm wired to a bomb, essentially," Stevens said, licking his lips. He was starting to sweat. "If you kill me, or if I kill myself, my heartbeat will stop. That will trigger the software to send a command to a remote device. That device is a bomb."

"I was planning to blow up this place anyway," Bolan shrugged.

"You don't understand," Stevens said. "It's not a conventional bomb. It's a dirty bomb—a single rod of combat-60 and just enough explosives to get the job done. Within a half mile, everyone lingering in the neighborhood can expect to get an acute dose of radiation. Go ahead and shoot, if you want to risk it."

"You're lying," Bolan said.

"Am I?" Stevens shot back. "Are you willing to risk the consequences of finding out?"

"There's nothing particularly elegant or sophisticated about a dirty bomb," Bolan said. "That's not your style. That's not the type of device employed by a man who designs his own special land mines. That's not the work of someone who's devoted his life to advancing arms development. The dirty bomb is the poor man's option, the terrorist's expedient leverage. I don't buy it."

"I'm warning you!" Stevens said shrilly. "I'll give you one chance to get away, but if you won't take it, I'll shoot myself and we'll all go up. This blighted city will be laid waste, a cancer growing at its center! Just say the word, soldier, and I'll pull this trigger and let the bomb explode!"

"That's quite a promise," Bolan said. "I wonder if you're the type of man who's actually capable of taking his own life? I've met men who were willing to do just that, in the last few days. They were brought into this specifically to take you out. Even hired guns like those people were better than you. At least they knew that a line existed, even if they were too willing to cross it."

"Shut up!" Stevens shrieked. "It's not fair!"

"Fair?" Bolan asked. "Who said anything about fair?"

"All I wanted to do was continue my work, make some money," Stevens said, staring through Bolan. "That's all. Was that so much?"

"Was it worth the deaths of all those people?" Bolan countered.

Stevens sat as if thinking about the question. Then he blinked. He looked at Bolan and something like resolve filtered past his blue eyes.

The .45 swung from his head to point at Bolan.

Bolan fired.

The single round from the AR-15 took Donald Stevens between the eyes, burning through him and ripping him open. He collapsed in a broken heap half in and half out of his chair. What was left of his last expression was one of shock. At the end, his type never could believe that death had come for them. Bolan had seen such expressions before.

Bolan walked across the office, bent over Stevens and ripped the bandage from the dead man's chest.

There was nothing beneath it. Stevens had been bluffing, as Bolan suspected.

The soldier phoned Burnett as he was exiting the building. The detective simply rammed the Crown Victoria through the fence and drove up to where Bolan stood surveying the building.

"Cleaned house already?" he asked. "What did you find?"

"Donald Stevens and a warehouse full of munitions," Bolan told him. "Plus plenty of the materials necessary to make the stuff."

"Knowing you, I'd have thought this place would be a mushroom cloud by now," Burnett cracked.

"You don't know how close you are," Bolan said, "and originally I had intended to level this place. On second thought, however, it's quite possible there's evidence here that Stevens missed when he was busy destroying his research. The equipment itself may be traceable to some source that is in turn traceable farther up the chain. It may be possible to find a link to Norris Labs. We're going to need heavy police presence to cordon off this area and secure the building."

"Don't you have any federal friends who can help?" Burnett asked.

"I can call in backup," Bolan told him, "but it will take time to get enough people here. In the meantime I need a wall of uniforms to keep this place locked down until we can start going through it piece by piece."

"I'll get on the horn and see what I can arrange," Burnett said. "I'll start with—"

Bolan peered at the detective, who had stopped speaking suddenly. "What is it?"

"Do you hear that?"

"Hear what?" Bolan's ears were ringing slightly from the firefight in the warehouse.

"Oh, shit, Cooper." Burnett looked up at him. "Get in!"

Two armored trucks rammed through the sealed overhead doors on the side of the warehouse, their engines snarling loudly in the late-morning air. The doors were split and shoved aside like scrap metal as the trucks roared free, tearing across the crumbling parking lot until the drivers spotted the Crown Victoria. Then they turned, their ugly metal snouts pointed directly at Bolan and Burnett.

"Get in! Get in!" Burnett screamed. Bolan ripped open the passenger door behind the cop and threw himself into the backseat. The detective was already burning rubber from the rear wheels as Bolan yanked the door shut behind him.

The powerful police cruiser surged forward, initially gaining ground against the trucks.

"Keep us in this area," Bolan said. "The more deserted, the better. We can't afford to draw them to a more populated area."

"Who do you suppose they are?"

"No idea," Bolan said, looking back. "Doesn't matter. Obviously Stevens had some security people in reserve. They either don't know he's dead, or he had some kind of arrangement with them in case he checked out. They're gunning for us now, and they've got more than enough power to do it."

Each truck was about the size of a Chevy Suburban, but with a body composed entirely of heavy angle plate. Slits in the windshield armor and on the sides provided gun ports and visibility, limited though the latter would be. On top of each truck was a turret that appeared to Bolan to house a PKT 7.62 mm machine gun. There was little doubt what sort of ammo the guns would be using.

"If we get tagged," Bolan told the detective, "we're going to burn in here."

"No pressure, though," Burnett said grimly. He gripped the

wheel with both hands, flooring the accelerator and watching the road intently. As they reached the far end of the parking lot, both men braced themselves for the impact as the Crown Victoria smashed through the chain-link fence. A piece of barbed wire caught on the rear bumper and dragged behind the car, trailing sparks.

Bolan watched through the rearview mirror, the AR-15 on the floor next to him, his Desert Eagle in his fist. One of the armored trucks slowed slightly and swiveled its turret. Bolan watched as a stream of 7.62 mm ammunition poured into the warehouse. The truck kept moving as it fired, and the lead truck was closing on the Crown Victoria. Bolan was transfixed as the second truck emptied round after round into the wall of the warehouse at ground level.

The shock wave, when it came, slapped against the rear window of the Crown Victoria hard enough to make the car vibrate. Bolan covered his face with his arm, just in case, but not before he saw the incredible explosion. It was not a single blast, in fact, but a layered series of smaller explosions building to a crescendo of destruction, an orgy of heat and light and debris. The warehouse was crippled, broken, shattered and then reduced to cinders by the force of the blast, which raised a plume of dark smoke that enveloped everything for half a mile.

Burnett struggled on through the gloom, doing his best to keep the vehicle moving despite the sudden darkness. When they finally drove out of the worst of the smoke and debris cloud, Burnett rolled down his window. He stopped and both men listened for the sound of the trucks over the idling of the car.

"Back to Plan A, huh?" Burnett said to Bolan, grinning his lopsided grin. He turned away suddenly. "There! I hear them again." He stomped the accelerator and the car lurched forward, the tires squealing briefly.

Whatever the heavy, armored trucks had for engines, they were more than up to the task of pushing the large vehicles after their quarry. Burnett drove and Bolan watched as the security forces started to close the gap between the vehicles.

"Burnett," Bolan said, reaching for the AR-15, "I need you to get us far enough ahead so I can get in position. Can you do that?"

"Watch me," Burnett said. He began driving like a madman, his foot on the floor, the Crown Victoria howling and fishtailing through turns around the abandoned and boarded-up buildings of the decrepit waterfront district. The trucks pressed but could not match Burnett's aggressive maneuvering, allowing him and Bolan to gain the extra combat stretch they needed.

"Okay," Bolan told the detective. "Now."

The Crown Victoria shuddered to a rolling stop on abused brakes as Burnett stomped the pedal. Bolan, holding the AR-15 by the front guard, threw himself out of the car, banging the hood twice with his right fist. Burnett stomped on the gas again and peeled away, as Bolan ran into position at the side of the road. The armored trucks were already bearing down.

Gunfire split the morning air and echoed off the decaying buildings of the deserted section of Camden. Bolan poured on the fire from his captured AR-15, focusing on the engine compartment of the lead truck. The DU rounds hit the truck grille and burned through, shredding the engine compartment and igniting a series of explosions within the motor. Bolan kept firing and clipped the front tires for good measure.

The entire front of the truck burst into flame. The front tires burst. The truck suddenly lost velocity, only to lurch as the speeding truck behind it slammed into the rear of the lead vehicle. The burning truck was slammed over on its side, where it skidded across the asphalt in a shower of sparks and burning metal.

Bolan charged around the wreck and flanked the rear truck as both vehicles came to a stop. The turret on the rear truck began to swivel in his direction. Swapping magazines on the run, he hosed the turret with more DU rounds, destroying the machine-gun and the metal mount to which it was attached. He thought he heard a scream from within the turret itself, but he couldn't be sure over the rattle of the AR-15. With the turret out of commission, he began shooting the cab of the truck. The DU rounds entered the armored cab effortlessly, pulping the men inside.

The AR-15 clicked on an empty chamber. Bolan was out of reloads for it, so he let it drop and drew the Desert Eagle from the tactical holster on his right thigh. He advanced on the burning lead truck. Two men were climbing from the cab, using the passenger-side door to scramble out onto the top of the wreck. Bolan covered them with his pistol. They were shaken from the crash and one was bleeding from a head wound. Both had pistols in holsters on their belts.

"Hands behind your heads!" Bolan ordered. "Move away from the vehicle slowly. Come to me and stop at the curb."

The two hired guns, both wearing urban camouflage fatigues, both white males in their late twenties, staggered over as Bolan had ordered. "Don't shoot," the one with the bleeding forehead said. "Don't shoot. We won't resist."

"On your knees," Bolan told them. Both men sank to their knees with their hands clasped behind their heads.

The Crown Victoria cruised up, the smell of hot rubber clinging to the hard-driven vehicle like a cloud. The engine ticked furiously when Burnett got out of the car. "Hey, Cooper. I thought you might need help," Burnett said, "but then I thought, well, hell, it's only you against two armored trucks with heavy machine guns firing explosive bullets that can pierce armor and buildings and set fire to everything in sight. Sounds like a fair fight to me."

Bolan scowled. "Get their guns," he said. "Carefully."

"Sure," Burnett said. He was careful to stay out of Bolan's line of fire, moving to one man and then behind him to the next, taking each of the sidearms the men carried.

"You want them?" He brought Bolan the two weapons, both Glock 17s.

"Identify yourselves," Bolan ordered his prisoners.

"Simmons," said the one with the head wound. "He's Appleton."

"Thanks for identifying me to the enemy, asshole," Appleton said.

"Oh, shut up," Simmons shot back. "You're not in Afghanistan, Joey. You never were, man."

"Enough," Bolan barked. He pointed the Desert Eagle's snout at first one, then the other mercenary. "So. What's your story? Simmons?"

"We work for Hills Protective," Simmons told him. "You killed Rawl. We were looking for some payback."

"What do you know about the operation in that warehouse?"

"We were told to destroy the place if security was breached," Simmons said grudgingly. "Stevens insisted on that. He said he didn't want anyone to benefit from his work, if he couldn't."

"Figures," Burnett put in.

Bolan spent a few more minutes interrogating Simmons and Appleton, but it was clear they didn't know anything useful. Their hearts weren't in the game, either. Both men seemed defeated. At Bolan's suggestion, Burnett contacted the local authorities, who sent a car to pick up the prisoners. Many more police and fire vehicles arrived, as well. Bolan imagined representatives from every conceivable state agency would be on hand by nightfall, combing over the cinders of the warehouse under the watchful eyes of the government agents sent by Brognola.

The soldier and the detective milled about with the other personnel on scene until Bolan was satisfied that the situation was sufficiently contained. Then they returned to the Crown Victoria.

"You know what I could use?" Burnett said.

"What?"

"Lunch."

17

The upscale luxury apartment building on the Delaware River sat in the midst of an affluent waterfront neighborhood in Philadelphia. Burnett pulled the Crown Victoria into the building's private multilevel parking garage, flashed his badge at the attendant and conferred briefly with the man. They found the parking spot reserved for Emilie Taveras, where a gleaming Hummer H3 was parked. Burnett gleefully parked the Crown Victoria to block in the Hummer.

"He could probably ram his way out if he tried," the detective admitted, "but it will buy us time."

"We don't know that this is Pierre Taveras's vehicle," Bolan pointed out.

"Trust me," Burnett said. "I doubt that Pierre's saintly, blue-haired mother is driving a Hummer at the age of eighty-nine. She's probably more the sports-car type."

Bolan ignored the detective's attempt at humor, but mentally conceded the point.

They had found a chain restaurant on the outskirts of Camden, a run-down place where the service was slow and the servers were sullen. Still, the food was good, reminding Bolan of how long a morning it had been. Burnett ate like a man who'd been fasting for weeks, explaining that mortal danger always gave him an appetite. The Executioner had to admit to himself that the cocky detective's sense of humor was growing on him, but vowed silently that he'd never tell Burnett as much.

Burnett lingered in the restaurant while Bolan returned to the car and placed a call on his secure phone. Barbara Price sounded pleased to hear that he had come through the latest operation unscathed. Bolan briefed her on what he'd seen inside the warehouse and listened as she relayed what the on-site teams were reporting.

The warehouse and the area immediately surrounding it were a total loss. Fortunately for everyone involved, there were no viable businesses and certainly no residences close enough to be damaged by the blast. There were some health concerns raised by the smoke cloud produced by the explosion, but Price told Bolan that EPA teams were taking air samples and had found nothing too harmful as of yet.

"We're running down the last of the players at large," Bolan told Stony Man's mission controller. "The only one left is Pierre Taveras and whomever he might have with him. Burnett tells me there's one place, a last-ditch safe house of sorts, that he might go. It's not far—right across the river in Philadelphia."

"What's so special about this location that your detective friend thinks he'll go there? Taveras has to be running pretty scared by now, with his organization shot out from under him," Price said.

"True," Bolan said. "But this place *is* special. It's where Taveras's mother lives."

Price nodded before remembering that Bolan couldn't see her. "Do you need any support? I could get Jack in the air."

"No," Bolan told her, "I don't think we'll need him. While there have been a couple of times during this mission that I would have liked to have him, I can't see diverting him now. Call it a point of pride, but I want to wrap this up on my terms. Burnett's proved very useful, anyway. We're going to drive into Philadelphia, locate Taveras if he's there and take him down."

"Do you mean to bring him in?"

"I'll do what I have to do," Bolan stated.

"Detective Burnett doesn't have any qualms about that?"

"He's a realist," Bolan said. "Besides, there's no way Taveras will come quietly. I've seen the type hundreds of times. A week ago he was the king of New York City, as he saw it, destined to unify the criminal element under one banner, a lord overseeing his Manhattan fiefdom. Today he's nothing but a criminal with no resources, no options and nowhere to go but—if Burnett is right—running to his mommy. He'll be like the worst caged and wounded animal you can imagine, racked with paranoia, ready to lash out at whoever comes to collect him. A man like that will die before he'll go quietly. He'll also be looking to take as many people with him as he can. Men like Pierre Taveras don't like to die alone. They prefer lots of company."

"Understood," Price said. "Good hunting, Striker."

BOLAN AND BURNETT left the parking garage and made their way to the main lobby, Burnett marveling at the well-furnished facilities. "I guess this sure beats being put in a home in your twilight years," he said. "Apparently Mrs. Taveras likes to live in style. I've known about this address since we first started putting together a dossier on Pierre, but I didn't put two and two together. The riverfront address pretty much screams money, I guess."

"It stands to reason." Bolan nodded. They walked through the lobby, Bolan scanning from side to side, front and back, checking for targets. Nothing seemed out of the ordinary. A younger man sat with an older couple, perhaps his parents, drinking coffee as they relaxed in a set of overstuffed chairs set around a low table in the lobby. There were a few other people milling about, too. This wasn't a retirement home, Bolan reminded himself, so there would be people of all ages in the building.

They bypassed the elevators at the far end of the lobby and

instead took the stairs. Burnett groused about the long walk to the twelfth floor, where the apartment was located, but he seemed as aware as Bolan of the dangers inherent to being enclosed in an elevator during a combat scenario.

As the stairwell door closed behind them, neither man saw the younger man at the coffee table pull a cell phone from his pocket and make a quick call.

Burnett was breathing hard by the time they made the twelfth floor. "You don't even look winded," he said, stopping to catch his breath with his hands on his knees. "How do you do it?"

"Practice," Bolan said. He opened the twelfth-floor stairwell door and peered out through the crack. "I don't see anyone," he said. "No guards, no visible cameras."

"Twelve-fifteen," Burnett wheezed. "That's the one we want."

"Looks like it's at the end of this hall on the left," Bolan told him.

"Well," Burnett said, straightening, "let's get him, then." He drew his Glock and press-checked it.

"Yeah," Bolan said. The Desert Eagle felt good in his hand. There was no need to check it again; he knew it was chambered and ready.

They moved quietly down the hallway. Bolan kept his eyes open for civilians. He did not want anyone walking into the line of fire. While the setting was much more affluent, the whole scenario felt a lot like the raid on Jonathan West's apartment. From the look on Burnett's face, he was thinking the same thing.

They reached the door to unit 1215 and Bolan motioned for the detective to take the left side while he took the right. From the side, well clear of the doorway, Bolan rapped on the door with his free hand, the Desert Eagle held at low ready.

"Hello?" an elderly woman's voice responded.

"Mrs. Taveras?" Bolan said through the door. "I'm sorry to bother you, ma'am. My name is Cooper. I'm with the Justice Department. Could we come in and speak with you for a moment?"

"Just a moment," the woman said. There was at the sound of a dead bolt moving and a chain being unhooked from the other side of the door. When it swung open, Emilie Taveras stood there, a frail old woman with blue-tinted hair and fingers gnarled by arthritis. "Hello," she said.

"Hello," said Pierre Taveras, who stood behind his mother holding a 9 mm Smith & Wesson pistol to her head. "Step inside, *hijo de puta.* Keep your gun pointed at the floor until you have closed the door again behind that *puto,* Burnett. Then drop your guns on the floor. Carefully. I love my mother. I would hate to have to spray her brains all over both of you."

The two men complied. Taveras motioned both of them to sit on the leather-upholstered couch in the living room. Then he whispered to his mother and she wandered off in the direction of her bedroom.

"Your mother takes being threatened pretty well, especially when it's her son doing the threatening," Burnett commented.

"She has been senile for many years," Taveras said, taking a seat opposite Bolan and the detective. He kept his Smith & Wesson aimed between them, occasionally swinging it from one man to the next as he spoke. On the glass-topped coffee table between them was a closed laptop.

"Do not doubt me," Taveras warned. "I would kill her in a heartbeat. She is old and her mind is mostly gone. It would be a mercy, I think. And I would rather kill her myself than trust what would happen to her after I am gone, after the money that pays for this place, for the home nurses that attend to her each morning, is all gone. Is that really so hard to understand?"

"That you'd put a bullet in the back of your own mother's head?" Burnett said. "Why, gosh, no. Any of us would do that. Right, Cooper?"

"I knew you would come," Taveras said, ignoring the detective. "I knew the men who had done so much damage to me, who helped lead my enemies to my doorstep so many times, would not stop until they hunted me to my final refuge. That is what you did, is it not, Detective Burnett? I should have killed you when last we met."

"Probably," Burnett said.

"And this one." Taveras nodded to Bolan. "He should be screaming his last at the point of July's knife right now. Yet here he is, this *bastardo grande,* alive and well, and July is dead. How did you escape, *pendejo?* Did this one—" he laughed as he nodded at Burnett "—come to your rescue? Now, *that* would be funny!"

"Cut to the chase, Taveras," Burnett said. "What do you want?"

"Want? Want? Why, I want to kill you both," Taveras said. "But first I think I will torture you until you go insane. That is what I want."

"De la Rocha thought he was going to do the same," Bolan spoke up. "It ended badly for him."

"Then we will sit and chat," Taveras said lightly. "We will get to know each other as enemies should. And while we chat, my men will be murdering every single person living in this building. How would that be, hmm?"

Burnett looked to Bolan and back to Taveras. "You're not serious."

"Of course I am serious," Taveras said. "What have I to lose? You and this one—" he jerked his chin at Bolan "—have seen to it that everything has been taken from me. I have very few resources left. I have no more of Stevens's precious bullets. I have a handful of men still loyal to me. I have no safe houses, no bases of operation. Even now, the lesser gangs of New York will be moving in on territory previously held by El Cráneo. My empire crumbles around me."

"Killing innocent people won't change any of that," Bolan told him.

"No? Perhaps not. But it will make me feel better. And it will make *you* feel worse, before I kill you both. A man in my position learns to take his pleasures when and where he can."

"You'll never pull it off," Burnett said. "There are hundreds of people in this building. You don't have the manpower to get them all, especially once it becomes obvious what you're doing. Look around you, Taveras! Everything changed with 9/11. People won't just stand by and be slaughtered. They'll come at you with everything they've got. You've got, what, a dozen men left, tops? It's not enough."

"You underestimate me even at the end, Burnett," Taveras said. Still pointing the gun, he reached with his free hand for the laptop, opening it. The sleep mode deactivated and the screen displayed the program running on the computer. The schematic of a multilevel apartment building was visible. Red blips on the screen moved slightly in key locations on the schematic. Perhaps two hundred other blips, those designated blue, were clustered among the rooms on the computer-generated diagram.

"What is that?" Burnett asked.

"This," Taveras said proudly, "was a little present from Stevens. He sold us much firepower, but also a bit of other technology, now and then. He was very proud of this little device." Taveras held up a small, pressurized canister. This gas is remarkable. It has no smell. It has no taste. It is invisible. But when it is released into, let us say, the ventilation system of a building like this one, it clings to living flesh and reacts with body heat. It creates a signature that one may track. Stevens told me the technology for the sensor is little different than a cell phone or, in this case, a wireless computer."

"Those dots," Burnett said. "Those are the people in this building."

"Yes," Taveras said. "And the red dots are red because my people each wear these." The drug lord held up a small electronic disc the size of a penny. "You see? I know where everyone is. I know where my men are. From here, and with this," Taveras said, tossing the disk aside and bringing out his own cell phone, "I can coordinate their actions. I can kill everyone in this building and see to it no one escapes. I am God here." He laughed, an edge of hysteria in his voice. "And I am a wrathful god, Burnett!"

"You don't have to do this," Burnett said. "You're only making it worse for yourself if you get caught. Cut a deal instead. I head the task force—my word carries a lot of weight. There's another way, Taveras."

"Another way?" Taveras scoffed. "In a cage? I do not think so. No, I think the way is revenge. Revenge for the many things you both have taken from me. Revenge for July. Revenge for Jesus, who was stupid but loyal. Revenge for me. You have insulted me. You will not live to tell the story. You will not amuse others with the tale of how you broke Pierre Taveras."

Taveras stood. With one foot, he shoved the glass coffee table aside, clearing the space between him and where Burnett and Bolan sat on the couch. Looming over them, he aimed the gun from Burnett to Bolan and back again. "Which of you," he said, "will die now, and which of you will die later? I find I need only one witness for what we are about to do here. I need very much to kill one of you first. The other can stand by and feel the pain of being helpless to stop my people."

"You don't have to kill innocent civilians," Bolan said, his voice full of menace. "Don't do this, Taveras."

"Of course I have to!" Taveras said, swinging the gun at Bolan. "What do you think Times Square was for? I must send a message. I must make it clear that I am willing to do anything. I must be feared. Why, this is the start of El Cráneo's return to power! The city will tremble at the thought of the Skull among them, and they will know that we cannot be stopped. We will—"

Bolan pushed off the couch with his arms and fired a vicious front kick into Taveras's shin, which was just within range. There was a snapping sound, and Taveras fell as his leg gave way beneath him. Bolan kicked him again in the face as hard as he could, snapping the drug lord's head back with an audible crunch. He landed on the corner of the coffee table, the back of his head driving through the edge of the table and shattering the glass top. The computer hit the carpeted floor in a shower of glass.

Taveras's eyes rolled up inside his head and he was still.

Burnett's jaw dropped.

Bolan hurried to secure Taveras's gun. Then he knelt, checked the drug lord's pulse. Finally, he searched the body, finding a money clip and a few other personal accessories, but nothing else.

"Is he dead?" Burnett asked.

Bolan nodded.

"Can't say I'm real sorry to hear that," the detective said.

"The feeling is mutual," Bolan said. "Grab the computer and make sure it's okay. We've got work to do."

18

Emilie Taveras was sleeping peacefully, oblivious to the death of her son in the next room. Burnett returned from checking on her and sat down at the kitchen table, where Taveras's laptop was open and running. He'd found the power cord and connected it. Taveras had apparently been fairly casual about things like battery power remaining.

Bolan stood behind him and watched as Burnett played with the monitoring program, changing views from room to room. The three-dimensional schematics of the building itself weren't something Stevens's sophisticated tracking gas would have been able to provide. The soldier suspected Taveras had to have provided the information somehow, planning all along to use the tools Stevens had given him to create a last line of defense in the one place he was likely to go if everything else went wrong. Taveras had been an egomaniac and an unstable, brutal man, but he had also been quite cunning. He and El Cráneo would not have risen to power, otherwise. It would have been just like Taveras to plot out such an elaborate strategy to protect himself—and to give him the means to strike back, using innocent people as leverage.

The soldier and the detective had no choice but to assume that any word of Taveras's death would trigger a response from the ten men stationed throughout the apartment building. Burnett had Taveras's cell phone in his pocket. So far no one had called, but either Taveras's men would check in with him regularly, or the drug lord himself would be expected to call his El Cráneo operatives. It was likely that those in the building knew Burnett and Bolan had come up, for Taveras had not been at all surprised by their entrance. It all added up to falling numbers. They would need to work quickly to avert Taveras's scheduled massacre.

Already working in their favor was the fact that the monitoring program could no longer be used to coordinate the attack. Too many people would die, however, if the El Cráneo gunmen simply started shooting. Bolan would not risk that if it could be avoided. There had been too much death already.

Bolan dialed Burnett's number from his secure phone, attaching the wireless headset he carried for the device. "Testing," he said.

"I've got you," Burnett said, holding his own phone to his ear.

"And I can hear you loud and clear," Bolan said. "All right, Burnett. You're my eyes. Keep talking. I'll be the red dot that's moving." He held up the disk that Taveras had discarded, placing it in a pocket of his blacksuit.

"I see you on the screen," Burnett confirmed.

"Remember that if I answer you I might give away my position," Bolan warned, "so in most cases just keep telling me what's happening. Assume I'm listening."

"Gotcha," Burnett said. "Time to clean house."

Bolan nodded. He drew the sound-suppressed Beretta 93-R, press-checked it and slipped out of the apartment. Burnett watched him go and then turned to the laptop screen, following the moving blip.

Bolan's first step was to take the stairs all the way to the lobby level. Taking out the El Cráneo shooters from top to bottom would give those on the ground level more time to become aware of what was happening. They were therefore more likely to escape, if they could, and Bolan could not have them running free in the surrounding area. El Cráneo would die, the threat ended for good. Bolan could not bring back the countless people El Cráneo had killed in their bloody rampages, but he could see to it they never took another life.

Bolan left the stairwell and moved quietly to the rear entrance to the lobby, opposite the elevators. He peered around the corner with one eye, careful to move slowly. The older couple and the younger man were still seated around the lobby coffee table. There was no one else except for a clerk in the apartment building office, visible through the glass door labeled Management just off the lobby.

"You've got a red dot with two blue dots," Burnett said in his ear. "Just forward of your position. There's a room to your left, to the rear of your position." Bolan glanced to the lobby door. "I've got a blue dot and a red dot there, too." Bolan frowned. He could see only one person inside the management office, seated at a desk.

Bolan walked casually through the lobby, counting the numbers in his head. At the last instant, the man seated with the old couple turned to see the Executioner approaching. His eyes went wide in recognition.

Bolan's Beretta came up and coughed once. The suppressed round slapped into the gunman's face and took him down. He slumped across the coffee table. The old woman brought her hand to her mouth but did not cry out.

Even as the thug was falling, Bolan was changing course, running for the glass-fronted office door. He did not even try the knob, instead simply kicking low with one foot to send the flimsy door rocking inward and banging off the drywall facing it.

The El Cráneo shooter rose at the sudden noise. He was standing over a pretty, young red-haired woman who was tied hand and foot with electrical cords beneath the desk, her mouth covered with duct tape. Bolan fired again in single-shot mode, the suppressed hollowpoint round striking his target in the head. The gunner slumped to the carpet, dead.

Bolan crouched next to the frightened woman, placed his finger to his lips and then removed the duct tape as gently as he could.

"Don't yell," he said. "I'm with the Justice Department. These men are part of a gang who've taken hostages throughout the building. I'm going to free you, but I need you not to call 9-1-1. Just leave, quietly, as if nothing is wrong. You've got to give me time to remove the rest of them. If they learn they've been discovered, they'll start shooting. Do you understand?"

The woman nodded.

"What's your name?" Bolan asked.

"Dana," she said.

"Well, Dana," Bolan said quietly, "I need you to do me a favor. There's an older couple in the lobby. I need you to take them with you when you leave and see to it they're okay. Can you do that?"

Dana nodded again. "I'll do my best."

"Good. Please go now, and go quietly." He finished untying her. She was a little wobbly on her feet, but she managed, moving quietly and briskly through the lobby and ushering the man and woman out without raising a fuss. As Bolan left the office, the old woman waved at him. Her husband tipped an imaginary hat. They were stronger than Bolan had given them credit for, he realized.

"I've got two red blips down, eight to go," Burnett said in his ear. "The trackers fade when a person wearing one dies, apparently."

"Makes sense," Bolan said. "Next?"

"The next two are two floors up," Burnett told him. "One's in unit…let's see here…it's going to be 205 and 216, if I'm reading this right. There's no one but the shooter in 205, but 216 has three hostages."

"Got it."

"Oh, and, Cooper? I've been getting calls from some of them. I mean, Taveras has. I've been doing my best Taveras impression." Burnett's voice grew more gravelly and took on a Spanish accent. "'I am okay. Stop bothering me.'"

"Not bad," Bolan said. "All right, I'm going."

There were a few residents moving through the apartment building, unaware of the drama unfolding around them. Bolan dared not tell them what was happening. If even one panicked resident called the authorities, the resulting chaos would alert the remaining gunmen and lead to possible carnage. Instead, the Executioner would have to neutralize the threat before anyone knew what was happening. He silently thanked Cowboy Kissinger for the custom suppressor fitted to the barrel of his Beretta machine pistol.

When he got to apartment 205, he tried the knob very slowly. It was locked. Bolan backed off two paces and triggered a suppressed triburst into the locking mechanism. He plunged after his shots with a side kick, shouldering past the door and bringing his Beretta on target as he entered the apartment.

The El Cráneo man inside was sitting on the couch, eating a sandwich. He jumped up as Bolan burst in, grabbing for the revolver in his belt. The Executioner shot him in the head, watching dispassionately as he fell. A quick search of the apartment revealed a dead man in the bathroom, his throat cut. This was obviously 205's resident. For whatever reason, he'd been killed when the building was initially taken. Bolan frowned and looked back at the dead man in the living room. A life for a life seemed just, to many, but the life of the El Cráneo thug was worth far less than that of any innocent civilian as far as the Executioner was concerned.

"Neutralized," he said aloud.

"Got it," Burnett responded. "No change in 216. Everyone's clustered in one of the rear rooms of the apartment, must be the bedroom."

Bolan didn't like the sound of that. He moved quickly to apartment 216. "Burnett," he whispered, "are they still in the bedroom?"

"Yes," Burnett told him.

"Stand by," Bolan said quietly. He took out his pistol-grip lock pick and worked it into the door lock. Then he eased the jimmied door open, creeping in as quietly as he could across the carpeted floor.

A scream sounded from the bedroom.

Bolan ran for it, ramming the bedroom door with his shoulder. There was a grunt from the other side as the door met the resistance of a human body. Then Bolan was through, almost tripping over the El Cráneo gunner. He aimed and fired a 3-round burst, stitching the fallen gunman. The man's eyes stared at the ceiling in death, his face a mask of shock.

Another man in his thirties and a boy of no more than five were bound with duct tape and lying on the floor next to the king-size bed. The man looked at Bolan with hatred in his eyes, while the boy merely looked terrified. On the bed, her wrists tied to the bedposts, was an attractive woman with auburn hair and brown eyes, wearing only her underwear. Bolan took in the shreds of what had been a blouse and a pair of slacks, lying on the floor. The El Cráneo thug's knife, a cheap switchblade, had also fallen nearby. The woman was sobbing, her eyes squeezed shut.

Bolan holstered his Beretta. He drew and opened his knife, using it to cut the tape holding the woman's wrists. She shrieked and shrank from him as he knelt over her. Bolan managed to get his arms around her, careful not to cut her with the knife he still held, and whispered in her ear as she trembled against him.

"You're okay," Bolan told her. "My name is Cooper and I'm with the Justice Department. You're okay. He can't hurt you." He gently set the woman back on the bed, where she curled into a ball trying to cover herself. Then he went to the husband and son on the floor, deducing their relationship from the expression on the man's face.

"Did you hear me?" Bolan said, cutting the tape from the man's wrist and letting him free the son. "I'm with the Justice Department. The man who attacked you is part of a gang of thugs in this building. I know where they are, but to get them all, I need your help."

"He was going to—" the husband started.

"I know," Bolan said.

"He tied us up and there was nothing I could—"

"Listen to me," Bolan said. He went to the corpse, found a Bersa Thunder .380 automatic pistol on the body and brought it over. "Can you use a gun, sir?"

"I used to target shoot," he said.

"Can you operate this?" Bolan held up the pistol.

"Yes, I think so," he said. Bolan handed it to him. The shaken husband ejected the magazine after fumbling for the catch. Then he racked the slide, ejecting an empty round. Bolan watched as he fed the round back into the magazine, reloaded the gun and chambered it. He did know what he was doing, it seemed. Bolan did the only thing he could do for any man forced to sit helplessly and watch his woman be attacked. He gave him a chance to get his manhood back.

"Look," Bolan said, "I've been in situations every bit as bad as what you just faced. I know how angry you are. You can help me and you can keep your family safe."

"What do you need me to do?" The man looked up at Bolan as his son clung to his leg, burying his face in the man's flank.

"Don't call 9-1-1," Bolan said. "Don't leave this apartment. Move a piece of furniture in front of the door after I've gone. Guard your family and don't let anyone in. Eventually, the police will come. Stay here until they do, because once they've come, it will mean this is all over."

"Thank you," the husband said. He rose and went to comfort his wife, the gun still in his hand.

Bolan left as he'd come, hoping they'd be able to do as he'd instructed. The sight of a family traumatized by Taveras and El Cráneo, by the gang's indifference to human life, filled him with righteous rage. He would not stop until he'd cleaned the building of these vermin.

Burnett's voice sounded in his ear again. "They're getting a little jumpy, big guy," he said. "I'm holding them off, but I think they're starting to get suspicious at being ignored. You'd better move. We've still got six in the building."

"Give me the locations."

"I've got one on the fifth floor," Burnett said, "moving around in apartment 518. I've got another on the seventh floor who seems to be pacing back and forth in the hallway, or just running laps around the building. Probably one of the nervous nellies who keep calling. I've got three of them clustered in apartment 901 in the living room. The last one's in apartment 1114, not moving at all."

"I'm moving," Bolan said. "Stay with me."

The Executioner took the stairs to the fifth floor, then walked quietly to unit 518. From the left side of the door, he pressed his back against the wall and started knocking quietly.

"Who is it?" called a voice.

Bolan knocked again, more softly this time.

"I said, who the hell is it?"

Bolan knocked again, even more faintly than before. As he did so, he drew the Beretta.

The door whipped open. A tall Hispanic man stood there, a big stainless-steel Ruger pistol in his hand. "Enrique, man, if you don't stop screwing around, I'm going to—"

Just what the El Cráneo man was going to do to Enrique was lost in the triburst from Bolan's Beretta. The hollowpoint bullets blew a cavity through the man's throat and out the back of his neck, causing his head to flop at an odd angle as he collapsed to the carpet below. Bolan stepped over the corpse, reloading, as he checked the apartment. It was empty, save for the dead El Cráneo member.

Bolan then took the stairs to the seventh floor. He eased the stairwell door open very carefully, listening for sounds of the nervous gunman Burnett had described. It wasn't long before he heard someone moving down the carpeted hallway, with the distracted pace of someone who was walking to walk, rather than walking to get somewhere.

Bolan lined up the shot on the man's center of mass as he rounded the corner. He fired once. The man staggered and backed up around the corner, falling to the floor beyond. Bolan came around to check him and found the man digging, not for a weapon, but for a phone.

"Fausto! Fausto, I have been shot!" the man shouted into the phone, just before Bolan put a bullet in his brain.

The Executioner snapped up the phone and put it to his ear.

"Jorge?" a voice said. "Jorge, all you all right? Jorge!"

Bolan closed the phone. "Burnett," he said aloud, "we're blown!"

"Go to 901," Burnett said. "They're starting to stir and there's three of them. Go, go, get them now!"

Bolan didn't waste time responding. He flew down the hallway, his feet pounding on the carpet, and ripped open the stairwell door. Then he took the steps two at a time, thundering up to the ninth floor, bursting through the fire door.

Room 901 was only a few doors down the corridor. Its door was opening and the El Cráneo men were emerging. Two had pistols, while one carried an Uzi submachine gun. Bolan threw himself on his stomach as the submachine gunner cut loose. Bullets filled the air above Bolan's head as he returned fire from the floor.

His angle was low. His shots slammed into the El Cráneo men at ankle level, chopping them down like saplings. They screamed as they fell. Bolan was immediately up, shoving himself to the side to avoid their wild shots as he let the empty Beretta 93-R fall from his hand. He drew the Desert Eagle and pulled the trigger in rapid succession, his .44 Magnum rounds finding their targets among the fallen men. When they stopped moving, Bolan kicked one of them over, checking the holes beneath him. The .44 Magnum bullets had dug into the floor but had not gone much farther after blowing apart the El Cráneo killers. Bolan let himself feel relieved; at least he did not have to worry that his shots would strike someone on the floor below. He holstered the Desert Eagle and then retrieved and reloaded the Beretta.

"Burnett!" he said. "I've got the ones from 901. What's 1114's occupant doing?"

"Nothing," Burnett said, sounding surprised. He's not moving at all. I've got a stationary blue blip in the kitchen, too, also not moving."

"Where's our last guy?"

"Bedroom," Burnett said after a pause. "Maybe he's asleep."

"He will be soon," Bolan said quietly. He checked 901 briefly, finding no bodies and nothing else of note. At least El Cráneo hadn't simply taken over several apartments by killing the occupants. It was likely the apartments sheltering only Taveras's gunman had been unoccupied when Taveras put his plan into action. The residents would be grateful they'd not been home to be part of it.

He took the stairs again, the muscles in his legs starting to ache. He found room 1114 and listened outside the door.

Nothing stirred inside.

He reached out and tried the knob. It turned. The apartment within was dark. Bolan took out his combat light and let its bright, white beam pierce the gloom. As he moved into the apartment, he swept the beam left, then right—

"Do not move."

Bolan froze. In the beam of his light, a thin man of average height with a craggy, pockmarked face and slicked-back hair was holding the naked blade of a butterfly knife against the throat of a middle-aged woman. The woman's eyes were wide with ter-

ror and she almost completely blocked a shot at the man behind
her, who was careful to keep most of his head behind hers. The
knife dug into the skin of her throat and had raised a thin line of
blood.

"If you shoot me," the El Cráneo man said, "if you *try* to shoot
me, you will hit her."

"Not necessarily," Bolan said.

"Then try," the thug said, smiling thinly, "but know that I will
drag this blade through her neck before you can do it."

"You're not wearing one of Pierre's little tracking devices,"
Bolan guessed.

"No," he said. "I did not wish to wear one. I told Pierre I
thought it wrong, like something from *Revelation*. I said I would
not wear it. He laughed at me but he said it was unimportant.
Now I am glad. I heard the shots. I knew what was coming. I
want safe passage from this place."

"Let her go," Bolan ordered.

"No," the thug said. "I like her right where she is."

"If you're a religious man," Bolan said, "you know what you
are doing is wrong."

"Who said I was religious?" the thug scoffed. "I did not want
Pierre's little mark of the Beast, no. But I am still going to hell.
There is no doubt about that. But I am not going today. You are
going to let me leave here."

"That's not going to happen," Bolan said.

"Who will stop me? You? I do not think so."

"Last chance," Bolan warned. "Where do you think you can
go? The police will be on their way here by now," he lied, "and
they'll have this place cordoned off."

"Then I will take her with me!"

"They'll never let you do it," Bolan said. "They'll know she's
as good as dead if they let you leave with her. Give up. Put the
knife down. You can still live through this."

"I am warning you!"

Bolan made the decision to fire. As many times as he had faced scenarios like these, he knew they could end only one way. Allowing predators to hold hostages only gave them more power. Bolan did not intend to let him escape. He would be damned if he'd let the gang member murder an innocent woman. Carefully, he reviewed the mechanics of the shot in his mind, calculating the path the bullet would have to travel.

He visualized bringing the Beretta on target. He had used the weapon for so long, had relied on it so much, that he could mentally picture every detail of the front sight, every slight blemish and nick. He could picture the luminous white marking on the front blade. Bolan allowed himself to enter the mental zone he had used so often as a sniper, as a warrior, as the man who had earned the name, the Executioner.

"Drop your gun!" the thug demanded, "or, I swear, I will—"

Bolan snapped the Beretta 93-R up to eye level and took the shot through the gunner's right eye, angling for deep brain. The shot was true, taking the man in the head without harming his hostage. The suppressed blast was almost anticlimactic. The butterfly knife fell from limp fingers as the El Cráneo killer simply switched off, dead on his feet. He fell to the ground. The woman looked down at him and then at Bolan, her hands to her face.

"Are you all right?" Bolan asked, going to her and checking her neck.

"I will be," she said.

"Is there anyone else here?"

"There's another one." She pointed to the dead man on the floor. "He's asleep in the bedroom. Oh, God! I thought they were going to kill me. I thought I'd never leave this place!"

Bolan paused long enough to take her by the shoulders and look her in the eye. "Listen to me. You're going to be okay. Wait here."

The soldier found the last of the El Cráneo murderers lying on the bed in the bedroom, a pair of headphones covering his ears. He appeared to be asleep. A sawed-off shotgun lay on the bed next to him.

Bolan stood over him, the Beretta pointed between the man's eyes, as he kicked the bedframe. The thug's eyes shot open and he automatically grabbed his weapon.

"Good night," Bolan said.

It was over.

Bolan told Burnett he was on his way back up, asking the detective to contact the local authorities, finally. The police would follow up, interview the apartment's residents and see to it the bodies were taken care of. Bolan, in turn, would need to get back to Stony Man Farm as soon as possible.

Back outside Emilie Taveras's apartment, Bolan knocked before letting himself back in. Burnett was just returning from the bedroom.

"Just checking the old girl again," he said. "Still asleep. If Taveras was right, she might never know anything happened."

Bolan jerked his chin to the corpse on the floor. "Not as long as we clean that up before she notices," he said. He went to the kitchen table.

"You look like you managed not to stop any bullets," Burnett commented.

"No," Bolan said. "I do my best work when I haven't been shot."

"Now what?"

"This computer could prove exceptionally helpful," Bolan said, picking up the open laptop and turning away from Burnett to take a closer look at it. "If Taveras was smart enough to use Stevens to create technology like he used here, he was probably keeping other records digitally. My people can take a look at this laptop, sift through it, even recover deleted data. There might be some hard evidence, or even just some clues, as to how all this came down, something to help us track down the person or people responsible. There are a lot of questions left unanswered. Someone has to answer for the leaks. There's a thread that connects everything. This might help us find it."

Bolan heard the hammer of a revolver being cocked behind him.

19

"I'm sorry about this," Burnett said. "I genuinely am."

Bolan did not turn. He set down the laptop. In the reflection of the darkened screen, he could see Burnett aiming a small stainless-steel Smith & Wesson .38 snubnose revolver at Bolan's head.

"You're the source," Bolan said. "The leak to NLI from within your department."

"Who better than the leader of the task force?" Burnett said. "Yes, it was me. I told you, Cooper. I had everybody wired for sound and video. Those bastards didn't make a move that I didn't know about in advance."

"But you let them kill innocent people anyway."

"The wiretaps were all illegal," Burnett spit. "After all, we couldn't trample the precious constitutional rights of a bunch of murderous drug dealers, could we? In order to know what was going on, I had to tap them, bug them, tape them, record them. But to do it right I had to go through a court system laced with judges, lawyers and lackeys who've been bought off! If it wasn't Caqueta, it was Taveras, and if it wasn't one of them, it was some lesser player who'd roll over for them. I told you, Cooper. If I played it by the book, I'd have been screwed."

"So you did it off the books and let them keep killing."

"Did I?" Burnett demanded. "Look around you, Cooper. I've done what none of my predecessors could. I've wiped out the two biggest drug gangs in New York City! I've put a *stop* to them. It was necessary. The ends did justify the means. Didn't you ever, just once, think it a bit odd that I was so cooperative? Show me another cop in the city who'd tag along while you committed the equivalent of mass murder. I don't know what government agency you really work with, but I can guess. You're some kind of CIA wet works character, aren't you? Some kind of government assassin. It's the only thing that makes sense."

"When did you go over, Burnett?" Bolan asked, finally turning to face the big man, careful to leave his hands at his sides away from his body. "When did you become a dirty cop?"

"You say that like it means anything," Burnett scoffed. "Look at what I've done, Cooper! At what *we've* done. You helped, after all. Hell, you did most of the work!"

"I didn't do it for you. I did what I did to stop the DU ammunition. To stop the killing. To stop the drug war in the city."

"And that's what we've done!" Burnett insisted. "Why can't you see it? It was a beautiful plan."

Bolan realized the truth. "You brought NLI into this," he said. "Then you put me on to them to take them out."

"Of course," Burnett said. "I told you. I had them all wired. When West and Stevens moved into town and set up shop, things started to get bad, to get bloodier than ever. Stevens, through West, was feeding both sides. I saw the future, Cooper, and it wasn't good. The gangs would eventually grind each other up, but they'd take a lot more people with them than they've done so far. They wouldn't stop, and their attacks were going to get more and more bold. I had to do something."

"You don't consider what's happened to be enough? A lot of people have died already," Bolan said.

"And that's too bad," Burnett said, his .38 never moving, "but it could have been a lot worse if I hadn't taken steps."

"Just what did you do?" Bolan asked.

"Isn't it obvious?" Burnett said, his voice edged with pride.

"What do you do if you want to end a war? You let both sides weaken each other. Then you make sure one side wins. Once you've done that, you can take out the side that's left. It's neat. It's orderly. It's simple. And it makes perfect sense."

"You convinced West and Stevens to cut off the Caquetas," Bolan guessed.

"Who else?" Burnett said. "I knew all about their connection, all about how they were getting the DU ammo. Every time Caqueta, Almarone or Taveras said a word about it, I heard it. All I had to do was put myself in touch with West."

"You cut a deal."

"Why not?" Burnett said. "It's what he expected. I let him bribe me, sure, but it wasn't the money. It's never been about that. I told him that to stay in business, I'd look the other way— but I made it very clear that I had a grudge against the Caquetas and wanted to see them hamstrung. He was happy to play up to Taveras, as I wanted him to do. In turn, he accepted that bribing me was the cheapest and most efficient way to stay in business here in New York."

"Why El Cráneo?"

"Hell, you met the Caquetas and Taveras," Burnett said. "Taveras was the stupider of them. The gangs were more or less evenly matched until I stacked the deck in El Cráneo's favor. But I knew Taveras was less likely to wonder why fortune had smiled on him. Caqueta and Almarone were more suspicious by nature, less convinced of their own divine right to conquer. They didn't suffer from Taveras's delusions and dreams of power. That made Taveras the better pawn."

"So you figured you'd let Taveras kill off the Caquetas and establish himself as king of New York's drug trade."

"Absolutely," Burnett said. "That way I could focus my efforts on just one organization. It's a lot easier to make arrests and win convictions when you're not splitting your resources between two fronts. What I didn't count on was you doing most of the work for me."

"That day in the hospital," Bolan said. "You killed that Blackjack operative. Why?"

"He was coming to report to me in person," Burnett said. "I'd told them where to find you, but specifically warned them off. They thought they knew better, figured they'd take you out. They sent an errand boy to inform me of this fact."

"So you stuck a fork in his neck?"

"You're not exactly a ninja, you know," Burnett said. "I heard you coming, in a big hurry. I figured it was either you or one of my officers. To be honest I thought it was one of my people coming to check on me, so I had to work fast. I had to silence my Blackjack messenger and then possibly even shoot one of my own people, depending on what he'd overheard in the hallway."

"You were going to shoot me?"

"This—" Burnett motioned with his eyes to the .38 "—is a backup gun, and completely off the books. When I kill you with it, nobody will be able to trace it to me."

"Where does NLI fit into this?" Bolan asked.

"You don't think I'm stupid, do you?" Burnett said, sounding annoyed. "When the first reports of DU ammunition being used in drive-by shootings in New York hit the wires, they sent representatives from Blackjack Group to start sniffing around. I'm the task-force leader, remember? They found me first if they found anyone. I made it clear that I was more interested in getting the ammo off my streets than finding out where it came from. I know big money when I see it. I let them know that I was open to an expedient solution, if they wanted to make one happen."

"So you let them bribe you, too."

"It's what they expected," Burnett said again. "Tell people you're just trying to do some good and they'll suspect you from

the beginning. Let them believe you're a money-grubbing bastard, and they'll have every faith in your low-down nature."

"You told NLI about Bryant Park."

"I did," Burnett admitted. "Caqueta and Almarone got the information from West's computer when they had him killed. Neither one of them is what you'd call a computer genius, nor were
their people. They found West readily enough, since he was
their contact to buy the ammunition anyway. They killed him to
send a message to Stevens, and tossed his place and searched
his computer to see if they could find anything of interest. They
talked all about it—and what they knew, I knew. The fools
couldn't see any way to capitalize on the Bryant Park meet, but
it was one of many loose ends NLI would be only too happy to
tie up for me. So I contacted Leister and let him know so he could
send a team to eliminate whoever was sniffing around. I also sent
them to West's apartment to destroy any evidence Caqueta and
Almarone had probably missed."

"And you let NLI know about the meet with Caqueta."

"It was too perfect to pass up," Burnett said. "It was a chance
to chop the head off the snake, and it worked beautifully."

"Then you fed NLI the information on Taveras. You were
herding Leister to me, so I could eliminate him for you," Bolan
said.

"Well, I couldn't very well have NLI's Blackjack boys spilling their guts about the dirty cop who was helping them, could
I?" Burnett said. "I knew from the moment you stuck your nose
in this that I could count on you to help me tie it all up. Originally I was going to have to trust that NLI's desire for secrecy
would outweigh any lingering doubts they might have about
letting me live knowing what had been going on. With you
storming around, knocking down their people like bowling
pins, it was easier to let you finish them than trust to fate
alone."

"But Leister wasn't a hothead. He came to talk to Taveras, to try to work something out. He was throwing around Blackjack's weight but didn't actually want to move on El Cráneo."

"He was smart," Burnett admitted.

"So you arranged for Taveras to hit Blackjack."

"I did," Burnett said. "All it took was an anonymous phone call and an appeal to Pierre's overdeveloped sense of pride. I told him Blackjack didn't respect him. I told him Leister was laughing at him. Then I told him where to find Leister's people."

"And after Leister was sufficiently motivated to come after Taveras, you made sure we were all in the same place at the same time. You showed me the video beforehand to herd Leister to me, make sure I'd take him out for you if the opportunity arose."

"Sure," Burnett said. "I had Leister's number, just like I had everyone else's. I called him. I told him SWAT was going to move on Taveras in the morning, and if he didn't want to lose the chance to silence Pierre before he talked, Leister should get his people moving. It stood to reason they'd hit that night. Leister thought I was just another frustrated cop who wanted to see the bad guys taken out by any means necessary. I told you, people have great faith in what they think are others' sinister motives."

"That's why you wanted to wait to go to the club," Bolan said.

"Absolutely," Burnett said. "I needed us all there at once. Get everybody on the same page and get them shooting one another," Burnett said. "All I had to do was try not to get plugged in the process. I wasn't so much worried about you. No offense."

"You betrayed Leister to take him out of the equation."

"That's right," Burnett said.

"How did you know where Blackjack was staging its operations?" Bolan asked.

"I knew it because Stevens knew it," Burnett said smugly. "The man was a scientist, not a criminal mastermind. All it took was some investigation into West's phone records to trace a route back to Stevens. Then I tapped his phone. His security people kept him up to date, so whatever he knew, I knew. It's a good thing, too. If I hadn't found that and covered it up, the whole operation would have been busted long before the war got hot enough to really produce any real attrition on both sides."

"So you let the killing continue. You could have stopped Stevens, but you aided and abetted him. You needed him to keep selling his ammunition. And you did it all to help this city."

"Why not?" Burnett said. "Originally, once El Cráneo was in power in New York, I was going to let Blackjack's hired commandos take them out. Taveras was a loose end who could possibly bring someone back to NLI, after all. Eventually NLI would get Stevens, too, either on their own or with my help. Once that was done, the city would be safe again, and I'd live out my days happily bribed by all concerned. You made things more complicated, but also safer for me. With you in the picture, I could let you take down NLI's paid guns—and of course, you nailed shut Taveras's coffin, too, which I couldn't have counted on. You've helped wrap it all up, Cooper. All I had to do was hold your hand and point you in the right direction."

"I'd have done what I did with or without your interference," Bolan told him.

"Probably." Burnett shrugged. "The only problem is, now you're a loose end. I took a lot of risks to see this thing play out, get everyone shooting at one another. I knew I'd have to be flexible if it was going to work out. If I pushed and pushed, eventually I'd get what I was after. Still, I had some semblance of a plan. Taveras was supposed to take care of you for me, not the other way around. When he got the drop on me outside the motel, I told him right then and there who I was and why he couldn't afford the heat for killing me. He didn't care who was waiting for him to kill, so long as he got his payback. I figured there was a good chance everything would fit."

"You sure like to gamble," Bolan said.

"Maybe." Burnett shrugged. "The whole thing would have

worked out nice and neatly. Stevens sent Taveras after Leister in New Jersey, so I just made sure we headed to the same location. I figured nature would take its course. Taveras wasn't good for much, it turns out. But he wasn't as stupid as I thought he was, either. That computer could have just about anything on it. If it has anything in it that could point back to me, or to any part of my plan, sooner or later, you and your people—or other folks in positions of power—are going to know what I did. I can't allow that. The chain has to end here, with you."

"That's very noble of you," Bolan said.

"If you think you're going to make me feel guilty," Burnett said, "you can forget it. I've buried better than you getting here, Cooper. I've had to look away while good agents got taken down so they wouldn't uncover what I was trying to do before it was finished. You're a decent man, and you're working for what I'm trying to accomplish, more or less—but you're not willing to see the big picture. You think there should still be some kind of rules. There aren't. There are only results, Cooper, and that's what I'm getting. I regret that it has to end like this. That doesn't mean I won't do it. You helped all this come down. Everyone else is gone now. Now it's just you. With a single bullet, I can close this case."

"You're going to gun me down right here?"

"No," Burnett said. "Too many questions will be asked if your body turns up. Some smart-assed forensics expert will find something I missed. The bureaucrats hate neat packages. They start looking for setups."

"Imagine that," Bolan said.

"Enough. Drop the guns, very carefully."

Bolan complied, easing the Beretta and the Desert Eagle to the floor and kicking them away at Burnett's command. "Now what?" he asked.

"You're just going to disappear," Burnett said simply. "It's better for everyone that way."

"Better for you, perhaps," Bolan said. "You know, Burnett—"
The Executioner struck.

While Burnett was focused on Bolan's words, the soldier let
his legs fall out from under him. As he dropped, his legs came
within range of Burnett. The detective's .38 boomed, but the bullet went high. Bolan was no longer there to be shot.

The Executioner fired his right leg into Burnett's shin with
all his might. Something snapped. Burnett went down, screaming, and lost the .38 as he did so. With his enemy so close and
his guns out of reach, there was one choice. Bolan threw himself onto Burnett.

The two men wrestled on the carpeted floor. Despite the pain,
Burnett had an advantage thanks to his size. As he and Bolan
fought for control of each other's limbs, Burnett managed to
wrench his right hand from Bolan's grip and put his palm on the
butt of the Glock still in its holster at his side.

As Burnett's hand closed over the plastic frame of the Glock,
he heard a metallic click.

Bolan, his left hand still pinning Burnett's left, bracing himself on the detective's chest, was pointing a tiny North American Arms .22-caliber minirevolver at Burnett's left eye. The
little single-action repeater was cocked. It almost disappeared
in Bolan's fist, but the black muzzle was unmistakable.

"Where did you get that?" Burnett asked quietly.

"I have a rule that I try not to break," Bolan told him. "I don't
kill cops. I'm taking you to face justice, Burnett. Of course,
you're not really a cop. When you sold out innocent people,
when you started committing cold-blooded murder for what
you thought was the greater good, you crossed the line. You
joined the criminals. You gave up your badge. You disgraced
yourself and your department. You're going to pay for that."

"Who are you to judge me?" Burnett demanded. "Who are
you to be judge and jury—"

"Who am I?" Bolan echoed. "I'm the one who fights for all

of them, all those people you watched die so you could save the city from itself. Now, get up. Flinch and I'll empty this into you."

Burnett's shoulders slumped. He was caught and he knew it.

It would not be easy for him on the inside.

Bolan considered his next step as he led the dirty cop away. No, he was not the judge, nor the jury.

He was the Executioner.

20

Mack Bolan stood on the steps of the New York Public Library. To either side, the lions sat regally on their stone pedestals. Undaunted, a New York City pigeon rested on the petrified mane of the restored statue behind which Bolan had sought refuge. The city repair crews had made their rounds with surprising speed, setting right again the ravages of the past few days.

Bolan was glad to see he'd done no lasting damage, even indirectly. The lions had stood since 1911 when the NYPL was dedicated. Originally named for the library's founders, they'd been rechristened Patience and Fortitude by Mayor Fiorello LaGuardia during the Great Depression. Those names had stuck. The statues had seen a lot in the last century—and they'd see still more.

The Executioner smiled and shook his head. You could hit New York hard and New Yorkers harder. You could kick them while they were down. You could punch holes in their landmarks and burn their buildings to the ground. You could not, however, keep them down. The city and her residents were here for the long haul. That was why Bolan fought. That was why he would always fight, standing between the people of cities like New York and the predators who sought their ruin.

As Bolan stood, he caught sight of Hal Brognola walking briskly up Fifth Avenue. The big Fed had his hands shoved into an open and very rumpled brown trench coat over a conservative suit. The man from Justice caught Bolan's eye and joined him on the steps, sparing a glance at Patience and Fortitude as he did so.

"Pretty inspiring," Brognola said.

"Had a busy night?"

"It hasn't exactly been a relaxing week for me." Brognola laughed despite himself. He sighed and looked at the Executioner. "Burnett's in custody and singing like a canary, trying to avoid the death penalty. He just might, at that, but I don't like his odds once he's behind bars. He's made enemies on both sides of the fence."

Bolan nodded.

"Burnett's task-force members have been rounded up, too," Brognola went on. "The department cooperated and we've got Justice oversight on the internal investigation. A couple of them have cracked and rolled over already."

"Good," Bolan said, still looking at the lions.

"Thanks to the material you sent us and what we've gleaned from Taveras's hard drive, the Man has ordered a federal raid on NLI and on Blackjack Group," Brognola said. "By tomorrow, both companies' assets will be seized and their people will be behind bars awaiting trial. God only knows the circus that will generate, but eventually we'll put them away."

"There are more direct methods," Bolan said neutrally.

"There certainly are." Brognola nodded. "Fortunately, that shouldn't be necessary."

"Blackjack's people might not go quietly," Bolan pointed out.

"They shouldn't be too much trouble," Brognola said. "Most of those working as contractors for the company will never be involved. The management ought to be eager to cut whatever deals it can. I suspect they'll come clean with a minimum of hassle. As for NLI, they're not field people. They've been terrified of the damage looming to the company itself. That damage is done. They'll show us their throats in an effort to stay out of prison."

"How will you know the sacrificial lambs they give you are the ones truly responsible?"

"We won't, necessarily," Brognola said sourly, "but it will be enough to contain the problem and, hopefully, prevent it from happening again. The Man wants to send a message from Washington to the military-industrial complex, as they say. If one of your people goes off the reservation, it's a lot more painful to cover it up than simply to come clean."

Bolan nodded. "Has anyone checked the Camden situation?"

"Preliminary reports and sampling are in. There's an increase in background radiation, a few traces attributable to the depleted uranium on-site. Nothing really major, though. Certainly nothing on the order of a dirty bomb. No Chernobyls to speak of, not this time. Stevens was definitely bluffing."

"The evidence is all squared away?" Bolan asked.

"Yes. The local authorities have been apprised of the situation. It's pretty buttoned up."

"Then I guess we're done here," Bolan said.

"I guess so," Brognola said. "I'll be happy to get back to Wonderland. I think I've met with everybody in city government except the dog catcher." He paused. "Striker?" he said finally. "The line gets thinner every day."

"The line between them and us?" Bolan said, turning to regard his old ally. "I've never thought so. Burnett did what he did believing that any amount of evil justified the ultimate good. He thought he could clean his city by letting evil fester, then cutting out the cancer he'd allowed to grow. It can't be done that way. How many have we seen who've done just that—people who've played God with the power they had over others, believing they knew better?"

"But not you," Brognola said.

"No," Bolan said frankly. "I've never done it that way. I simply take the war to the predators' doorsteps. I send a message, too, Hal. The message is that when you prey on the innocent, you *will* die. It's never been any more complicated than that."

"Burnett and those like him?" Brognola offered.

"They became what they fought," Bolan said. "They became predators who spilled innocent blood, or allowed it to be spilled or just stood by knowing it was to be spilled, simply because they thought it was expedient. They joined the ranks of the predators. They became the rot eating society. That's where I come in. I burn it out so it can't hurt anyone else. I burn it out my way, on my terms."

Brognola looked at the Executioner for a moment longer. Then he shoved his hands into the pockets of his trench coat and looked back to the street. "Striker," he said, "you're not telling me anything I don't already know. But it's good to hear it once in a while."

"I know, Hal," Bolan said.

The big Fed nodded and walked off. He was quickly swallowed by the stream of pedestrians moving past the library. Bolan offered the lions one last glance before he, too, moved off among the crowd.

The Executioner had a war to fight. As long as men like Caqueta, Taveras and even Len Burnett were willing to take life without justification, Bolan would not stop. He would fight for all those who could not fight for themselves and for all those who had died along the way. Walking briskly among the New Yorkers, Bolan set his sights on the road ahead and on the challenges before him.

There was work to be done.

There always would be.

Look for

THE SOUL STEALER
by AleX Archer

Annja Creed jumps at the chance to find a relic buried in the long undisturbed soil of Russia's frozen terrain. But the residents of the town claim they are being hunted by the ghost of a fallen goddess said to ingest souls. When Annja seeks to destroy the apparition, she discovers a horrifying truth—possibly leading her to a dead end....

Available May 2008 wherever you buy books.

GRA12